DO YOU REMEMBER THE FIRST TIME?

Jenny Colgan was born in 1972 in Ayrshire. After Edinburgh University, she worked for six years in the health service, moonlighting as a cartoonist and stand-up comic. She is the author of four previous bestselling novels: *Amanda's Wedding*, *Talking to Addison*, *Looking for Andrew McCarthy* and *Working Wonders*, all of which are in development for film and TV. Jenny is married, lives in London and is working on her sixth novel. For more information, visit her website at *www.jennycolgan.com*.

Acclaim for *Working Wonders*:

'Funny, magical and moving, this is a rewarding read.'
Time Out

'We laughed a lot.'
Heat

'A delicious comedy. Will melt even the hardest of hearts.'
Red

'Colgan's witty book perfectly captures the frustrations and petty vexations of office life.'
She

'Hugely entertaining and very funny.'
Cosmopolitan

'A funny, clever page-turner.'
Closer

'Fans of *The Office* will love this witty tale.'
Woman's Own

'A quirky tale of love, work and the meaning of life.' *Company*

'If you think David Brent causes mayhem in *The Office* wait till you see what town-planner Arthur and his team get up to in Jenny Colgan's comic romp.' *In Style*

Looking for Andrew McCarthy:

'Colgan is on top form in this, her latest outrageous romp.' *Cosmopolitan*

'Jenny Colgan is one of the leaders of the pack and this, her third novel, will delight her legions of admirers. Fast-paced, funny, poignant and well-observed it reads as a pastiche of the movies she loved . . . If a time capsule were buried to capture the world at the turn of the 21st century, this would be a candidate for inclusion: her sense of time and place are that authentic.' *Daily Mail*

'*Looking for Andrew McCarthy* will strike a chord with anyone who did their growing up in the 80s. Wonderful, warm and resonant for anyone who ever wondered what happened to teenage dreams.' *Hello*

'*That's Life* meets *This Life*, with *Once in a Lifetime* thrown in, all talking heads, witty one-liners and angst-ridden relationships . . . Did I like this book? Well, d'uh! Do hedgehogs have quills? A pure belter of a novel.' *Glasgow Herald*

'Colgan's enjoyable new bestseller investigates the notion that having it all can sometimes mean having precisely nothing at all.' *Marie Claire*

By the same author:

Amanda's Wedding
Talking to Addison
Looking for Andrew McCarthy
Working Wonders

JENNY COLGAN

Do You Remember the First Time?

HarperCollins*Publishers*

This novel is entirely a work of fiction.
The names, characters and incidents portrayed in it are
the work of the author's imagination. Any resemblance to
actual persons, living or dead, events or localities is
entirely coincidental.

HarperCollins*Publishers*
77–85 Fulham Palace Road,
Hammersmith, London W6 8JB

www.harpercollins.co.uk

A Paperback Original 2004
3

Jenny Colgan asserts the moral right to
be identified as the author of this work

A catalogue record for this book
is available from the British Library

ISBN 0 00 715385 6

Typeset in Garamond 3
by Palimpsest Book Production Limited, Polmont, Stirlingshire

Printed and bound in Great Britain by
Clays Ltd, St Ives plc

Acknowledgements

Ali 'the Top' Gunn, Lynne Drew, Maxine Hitchcock, Fiona McIntosh, Jane Harris, Martin Palmer and everyone at HarperCollins, especially the reps; Nick Marston, Tally Garner, Camilla, Carol Jackson, Stephanie Thwaites and everyone at Curtis Brown; Rachel Hore, Deborah Schneider and Emma Draude.

Katrina, Karen, Shappi, Salty Sandra, Danuta da Rhodes, the Writer's Blockettes, without whom this wouldn't be half as great a job as it is; Mueller and Roni; Alex (especially for the website); Kate Rusby and John 'the piano's my main instrument really' McCusker; Robin, Dominic, Michael and Mary Colgan. No thanks to Darius Danesh Management . . . next time we are definitely sticking with Justin Timberlake . . .

To Mr B, who
makes me feel
sixteen every time
he walks in the room. (The good way).

Chapter One

The rain was beating down on the windscreen, as we tried to navigate (rather damply) along the winding country road.

'I hate the country,' I said gloomily.

'Yes, well, you hate everything that isn't fifteen seconds from an overpriced cappuccino,' said Oliver crossly, although in his defence he had been driving from London for six hours.

'I don't hate everything,' I said. 'Only . . . those things over there.'

'What things?'

'Those . . . oh, you know.'

'Cows?'

'Yes, that's it.'

'You can't recognise a cow?'

'Remind me.' He used to think this was really cute.

'It's where your latte comes from,' he said, sighing.

Oliver does like the country. He was born, bred and boarding-schooled here. He couldn't understand why someone who'd lived their whole life in London wouldn't want to get out of it once in a while. I had patiently explained to him several times the necessity of all-night Harts the Grocers, proper bagels, and the choice, if one so wished, to pay six pounds for a bottle of mineral water in a nightclub, but he would bang on about fields and animals as if they were a good thing.

I examined his profile in the dimming light. He looked tired. God, he *was* tired, very tired. So was I. Olly worked for a law firm that did a lot of boring corporate stuff that dragged on for months and was fundamentally big rich bastards (Ol excepted, of course) working out ways to screw other big rich bastards for reasons that remained mysterious, with companies called things that sounded like covers for James Bond. I worked as an accountant for a mega firm – there were thousands of us. I tried to tell people it was more fun than it sounded, but I think after eleven years they could tell by my tone of voice that it wasn't. It had seemed like a nice safe option at the time. It was even fun at first, dressing up and wearing a suit, but recently the sixty-hour weeks, the hideous internal politics, the climate of economic fear, and the Sundays Ol and I spent with our work spread out over the kitchen table were, you know, starting to get to me. I spent a lot of time – *so* much time – in the arid, thrice-breathed air. When we were getting to the end of a deal I'd spend twelve hours a day in there. That was about seventy-five per cent of my waking seconds. Every time I thought about that, I started to panic.

It wasn't that we didn't have a good lifestyle, I reflected, peering out through the rain, and thinking how strangely black it was out here: I hadn't had much total darkness in my life. I mean, we both made plenty of money – Olly would probably even make partner eventually, as he worked really hard. But the shit we went through to get it . . . Jeez.

We took nice holidays, and Olly had a lovely flat in Battersea that I practically lived in. It was a good area, with lots of bars and restaurants and things to do, and if we got round to having kids, it would be a good place to bring them up too. Parks nearby and all that. Good schools, blah blah blah.

Good friends too. The best, really. In fact, that was why we were here, splashing through the mud in the godforsaken middle of nowhere. My oldest friend from school, Tashy, was getting married. Even though we'd both grown up in Highgate, she'd come over all *Four Weddings* when she and Max got engaged, and insisted on hiring some country house hotel out in the middle of nowhere with no connection to either of them.

I was glad she was getting married, give or take the bridegroom. We'd planned this a lot at school. Of course, not until we were at least twenty-two (we were both now thirty-two). In the manner of Princess Diana, if you please (although I'd been to the dress fitting and it was a very sharp and attractive column-style Vera Wang, thank you very much), and we'd probably be marrying Prince Edward (if we'd only known . . .) or John Taylor.

Olly caught me looking at him.

'Don't tell me – you want to drive.'

'Do I fuck.'

He grimaced. 'Look, I know you're tired, but do you really have to swear so much?'

'What? We're not driving the Popemobile. We're all grown-ups.' I wrinkled my nose. 'How would you start to corrupt a lawyer anyway?'

'It's just not nice to hear it.'

'From a lady?'

He sniffed and stared through the windscreen.

I hate it when we get snippy like this, but really, I was exhausted. And now we'd have to go in and be super jolly! And Fun! All Evening! So I could keep Tashy's spirits up. I wondered who else was going to be there. Tashy was a lot better at keeping in touch with people than I was. When really, all I wanted to do on a Friday evening was pour an enormous glass of wine, curl up in front of the TV and drift off before the best of Graham Norton, which might, just might, mean I woke up rested enough either to go to the gym or have sex with Ol (not both).

Oliver stayed quiet, staring out into the darkness. I turned up the radio, which was playing 'Colourblind' by Darius. Eventually he couldn't stand it any longer.

'I can't believe you still listen to music like that.'

'I'm breaking – what – the after-thirty pop music bill of rights?'

'It's just so childish.'

'It's not childish! Darius wrote this all by himself!'

Ol gave me a look. 'That's not what I mean.'

'I'm not listening to Dido, OK? It's not going to happen. I'd rather die.'

'At least she's your age.'

'And what's that supposed to mean?'

Ol shrugged it off, and I let him. I knew why we were squabbling anyway, and it was very little to do with the respective ages of pop musicians.

It put a lot of pressure on a couple, especially our age, when one's friends baled out and got married, I reckoned. I

4

mean, who was next? I was worried it was going to be like musical chairs, and we'd all sit down at once, wherever we happened to be.

'Turn here?'

I looked at Ol, who knew already I wouldn't know. He turned anyway, and a hedge brushed the window. It was very dark.

I mean, everyone was rambling along, having fun, working their guts out all week to get ahead, and pissing away the weekends for fun . . . then suddenly, ding dong, the first thirtieth birthday party and engagement bash invites had fallen on the doormat all at the same time, and we kept finding ourselves trailing round Habitat, buying the same vase over and over again.

I knew Tashy would try to do things slightly differently – everyone does, even if it's just a new place to stencil their initials ('Aren't the salt and pepper cellars in the shapes of our names adorable? And so reasonable!'), but it was still a wedding, wasn't it? There'd be a traditional Church of England service, the one everyone likes with the 'have and holds, for richer for poorer' stuff in it, even though our Sunday religion is strictly the *Observer* and the *People*; there'd be champagne on a lawn somewhere, there'd almost certainly be cold wild salmon at some point, and twelve-to-fourteen hours of pointless drinking before we had to stumble back to some horrid b. & b. somewhere for three hours before pulling ourselves out of bed to stuff full English breakfasts down our necks before piling back on to the motorway, leaving the bride and groom somewhere in a plane en route to the next forty-five years of togetherness, early nights, screaming babies and moving to Wandsworth because the council tax is cheaper and the schools aren't too bad.

Which was fine, of course. Lots of people did it. In fact, at the moment, it seemed a hundred per cent of everyone was doing it. I glanced at Olly. I had a funny feeling in the pit of my stomach that he might be thinking it was about time that he, too, did it. Just little things. Like he took over my bill paying because it would make it more convenient. (It did too; for an accountant I'm shocking with my money, like all those dipso doctors telling you to cut down on the booze. I always leave it till somebody's threatening to come round and total my kneecaps.) Or, maybe we should get a kitten? (If I wanted a small malevolent creature crawling round my kitchen demanding food I'd have a baby, thank you.)

Of course, my mum loved him. He was nothing at all like Dad; he was smartly spoken, and well off – oh – and hadn't left her.

'Not long now,' Olly said then, rubbing my knee in a making-up gesture. And I believed him. It wouldn't be long. Until Olly and I did what Tashy and Max were doing, and all our other friends were doing. Which should make me a lot more excited than I felt.

I shivered involuntarily.

'Are you cold?'

'Do you ever feel old, Ol?'

'Erm, cold or old?'

'Old.'

'Oh,' he said. 'Yes, of course. Well, I suppose, not really. I mean, I thought it might be a bit strange when I turned thirty, but it was all right really. I'm pretty much where I expected to be, don't you think?'

I was surprised at this. 'What do you mean, where you expected to be?'

'You know – by this stage in my life.'

'You mean, when you were younger, you thought about how close to a corporate law partnership you'd be in your thirties?'

He shrugged. 'Well, I took the A levels to get on to a law degree course, so I suppose I must have done.'

'You didn't just take your A levels because your parents wanted you to, but secretly you were going to be a rockstar or a footballer?'

'No! I think I knew by the time I was sixteen I wasn't going to make it as a footballer.'

'Really? I didn't give up on being a gymnast until last year.'

'The only gymnastics I've ever seen you do is accidentally falling out of bed.'

'That's not the point, is it? Don't you ever wonder about how we ended up just here?'

Olly was slowing to a junction, and as he stopped he turned to me and took my face in his hands.

'And what's so wrong with right here?'

The lights of the country hotel were twinkling ahead. Inside were old friends and good company. Here at my side was a decent man. Nothing was wrong at all.

* * *

'Flo! Ol!'

Tash had that massive, slightly manic grin people get when they've been welcoming people for hours. She looked splendid, as well she should, given the draconian diet she'd

7

been on for the past six months 'so my bingo wings don't flap all through the service'.

I gave her a huge hug.

'Elle Macpherson or Martine McCutcheon?' she asked, turning round 360 degrees.

'What, are you kidding? Kate Moss,' I declared.

She beamed even wider. 'Excellent.'

We'd been spending quite a lot of time, in the last few months, going through celebrity magazines and slagging off people getting married. We particularly liked those who go rather – ahem – over the top, like Posh Spice and Catherine Zeta-Jones. Max thought we were being incredibly childish. Oliver didn't know about it, in case he thought I was trying to give him hints, which I wasn't, in a way, although I was also getting to the point where I thought it might be a bit embarrassing if he didn't ask, which I know isn't very romantic.

Tashy is small, occasionally a bit chunky, but thanks to the no-fat, no-bread, no-booze, crying-oneself-to-sleep-with-hunger-pains regime she's been on lately, there was not a pick on her. Her hair was currently extremely glossy and straight, though was, once upon a time, very wild and curly, and her sparkly green eyes betray her past when she went through a career a week and was constantly getting into scrapes. Now she'd settled into being a software designer, which sounded more glamorous than it was (and doesn't sound *very* glamorous at all, really), and was marrying Max, who also worked in computers and who was tall, bald, and very, very dull, but a much better bet, on the whole, I suppose, than the good-looking unruly-haired rogues Tashy had spent most of her twenties waiting to call her,

8

then get off with somebody else. And her boho lool
gone too. Feather earrings and deep plum clothes had
way to a slightly more appropriate look for a nice middle-
class North London girl. In fact, Good God, was she wearing
Boden?

She grabbed me by the arm. 'Come on! Come on! They
can't mix a Martini, but I'm getting married so we're starting
on the champagne we towed back from France.'

'Yes, but you're getting married tomorrow. Isn't not having
a full-on death hangover meant to be part of the whole big
idea?'

'Oh, sod that. One, I'm not going to get any sleep anyway,
and two, someone's coming in with that full body foun-
dation spray thing Sarah Jessica Parker uses. Believe me, you
won't be able to tell if I'm alive or dead underneath it. You
won't believe the work that goes into making all us haggard
over-thirties brides look like freshly awakened virginal
teenagers.'

'You want me to take the bags up then?' said Olly, standing
grumpy in the chintzy hall, which was filled with copper
kettles and random suits of armour.

'Well, do you mind?' I said guiltily.

'Then what am I supposed to do whilst you two go off
and cackle like witches for three hours?'

I stared at him. I looked into his big likeable face. Why
was everything he said tonight really irritating me?

'Can't you go and talk to Max?'

Olly dislikes Max in the way that you're always a little
chippy about people in whom you recognise a bit of yourself.
Plus, he loves Tash to bits and has always been overprotective,
vetting anyone she goes out with.

9

'Is that Ol?' came Max's loud voice from the bar. 'Thought I recognised that clapped-out XR5.'

'I've got some work to catch up on,' said Ol. He yawned ostentatiously, winked and headed upstairs.

'Don't work too . . .' my voice petered out.

* * *

I heard the general sound of merriment through the big oak doors that led to the original ye olde trusty inne section, and sighed.

'Can we not go to the bar?'

'I think if there was ever a good minibar-emptying excuse it's tonight,' said Tash.

I rolled my eyes. 'Yes, because we usually require a parental consent form.'

'How's the lovely Ol then?' she asked as we quietly crept upstairs to avoid the revellers. 'Getting in a romantic mood?'

I think it's a bit insensitive to ask after someone else's love life when you have a big white dress hanging on the back of your door.

'It's fine,' I said. 'I think we must have one of those relationships where you bicker a lot to show you care.'

'Is that true?'

'Yes. People who are too affectionate are overcompensating,' I said blithely. 'Apparently.'

'OK,' said Tash.

'I took a test in a magazine.'

'OK!'

I bounced on the bed in her honeymoon suite. 'Well? Are you excited then?'

'Do I look excited?'

'Not as much as I'd expected, actually.'

She threw herself dramatically on the bedspread to me, widening her eyes. 'Oh, Flo, I just can't believe it . . . you know. It's the dreamiest thing that's ever happened! I'm the luckiest girl in the whole wide world.'

'Oh, shut up. You know what I mean, though. You must be a bit nervous, or something.'

'I am. I really am. It's just, what's as exciting as it's cracked up to be? Nothing.'

'Getting into our first nightclub?'

'Yeah, we were twelve.'

'It was very exciting.'

She grinned. 'Still. It is quite cool.'

'You're actually doing it!'

'I know!'

'That's better.'

I rolled over onto my stomach. 'So is it not going to be what we always thought it was going to be?'

Tashy stuck her lip out a little as we remembered the many hours we'd spent sprawled over her bed (I always liked going to hers; her slightly sluttish mother let us eat in front of the TV) in pretty much the same positions, discussing how it would be.

'Well, I suppose I've had sex already . . .'

'You haven't! You filthy bitch!'

'So that's out of the way. And, also, he's not royal and there aren't six million people lining The Mall with flags to cheer us on our way.'

We were quiet for a moment, and I jumped off the bed and ceremoniously declared the minibar open. It even had Baileys in it. Ooh, we used to love that. Sugary milk!

'Hey — remember these?'

Tashy eyed one up balefully. 'A feature of my first night of unmarried intercourse . . . and, possibly, my last.'

I tore them open and we toasted each other.

'To true love,' I said.

'Aha-ha-ha.'

Actually, I'd meant it. I took a swig.

'Just think — you'll never have to make love to a man who slaps you on the rump and calls you a filly ever again!'

'Neiighhhh!!!!'

'Or date ANYBODY SHORT.'

Olly and Max were both very tall. These were our minimum requirements. We'd always reckoned that short men for girls were the equivalent of that horrible joke blokes tell — 'What have fat girls and scooters got in common? They're both fun to ride, but you wouldn't want your mates seeing you with one.'

'Or snog anyone for a dare.'

'Or sympathy.'

'Christ, yeah. Remember Norm?'

'It was charity work,' I replied indignantly. 'Helping the less blessed in the world.'

Norm had been something of a mistake, something of a long time ago.

Norm had been a snuffling pig, outright winner in an ugly pig competition.

'Anyway, why are you starting, Bridezilla? What about Pinocchio?'

Pinocchio told a lot of lies and had a very long narrow woody.

'Pour me some more Baileys immediately,' demanded Tashy.

'I don't want to give you a headache.'

'Are you joking? We've booked singers from the local choral society to sing the hymns. No one's getting out alive without a headache.' She rolled over.

'It's turning out all right, though, isn't it?'

'We thought that at sixteen.'

'Oh yeah, when we hadn't gotten pregnant. God, we knew nothing.'

'I think we thought that was it, didn't we? That we'd cracked it.'

'And at any moment, the knight in shining armour was just outside putting money in the meter . . .'

'Can you believe both of our Prince Charmings are going bald?' said Tash meditatively.

'Yours fastest,' I said defensively.

'It's all the testosterone building up from me being too tired to shag him after planning this damn wedding.'

'Does not shagging them make them bald? We could have saved Prince Edward after all.'

'No we couldn't.'

The thing is, when your friends fall in love – seriously – it gets very difficult to discuss the boys with them any more. It's fine to completely and totally dissect someone you've seen twice because they look a bit like Pierce Brosnan and can get gig tickets, but once it creeps into the full time – watch telly with, wash socks of, etc. – it becomes impossible. It's like discussing somebody's naked dad.

Max was just so sensible, so safe. He just . . . he just didn't get it. And he didn't seem to know the lovely Tashy I remembered, haring down the seafront at Brighton with her heels in her hands at four a.m., or marching us off through

Barcelona because she thought she knew the way and was buying the sangria, or dancing all night on top of a bar, or taking her stuffed rabbit on holiday until she was twenty-six . . . I know people think this about all their friends, but Max . . . he was all right, but I didn't really think he was good enough for my her. I wanted someone who could match her, dirty giggle for dirty giggle, not someone who could help her work out her SERPS contributions and had strong views on the education of children.

Of course I knew this was how it was going to work. We'd even devised the Buffy scale of life relationships: you start off wanting Xander, spend your twenties going out with Spike and settle down with Giles. Which seemed to mean Tashy had never had a chance at an Angel. And, I suppose, neither had I. I didn't believe in angels, anyway. I didn't believe in much.

* * *

We leafed through a celebrity wedding edition of *OK!* magazine for the last time together as single girls. For one of us at least (and me too, of course, I'm never having bloody gold-rimmed parasols), the chances of ever having an elephant attending our wedding, being carried in on the shoulders of gold-painted slaves, spending over $2,000,000 on flowers, marrying someone older than our dads because they were very, very rich indeed, insisting all the guests wore a certain colour and weren't allowed to talk to you, the press or the special bought-in soap celebrities, were about to vanish for ever.

We sighed as we flicked over to some other minor star, who had designed her own dress (which showed, in that it looked exactly like the highly inflated numbers we used to draw in primary school, complete with more flounces than Elton John playing tennis), and had fifteen flower girls, including seven she barely knew but who happened to be in a similar television show – plus one girl who was so ugly she had to be close family, but had been zipped into skin-tight, bust-squeezing fuchsia anyway, next to the telly lollipop girls, looking like the unhappiest whale in captivity.

'"I haven't been able to sleep for months with the excitement,"' I read the bride said. 'Really? Do you think? Months?'

Tashy glanced at the gushing copy. 'They've only been together for six months. It'll all be over by Christmas. She'll be able to give hundreds of interviews about her heartache. It'll make her feel really famous. No wonder she's excited.'

'Huh,' I said. 'Plus, you know, celebrities: they have to fall in love ten times harder than the rest of us.'

'I know,' said Tashy. 'It must get really boring for Jen and Brad. They've been married for ever and people keep asking them if they're still as divinely in love as they were when they first met. Well, they aren't. *Nobody* is,' she said, addressing the magazine sternly.

'Do you remember when we were bridesmaids for Heather?' I asked suddenly. Heather is Tashy's big sister. She'd had to ask me too because we were so inseparable. We had had an absolutely great time. It was the eighties, so our dresses were enormous. We were allowed to wear a huge amount of blue makeup, white tights, and dance with all the boys wearing shiny Jonathan Ross suits. As Heather pointed out later, in a rare wistful moment after the divorce, we'd had much, much more fun than she had. At the time, we wouldn't have

15

believed that to be possible. We thought she was the most beautiful and enviable living thing we'd ever seen.

'Oh, yeah. Don't. I asked her if she wanted to be my matron of honour, and she snorted and said, "Thanks, but if you want to get involved in all that garbage, please do it without me, Natasha," and went back to doing yoga and eating muesli.'

'It is a real shame he got the sense of humour in the divorce,' I said, and Tashy nodded glumly.

Then she popped her head up from the magazine. 'Um.'

'What?'

She jumped up and got us another Baileys.

'What?' I said.

'Well, you know when you were talking about us being stupid at sixteen?'

'Mm?'

'You'll never guess who my mother ran into at the post office. Invited the whole family.'

I rather love Jean, Tashy's mother. She is giggly and dresses too young for her age and drinks too many gin and tonics – all the reasons she embarrasses the bits out of Tashy. It's amazing how, even though we're both in our thirties, we still turn into sulky teenagers when confronted with our mothers. It had been worse recently, with all the wedding arrangements for Tash, and there had been at least two occasions when Tashy had slammed out of the house shouting – and she was ashamed to relate this, even after a couple of glasses of wine – 'Stop trying to control my life!' She had also decided that since she and Tashy's dad (they were divorced, and got on a lot better than my parents) were paying for most of this enormous bash, they got final say in just about all of it, which included the guest list, the napkins, and those tortuously crap little sugared almond things. ('Why am I crying over sugared almonds?' Tashy had asked me. 'I'm not going to talk to her for a week. Cow.') She is so different from my mother, who does indeed have nightmares after *Crimewatch*.

But this wasn't solving the problem.

'Who?'

'We're over it now, right?'

And I knew straight away.

'This is why you stashed all this Baileys up here, isn't it? To soften me up?'

She nodded shamefacedly.

'You invited Clelland.'

* * *

'His whole family,' said Tashy, at least having the grace to look a bit embarrassed. 'You know our parents were friends first, before any of us lot even went to school. All those seventies kaftan parties. Probably all throwing their keys in bowls.'

'Let's not think about that,' I said. I might be an ancient grown-up, but I still didn't like to think about my parents doing it. And also, my heart was pounding, and my ageing brain was trying to take this on board.

'Anyway, they lost touch, but my mother ran into his mother at the post office – seriously, if she thinks she's going to be thinner than me for this wedding then she's got another think coming, upstaging bitch – so, anyway, they get talking and, of course, Mum can't stop shooting her mouth off imme-diately and—'

'Hang on,' I said, interrupting her nervous chatter and sitting dramatically upright. 'Clelland is coming?'

'Um, yeah.'

'OK, so can we forget the boring post office stuff . . . ?'

'Gee, gosh, you're right, Flo. How selfish of me. It's not like I'm busy or anything.'

'It's just . . . God, you know, I could have done with some warning.'

'Me too,' said Tashy. 'I don't think they'll even all fit under the marquee.'

Of course, even though she'd been through it, I couldn't really expect Tash to take this as seriously as I did. And, of course, Clelland isn't his real name. Nobody's called that, except probably some American soap star. Our parents were friends, and his dad is John Clelland, so he is too. The grown-ups called him little John, which he hated with such a vibrant passion he refused to answer to anything except for his surname until we got used to it. Then we discovered that porn book *Fanny Hill*, author John Cleland, and it was even worse.

That's Clelland. Passionate about things. He had been my first crush. Tashy's first crush had displayed her painstakingly homemade Valentine card all over the sixth-form common room to loud and lewd guffaws. Mine had been completely unaware of my existence for months. I'd really envied Tashy.

He was tall for his age, dark-haired, with expressive eyebrows: he was studious and intense-looking. He stalked around on his own a lot, which at the time I thought made him romantic and individual rather than, as I supposed now, horribly lonely and 'going through an awkward stage', as my mother puts it. And he had double English on Mondays and Thursdays, which was good, as, crossing over from chemistry, I could accidentally be there to say hello to him, Tashy stumbling along beside me, giggling her head off. He had to say hello to me because our parents knew each other, even though he was two years older and thus anything else would have been completely *verboten*.

At family parties he would sit in corners, dressed all in black, grumpily reading Jean-Paul Sartre or *The Lord of the Rings*, listening to Echo and the Bunnymen on his Walkman, refusing to eat meat from the barbecue, and the adults would all cluck and giggle over him and I would be furious with them on his behalf, but never brave enough to go up and say more than hello, red-faced and twisted up inside.

So, for a long time I was just one of the annoying people buzzing around him, trying to get him to clean out his bedroom. Until the year I turned sixteen. Big year that one.

And now I had one day's notice to see him again. Sixteen years on.

* * *

At my birthday just a few weeks before, when I turned thirty-two, we went to Bluebird, and had a nice posh dinner out and drank Veuve Clicquot and everyone talked about someone we knew who was getting divorced, which made us feel better about most of us not even being married yet, apart from Tashy, who was about to get married and looked green for most of the evening. Then someone kicked off about house prices, and none of the women would eat the delicious bread, and the smart sex toys and silly things people had bought me started to look a bit stupid, and I started to feel almost impolite to insist that everyone came out and spent what turned out to be an absolute ton of money to celebrate with me for seemingly no reason. Then we got home and I was unreasonably rude to Olly and spent half an hour with the magnifying mirror counting wrinkles, then I wondered if I was ever going to have a baby and then I went to sleep. It wasn't always like that.

Tashy and I had planned my sixteenth birthday party with almost as much precision as we planned this wedding, and with a lot more excitement. There was going to be some sort of sparkling wine, a punch. 'I'm making it!' said Dad sternly. 'I don't want anyone being sick.'

'But you're not going to stay upstairs!' I whined.

'Of course we are. Do you think we've never been to a teenage party before? We'll be patrolling upstairs. With guns.'

'PLLLEEEEAAASSEEE! It'll be the worst birthday party ever.'

Finally, bless them, they'd borrowed Clelland's little brother's baby monitor and set it upstairs, then gone to the pub next door with it practically stapled to their ears. I was the only one who threw up.

There was a reason I was looking forward to this party. I had my first ever boyfriend.

Clelland had actually been away most of that summer. I'd moped around like a nightmare, working in the Co-op and contriving to make my parents' lives a misery. Then, right at the end of one afternoon . . . he'd walked in, brown, thin, and heartstopping.

'Hello,' said Clelland, looking up from his bag of vegetables, which he had to buy and cook himself, in his parents' efforts to get him out of this stupid vegetarian phase he was going through (I thought this was thrillingly noble).

'Hi there.'

I gulped. My international crush – more than Paul Young, John Taylor and Andrew Ridgeley in one – was here, standing right before me . . . looking fit and tanned. I had to be cool. I had to be!

'Haven't seen you around,' I said dully.

'Hi,' he said, swallowing too. 'Well, I went off travelling for a bit.'

'Really?' I stuttered. 'Nice.'

'Not really.' He shrugged unconvincingly, looking around the dingy dungeon and nylon uniform I'd clearly spent my summer in. 'But I met a few people, you know. Students and stuff, hanging out. Then we all went to Spain, found this really cheap place, we worked as grape crushers and slept out under the stars. They let us drink as much wine as we wanted. Then we took the money we made and all went to Glastonbury for five days. But it wasn't that great or anything.'

'Good!' I said. 'I mean, sorry you had a rotten time.'

'Yes? What's been happening?'

'Well, erm . . . Ratboy kicked in the bus shelter and they had to put a new one up. Then he kicked it in again.'

Clelland bit his lip. 'What time do you get off?'

I felt as if I'd been punched in the stomach.

'Um . . .' I said. I genuinely couldn't remember.

We walked home that evening in the warmth, and he bought me a bag of chips and we lay on the heath and ate them looking at stars maybe not quite as good as those over Spanish vineyards, but I liked them. Then we kissed and kissed and kissed, salty sticky kisses for hours and hours and hours in the way only teenagers can, entwined like two vines

21

growing together. Then, finally, when the adults – the seedy, the dispossessed – started to arrive, we slowly headed for home, my insides turning somersaults all the way.

We had a few glorious weeks. Kissing, reading, talking, slumping around complaining about our parents, drinking cider, pretending not to know each other if we ran into anyone from school in town, not having sex. Actually, that rather amazes me now. I assumed everyone was like me, and now I find that even my most respectable friends (in fact, the posher they are the more like rabbits they start) were romping in the hay from their early teens whilst I was pushing his hand away, desperate to do more, but desperate not to put myself out on a limb.

Good Lord, I was useless. And look what I missed out on, thinking all the boys would be so great. It took years after that to get the hang of it, and truly, I would have loved to have maturely and pleasingly enjoyed adult relations when I had a pin waist, boy's bum and upper arms that pinged. Life is a bitch.

But then, I thought it was perfect. We went down to Brighton, tentatively hired a scooter, and I felt that I was living *la Dolce Vita*. We kissed on rocks, behind trees, on trains, everywhere possible, and the sensitive introverted lad turned out to be funny, gentle, idiosyncratic and only inclined to go on about George Orwell, Hunter S. Thompson and Holden Caulfield when I wasn't paying attention. We adored each other. Until –

'Aberdeen?' I stared at him.

He was trying to look sad and not excited by going to university at the same time.

'It was clearing. You know. I almost didn't get to go at all.'

22

'Where is Aberdeen? Is it on an island or what?'

'No, it's in the North of Scotland.'

'Do they speak English?'

'Yes, I believe so.'

I stared at him in disbelief.

I left him in the sitting room, went out to the garage, took out my dad's old road map and traced down the two boxes on the grid where places meet.

Aberdeen is five hundred and eight miles away from London.

'Aberdeen,' I said, taking a deep breath and trying to speak slowly, even though my heart was beating fit to burst and I wasn't sure whether or not I was about to start crying, 'is the furthest away from London you can possibly go.'

'I know,' said Clelland, half smiling that funny little crinkly smile. 'It's either that or the local technical college.'

'You're leaving me,' I said, and all the poise I'd sought to hold on to had lasted less than fifteen seconds. At the time too, though, I couldn't help but be slightly aware of the drama of it all.

'Oh, Flora sweetie...' He took me in his arms. 'I'm going away. I'm going to university. It wouldn't matter where I was going. We're only young, you know?'

The lump in my throat was like trying to swallow a rocket. 'But we're in love!'

He hugged me and held me close. 'I know. I know. You and me. Taking over the world, remember?'

'From five hundred and eight miles away.'

He looked pained; he must have known then, or at least had an inkling, about what happens to childhood sweethearts when one of them moves on. And I think I saw it too.

'I'll be back at holidays,' he offered lamely, as if trying to meet me halfway.

My mother caught me pounding up the stairs to my room.

'What's the matter, darling?'

'NOTHING!' I shouted in true teenage style, completely oblivious to any concept that she might understand what was happening – only too well, as I was to discover in a year or two. How could she? How could anyone know? Nobody had ever been in love like I had. No one was as special as Clelland. Nobody could see.

From my window I watched him as, after waiting half an hour, he slouched awkwardly down the garden path, and I wept with the magnificently dramatic thought that I would never see him again.

Oh God, the party. I tried to call it off, but Tashy and my mother had persuaded me that of course Clelland would show up. Plus we'd invited everyone.

The thing is, popularity is a tricky thing. It's infectious. We couldn't help it. It was the local comprehensive, it was pretty rough and, for some reason or another, that year everyone had decided to hate us.

I hadn't thought it would extend to a party, though. After all, everyone likes parties, don't they?

I was wearing a faintly daring red dress from Clockhouse, which I absolutely adored and spent the entire evening pulling down and panicking about whether I looked fat. (As the photos show, I looked teeny. Why on earth didn't I realise how lucky I was before I had to wear long sleeves with every-thing and couldn't brave the miniskirt any more?) How depressing. When I see all the teenagers these days marching around wearing next to nothing, Britney-style, I don't think, ooh, look at that awful paedo-fodder. Well, sometimes I do a bit. But mostly I think, go for it, girls, because as soon as I became a student I went straight into dungarees and baggy jumpers mode, and I never got that body back again.

Tashy had done my makeup, which involved something we'd read in *Jackie* magazine. We tried to copy it laboriously and somewhat unfortunately, and I had two pin-sharp lines of pink blusher up each cheek and very, very heavy blue eyeshadow. Actually, it would probably be all right now; I'd probably look like Sophie Ellis Bextor. If she was thirty-two and average-looking, instead of twenty-four and some kind of alien high priestess.

I'd put on my nicest bra, brushed my teeth a thousand times and was desperately, desperately hoping that only one boy would ever walk up the garden path.

Not a single person came.

We sat and drank the punch and ate the crisps, and couldn't even speak to each other. Tashy and I clung and tried to pretend not to cry. I looked at my best friend and felt my heart shrivel and die. This was life's test. We were failing.

'After this, school is going to be *so* much better,' vowed Tash fiercely. We considered wrecking a few things anyway, just so my parents would think some people had arrived. But we didn't. We ended up watching *Dynasty*. It was the longest four hours of my life. My mascara ran down and soaked my Clockhouse dress.

A few weeks later, my dad left us. About this time of year, in fact, as far as I remembered. Well, that would be a nice anniversary for my mum tomorrow.

* * *

Tashy was still talking, but I wasn't listening. I was remembering the night I turned sixteen.

'Your problem is, you think you only have one true love,' Tashy was saying, bringing me back to earth.

'Yes,' I said.

'NO!' she said. 'That's not it at all! What I mean is, it won't feel quite the same, but that's just because it's not new any more. It's just different.'

'Less exciting.'

'Well, you can't experience everything as if it's the first time round forever.'

'That's why being grown up is so sucky,' I said. 'I can't even remember what it was like the first time I read *The Lion, the Witch and the Wardrobe*. But it was the most exciting thing that had happened to me at the time.'

'Oh, you wouldn't want to be sixteen again, would you? It was hell. Oh God, do you remember that party . . . ?'

'No,' I said. 'It *was* hell then,' I agreed, thinking about all the times Tashy and I had sat eating lunch, worrying madly about whether one breast was growing faster than the other and whether Loretta McGonagall was talking about us (she was) and whether we'd get invited to Marcus's party (no, even though we asked him, the bastard. Just because we didn't wear stiletto heels and make out. Well, of course that was the reason). 'If I had to do it all again with what I know now I wouldn't make such a hash of it.'

Tashy sat up. 'You haven't made a hash of anything!' she said. 'Look at you. Good job. Smart car. Lovely bloke.'

'Yeah, yeah, yeah,' I said, staring at the ceiling. 'Do you remember what you and I said we were going to do when we finished school?'

Tashy thought for a moment and then laughed out loud 'Oh, yes. We were going to buy a car, travel through Europe, drawing cartoons and portraits, end up in Paris, rich and famous, live in a garret, buy a cat, then . . . let me see . . . I was going to marry a prince of some sort, and you were going to move to New York and look a lot like Audrey Hepburn.'

Since I've turned thirty I've become a bit pissed off with Audrey Hepburn. We all grow up with her, and it can't be done. Get your tits fixed and you could look like Pamela Anderson. Get cow arse injected in your lips and you could probably handle Liz Hurley. Wrinkle your nose and brush your hair a lot and you might get to marry Brad Pitt. But nobody, nobody but nobody, has ever looked as beautiful as Audrey Hepburn, and it causes untold misery in the interim. Have you seen the actress that played her in a mini-series? She looks like a cross-eyed, emaciated, buck-toothed wren compared to Audrey, and that's the best they could get from the population of the whole world. Anyway.

'Anyway,' I said, 'call me crazy, but maybe I'd have planned for that better by not immediately going to university to study accountancy then working for a company for ten hours a day for eleven years.'

'I am calling you crazy,' said Tashy. 'There are hardly any princes left in Europe, and we don't want Albert, thanks.'

'Hmm,' I grumped.

'Flo, we did everything right, you know. Everything we were told. We looked after ourselves. And this is our reward. Good lives. Fun.'

'If I was sixteen again . . .' I said wistfully.

'What?'

'I'd shag Clelland to within an inch of his life.'

'I wish you had,' said Tashy. 'Then you could have found out he was a weedy little indy freak, as nervous and teenage and odd-smelling as the rest of us, and then you could have stopped going on about him every time you got drunk for the next decade and a half.'

'I do not!' I protested. 'And anyway, you do not have a romantic soul,' I said, pointing at her.

'Yeah? Well, what's that, BABY?'

And she pointed to the dress hanging on the back of the door.

* * *

'You seem distracted,' Olly said as I slowly ironed my Karen Millen trouser suit. I'd loved it when I bought it, but did it now seem a bit . . . matronly? Old? Not exactly the kind of thing I wanted my first love to see me in?

'Not at all,' I said, in a completely distracted kind of a way, staring straight out of the window.

'Are you pissed off your best friend's getting married?'

'You know, I've heard of people who got married and survived,' I said. 'Not many, though.'

'Well, don't worry,' he said, looking at me with a twinkle in his eye, and suddenly I got a really strong feeling that he was planning something. In fact I knew he was. And I wasn't sure how that made me feel. It might have made me nervous, if I wasn't already incredibly nervous at the thought of coming face to face with Clelland again. Ridiculous, I know; so immature. It was just, I'd never run into him whenever I'd gone back home for Christmas or anything and . . . well, it was just interesting, that was all. He wasn't on his Friends

Reunited page either. Not that I checked a lot. I checked all the time, mentally giving points to people I thought were doing worse or better than me.

'For God's sake! Those bloody dry-cleaners have shrunk my trousers. Useless bloody bastards. I'm going to sue them.' Olly sucked his stomach in.

'Yes, dear,' I said, suddenly realising, as I stood there with an iron in my hand, how much I was starting to sound like my mother.

Chapter Two

It was a lovely day for a wedding, if you like that sort of thing. This was about the eighteenth I'd been to this year, but it was still very nice. I suppose it was a bit different, being Tashy's. I was very glad Tashy hadn't pushed me about being the bridesmaid. When we were sixteen it was all we talked about, but brides over thirty have enough problems looking young and innocent as it is, without an Ancient Mariner hanging grimly by her side, trying to make light conversation with the ushers and ignore the whispers ('Such a shame she's not gone yet . . .'; 'They do leave it so late, the lassies these days . . .') and Tashy's young niece, Kathleen, would do a perfect job of looking fresh and sixteen and completely overexcited, though trying to be too cool to show it – not entirely unlike we had been, it had to be said.

The church was cool and pretty as we slipped into seats near the front row, nodding and waving to everyone. No sign of *him*, and my parents weren't coming till later. There is something incredibly evocative about a traditional English wedding ceremony, and this one was done beautifully; so much so that when they started up the Wedding March, I choked back a tear. Olly gave me a meaningful look.

Tashy looked wondrous, of course. She has excellent taste, and that eat-nothing-that-doesn't-taste-of-poo diet had certainly worked. Her ivory sheath was incredibly tasteful, with gorgeous embroidered shoes just peeping out the bottom, matching the long lilies she held. I wondered briefly if she was going to burst out of her dress later after going into a crazed frenzy at the vol-au-vents table, then remembered that the point of a wedding is that you watch everyone else consume vast screeds of booze and nosh you've paid for but can't partake in, in case you do something rash, like enjoy yourself. But here, in the peace and stillness of the old church, I couldn't be cynical.

The vows were very traditional, and Max looked all right too, gruffly uming and erring over the responses – not that anyone was looking at him, of course. Even when we were kids, grooms always had something of an interchangeable quality to them. It was Barbie who was important. Ken was neither here nor there.

My eyes had kept scanning the pews for Clelland, just in case, but I couldn't see him. Maybe he was that bald geezer over there . . . or that enormously fat chap wearing the colourful waistcoat . . .

'God, how long is this going to go on for?' whispered Oliver with a wink, although he had just been singing 'Jerusalem' loudly and off key, and was clearly having a sensational time. I swallowed, guiltily.

* * *

31

'I hope there aren't too many prawns,' Olly was saying as we walked into the large marquee, which was bedecked with flowers and ruffled decorations. The sun was glinting off lots of very clean silverware and shiny glasses, waiting to be replenished on into the night. One billion photographs later and I still hadn't seen Clelland.

'Or anything with nuts. Or salad cream.'

'I'm sure the Blythes are far too posh for salad cream,' I said, and squeezed his hand chummily.

Olly was the pickiest eater I'd ever met in my life. I thought they thrashed that out of you thoroughly at boarding school, but I was obviously wrong, because he refused to eat most things that weren't cheese or fish fingers, on various spurious grounds.

'Well, you know viscous things upset my stomach.'

'All fluids upset your stomach.'

'Glooky ones most of all.'

I took a quick look at the hors-d'oeuvres coming over. Excellent – sausages on sticks, with a slightly pretentious veneer of sesame seeds over the top. He'd be able to cope with those, once he'd picked off the seeds. And I guessed I'd better make my way over to the bride as well, once I got half a—

My heart stopped in my throat. There he was, about ten feet away from me. Clelland. Looking exactly the same. In fact, if anything, he looked even younger. Then he turned his head away and disappeared into the crowd.

'Oh my God!' I said.

'I know. Sesame seeds,' said Oliver unhappily.

'No, no. It's just, I've seen an old friend. I have to go and say hello to . . . them.'

'OK. I'm off to pat Max hard on the back as a kind of non-gay way of saying well done,' said Oliver.

I walked over to where Clelland had been. But even as I got there, I felt something was wrong. Was my mind playing tricks on me? How could that be such an exact replica of someone I hadn't seen for sixteen years? I mean, people change in sixteen years, don't they? It would be completely impossible for it to be otherwise. I mean, of course, I'd hardly changed, thanks to the miracles of modern cosmetics. . . well, maybe I had a bit. Suddenly I gulped and smoothed down my hair. Did he have a picture rotting away in his attic?

I spotted his dark jacket again. He was talking to one of the waitresses with his back to me. I took a deep breath and walked up to him.

* * *

'Erm . . . hey there!'

The man turned round. And at once I realised my mistake. The likeness, though, was absolutely extraordinary. The figure stared at me. This wasn't a man at all, hardly more than a boy.

'Sorry, but . . . oh, you look familiar.'

'I'm Flora Scurrison,' I said warily.

His face was furrowed in concentration for another minute, then he broke into an enormous smile. 'Oh my God! Don't you remember me?'

Something was ringing at the back of my mind.

'It's Justin!'

Justin, Justin . . .

Suddenly it hit me.

'Oh my God.'

'Yeah!'

'You're Clelland's little brother.'

The one with the baby monitor.

'Yes! I recognise you from the photos.'

'I am SO OLD,' I said, almost without realising it.

'Everyone keeps coming up and telling me how much I've grown. I am nearly seventeen, actually. Quite grown up.' He looked petulant all of a sudden and I was reminded overwhelmingly of Clelland.

'You look a lot like your brother.'

'I do not.'

'He does not,' said a deep voice.

I looked up.

'Hello, Flora. Justin, scram.'

'You always treat me like a kid,' scowled Justin.

'That's because you sulk and whine all the time.'

Justin sulked off, whining.

'He'll be OK. He needs to eat about nine times a day, so the buffet's probably the best place for him.'

Clelland was . . . well, it was impossible I'd have mistaken him for anyone other than himself.

He had filled out, of course; he couldn't possibly be as absurdly skinny as he had been; that would have been David Bowie and nobody else. But his black, unruly hair was just the same as ever.

'I thought he was you,' I said, not trusting myself beyond a short sentence.

'God, really?' He glanced behind him at his brother, mooching off. 'Was I such a slouching runt at that age?'

'Worse!' I gave a very peculiar slightly strangulated laugh. 'At least he's not wearing a Morrissey T-shirt. Every day!'

'I loved that T-shirt.'

'I know.'

I held out my hand. 'Clelland, it's good to see you.'

'Oh God, it's John. Please. Nobody calls me that any more.'

'No, really? I thought you swore you'd never get tied down into "bourgeois tying-down name fascism".'

'Yeah? And do you still spell your name P-f-l-o-w?'

'No,' I said, going scarlet.

'So. . . what have you been up to?' He looked. . . he looked great. And wryly amused to see me.

'Oh, lots of things,' I said, as he easily lifted two glasses of champagne off a passing waiter.

'Yeah?'

'No!' I said. 'Well, I went to university then got a job and moved back to London.'

'That's three things.'

'Over quite a long period.'

We stood for a moment.

'What have you been doing then?' I asked awkwardly.

Oddly, I could see over my shoulder, Justin had bumped into Olly at the buffet and was pointing out foodstuffs to him.

Clelland – John, but I really couldn't think of him any other way – shrugged.

'Well, I went to Aberdeen.'

'I remember that,' I said quietly.

'Yes, of course,' he said, looking slightly awkward for a second, which came as a big relief to me. From the way our conversation had been going, I was beginning to wonder if I'd made up the whole romance in a psychotic episode and

35

we were distant acquaintances greeting each other at a Rotary Club dance.

'Then I joined VSO for a couple of years – get out and see the world, you know.'

'Oh yes. Where did you end up?'

'Africa.'

'Wow, that's amazing!'

'Complete and utter shithole. I hated every second of it. I wanted to catch malaria so they'd have to send me home.'

'God, I haven't wanted you to die for ages,' I said, before my brain had properly engaged. It was not a good moment. Olly stumbled over.

'Jesus, Flo, I can't eat a damn thing. Do you know they have almonds in the salad? You'd think they'd put on a few fish fingers just in case. This is going to be even worse than the Stricklands' wedding, and that made me sick.'

'You were drunk.'

'God, yeah.'

Clelland raised his eyebrows.

'This is Oliver,' I introduced him. 'My, er, boyfriend.'

Why the 'er'? I was conscious that perhaps I wasn't sounding as thrilled as I could.

Clelland put his hand out. 'Hi.'

'Hi,' said Olly, holding out his hand.

'Clelland's an old school friend.'

I'd never told Olly about Clelland. At first it was because I was obeying the 'don't tell new boyfriend about exes; they must think you're a virgin' type bullshit law. And then . . . well, some things are private. Also, I think if we knew all about how people behaved when they were teenagers, no one would ever go out with anyone.

'Nice to meet you,' said Olly gruffly.

Looking at them both, I felt very strange suddenly. comparing them. Definitely not. This was not a competitive thing. Clelland still had a chance to appear a complete prick.

'Olly's a lawyer,' I said helpfully.

'Really? And I shook your hand?' said Clelland, and smiled.

I'd hardly ever seen his smile. Not something suburban rebels do very often, smile. They talk about suicide and Leonard Cohen quite a lot. It was lovely. His teeth were slightly crooked, and the incisors pointed in.

'Oh gosh, yes, sorry about that. But we only really screw you if you're a multinational, our lot,' said Ol. 'Just the sixth circle of hell really.'

'So you're not one of those chaps that advertises on telly for fat ladies who fall off their chairs at work?'

'No. Although I help Flo, you know, when it happens at home,' he said with a grin.

'Yes,' said Clelland in the way people have to when someone makes a slightly off-colour remark. I couldn't tell if he thought it was funny either.

'What line are you in then?' said Olly, half eyeing a wait-ress carrying a bowl of prawn toast. He reached out a hand and took four.

'How come you can eat sesame seeds on toast and not on sausages?' I said without thinking. Both the boys looked at me.

'Because it's toast,' said Olly, as if explaining to a four-year-old. 'Anything can be done with toast.'

Clelland stuck his bottom lip out at me.

'Um . . . I'm an ethical logistician.'

'A what?' I said.

'Oh. Do you perform on stage a lot?' said Ol. 'Puppets and so on?'

'No . . .'

'OK, what is that then?'

'Well, I try to direct aid through the best routes. Try to play down the possibility of it being hijacked by armies, that kind of thing.'

I admit it. My heart leaped. This was exactly the kind of thing I'd have dreamed he'd be doing. Well, that or some sort of tragic *Moulin Rouge*-style poet, obviously, but this – heroic, good for the world, manly – I had a vision of him standing on top of an elephant, for some reason. Then, I'm ashamed to say, one of me looking like Meryl Streep in *Out of Africa*-style linens, saying, 'I hed a ferm in Efrica . . .'

'I hate it,' said Clelland. 'It's a pissy job.'

'Really? It sounds interesting,' said Olly.

'Everyone says that.' He ran his hand through his dark hair. 'It's bloody endless government bureaucracy, and as to how much good we even do at the end of the day I couldn't tell you. Certainly doesn't seem to make anything any better. God, I'm sorry. Am I being really depressing at a wedding? Was I always like this?'

He looked directly at me, and I couldn't meet his eyes. Get a grip, I told myself fiercely. Any minute, surely, Olly was going to spot the hot vibes coming out of my head and give me serious trouble.

'You were worse,' I said.

* * *

At Heather's wedding, just before my birthday, I had flirted madly with the best man, danced up and down with the ushers and ended up sharing a bottle of champagne down by the fountain with a grumpy-looking Clelland, who was talking about the bollocksy bourgeois imperative of forced enslavement. It was all rubbish, of course. It's just coincidence it came true for Tashy's sister.

'I'm never getting married,' he'd said, and my little teenage heart had dropped. What was I thinking? That we were going to run away to Gretna Green? Why did I think men two years older than me were grown up? Because I didn't know anything else, I suppose.

'Oh,' I said, fingering the fading roses of my bouquet. I dabbled my hand in the fountain in what I hoped was an alluring manner.

'Ritualised enslavement,' he grumped, pulling me to him. 'For men and women.'

His long thin hand brushed across the top of the lace on my dress. I shivered. We had done heavy, long-distance, serious snogging, but I still had a very heavy layer of being-a-non-slut, anti-aids parental-warnings, throw-it-all-away-pregnant-schoolgirl outright fear morality hanging over my head and hadn't let him go any further than the waistband of my C&A knickers.

'You're lovely,' he said. I beamed. He took this as an excuse to slide his hand up the sixteen layers of tulle I was wearing. Unsurprisingly, he got fatally lost on the way, and the whole romance of the fountain started to peter away as we kissed onwards, he groping desperately somewhere heavily hemmed only slightly north of my knees.

The more he pawed around, frantic, the more awkward and embarrassed I became. This wasn't how they described it in our purloined copies of *Cosmopolitan* at all. And there certainly wasn't much of this going on in *Lace*, or *Sweet Valley High*.

'Oh God,' said Clelland in lust and frustration.

I gulped, still at the stage of kissing when you're very conscious of what to do with your saliva.

'Erm . . .' I said.

Then he found it.

'Ooh!' I said.

He looked at me, but with a misty expression in his eyes, like he couldn't really see me.

I gulped again. 'I can't,' I said firmly.

'What – never?' he said, focusing on me.

'I don't know . . .'

'I'm sorry,' he said, 'but you are m-my girlfriend, Flo, and I-I thought . . .'

He was so red-faced I thought his head might explode. This new stutter wasn't helping either.

'I . . . I don't think so.'

'Of course,' he said.

'Everyone! Bridesmaids! Ushers!' I heard Tashy's mum calling from the house. 'Come on! We're cutting the cake!'

We looked at each other, two frightened deer.

Clelland went to withdraw his hand but before he could I had stood up quickly. I was as pink as my skirt as I ran to the house, leaving him there looking after me, confused.

* * *

Heather looked a picture, her hair as enormously rigid as it had been that morning, but now teetering unpredictably to the left.

She held her hand over Merrill's. The cake was a ludicrous,

six-storey pink and white nightmare, flowers curling crisply round every corner. I shut my eyes tight.

'What are you doing?' whispered Tashy, who I'd been relieved to find when I came in.

'Making a wish when they cut the cake.'

'You don't make a wish when you cut a cake at a wedding. You're thinking of blowing out candles at a birthday.'

'You do too make a wish,' I said, cross with her.

'Even if you did, it wouldn't be your wish, would it? It would be theirs, asking for lots of children or something. Yuk! Imagine Heather making babies!'

'Yuk!' I said, smiling and felt slightly better. They raised the knife. I shut my eyes anyway.

'I wish . . . I wish I was grown up, and love was easy.'

* * *

Funnily enough, when the photos had been taken and the glasses raised, I did feel different, in a strange way. I put it down to that miraculous change that's meant to happen to you when you're coming of age, like getting your national insurance number, but which I'd never felt before.

Now, however, a boy had touched me. I was a woman. I had made a woman's choice. I was going to behave like one. And also, of course, I was desperate not to lose him.

I walked straight up to Clelland, looking so out of place in the black shirt he'd insisted on wearing, dragged him on to the dance floor and kissed him like a woman should.

It wasn't until years later it occurred to me how unbelievably childish and embarrassing this might have been for our respective families.

* * *

And, of course, families never let you forget. My dad had just arrived at Tashy's wedding, late and a bit pissed. He came roaring up to Olly, Clelland and me.

'Hello, young Clelland! Good to see you! Tell me, you promise not to smooch our girl here for the whole of the evening, will you? Like at some weddings I could mention.' He slapped him on the back and snorted with laughter.

Olly's ears pricked up.

'Dad!' I said in an agony of embarrassment. 'That was years ago.'

'I'll try,' said Clelland, looking amused.

'Hello, Mr Scurrison,' said Olly.

My dad is a bit rude to Olly. I don't know why, but then my dad pretends not to dislike anyone, whilst holding deep personal convictions about people as varied as Jim Davidson and Tony Blair.

'Ah yes, hello, Oliver. Didn't see you there. Are you losing weight?'

This wasn't fair. It wasn't Olly's fault he was getting perhaps a little more than a bit of a tum. We all worked long hours, and if you eat practically nothing and then have to fill up on sausage – well, things can get a bit out of hand. He looked fine in his three-piece suit, though.

'Um, no. How are you doing?'

'I'm fine, fine! Just keep me out of Flora's mother's way now.'

I grimaced. I realise it's important to Dad to feel that the fact that they've split up is a bit of a jolly 'Ooh, Vicar, where's my knickers?' farce, but I don't have to like it. I was the one ringing home from my first term at university and listening to forty-five minutes of uninterrupted sobbing

42

from my mother. I'm the one that has to be contactable every single night now, or she calls the police. Being an only child to a neurotic mum can be even less fun than it sounds. And it was his fault.

Why do so many people split up like that? 'We're just waiting for the kids to leave home.' What does that even mean? 'We're waiting until our children take their first fluttering steps out into the world, forging their own personalities and identities and living alone for the first time, then we're going to crack their worlds apart.'

I've forgiven my dad. You don't, of course, have much of a choice, unless you want it to turn into a blood feud that cascades hatred down the generations. All I can say is, she was twenty-nine and it lasted six months and, of course, he wanted to come home afterwards. He told me it was his last chance; his last way to do something different and that I'd understand when I was older, and you know, sometimes, looking at my life, if I'm being honest, I probably can.

I was twisted when my mum wouldn't take him back. Part of me just wanted everything to suddenly evaporate so that they would go back to the way things had been or, better, the way I'd have liked them to have been, more *The Good Life* than *Butterflies*. But I was glad she wasn't doing it. I was glad she was standing up to him. Because, although I didn't exactly have twenty years of marriage behind me, and I didn't know much about life (though then I thought I knew pretty much everything), I would have liked to have been as firm as she was with the love of my life.

I could see her now, coming in, but decided to duck from

her until I'd got rid of Dad. Watching her in silhouette I was struck by how old she looked; my dad just looked like a jolly, chubby, balding, middle-aged man, of which there are approximately ten million in Britain; good yeoman stock. My mother was painfully thin for her age – I was always trying to get her into milkshakes because of that brittle bone thing – and walked as if she was in pain. If you looked closely she was beginning to get a hunchback. Once your world is cracked open, you can't go back, I think. She never could. I can barely remember the carefree, normal way me and my mother used to relate when I was a teenager – normally, with sulks and huffs and slamming doors. I didn't behave very well either. But now, she was more like a house-bound grandmother, and she trusted nothing.

* * *

God, Tashy was brilliant back then. I couldn't decide which was worse: losing my dad or losing Clell. In fact, I was so wrapped up in my own misery, I was hardly there for my mum at all, something I will never forgive myself for. Tash and I had a grand tearing-up of Clelland's letters (which I still read anyway; he was having a great time. I only ever got three, 'cos I couldn't reply to any of them. What with? 'Dear Clelland. My life is shit. Love Flora?'). I got my head down and got out as quickly as I could, and I'd been trying my best to have fun ever since. Looking at Ol, I wasn't sure it was working.

It was a bad age for me. I thought it was because nobody could ever love me that I would always be alone. After all, if you love only two men, and they both leave at the same time, it doesn't bode well.

* * *

There's a reason we never forget our first loves, as Tashy has patiently pointed out to me many, many times. Our young little hormone-seething bodies have never felt anything like this before. Your brain doesn't know what's happening to it. After the first one, at least you've got some forewarning of the triple whammy that's going to happen to your head, your heart and your groin. You understand what is going on, even if that doesn't give you much more power over it than you have at sixteen.

And, as has also been noted, if your first love kisses you hard on the lips then disappears (or goes to Aberdeen – technically the same thing), and travels all over the place in the holidays, and then you go to Bristol, it's hard to get a proper handle on the whole deal. You haven't watched them grow fat or old, or watched them mess things up or, heaven forbid, stayed with them and watched the infatuation curdle. And as you grow up and learn the inevitable compromises of real love, it's hard not to remember the unlined face and innocent excitement, especially if you think the other person might feel the same.

Or, of course, even remember you that well.

* * *

We were standing to watch the speeches. Oh God, Max, no, please.

'Why is a woman like a computer?' he began ponderously, and there was a palpable shift in the audience as everyone prepared themselves to laugh at something that wouldn't be in the slightest bit funny.

45

'You can turn it on whenever you like . . .'

Clelland kept sneaking glances at me standing beside him, and – I couldn't help it – I was curious too.

'Three-and-a-half-inch floppies . . .' droned Max.

'I thought it was you!' said my mother, loud and too bright. She appeared from nowhere, with too much powder on, looking nervous.

'I'm your daughter,' I said rather sharply. 'Who could you mistake me for?'

'Goodness, I don't mean that. I just meant . . . where were you? I was worried.'

She looked around anxiously. I did too, instinctively checking where Dad was. She started to quiver if he got too close.

'Just chatting to people,' I said. I didn't want to reintroduce Clelland to her. I'd spent enough emotional time with my mother; I didn't like her getting upset over me.

'All right. Well, don't go too far, will you, darling? I hardly know anybody here. I can't think why Tashy invited me. All these young people!'

'Don't be silly, Mum. You know Tashy's mum and dad!' In fact, Jean chose that moment to put her hand up and wave. 'There you go!'

'But they're the parents,' my mother said as if talking to an idiot. 'They're very busy at weddings. Well, so I hear. Who knows, eh?'

I'd been waiting for the first one of these. I was amazed it had taken so long. I realised Clelland was close enough to hear every word of this.

'Erm, yeah, Mum.'

'You and that lovely chap. So good together. And you've been together so long! You must be next. Oh yes, there'll be a wedding soon for us, I think. Darling, think about it! It'll be such fun! We can do it all together.' And she tapped my arm in what she clearly thought was a reassuring manner. I saw Clelland raise his eyebrows.

'Ah! There you are, Olly! Hello, darling! It's Mummy!'

Unlike my father, my mother adores Olly and, it has to be said, he's very good to her. I think he does know that because I don't have any brothers he's the only man in my mother's life at all apart from the postman, and so he treats her well. She is a bit – well, very – clingy.

This 'call me Mummy' stuff has to stop, though. It really has to stop.

'Hello, Mummy,' said Ol, bending down and giving her a hug. I think perhaps what annoys me most is that sometimes I think Olly gets on with my mother probably better than I do. And vice versa. I often think they'd probably do better on their own.

My mother turned round. 'I won't say a word, dear!' she mouthed to me.

Clelland leaned over. 'Aren't you going to reintroduce me to "Mummy"?' he said, with a glint in his eye.

'She probably didn't recognise you,' I said. 'What with all the disappearing and everything.'

'What do you mean?'

'You. Disappearing. To Aberdeen. Remember?'

He started. 'I remember you not replying to any of my letters.'

'It was a busy summer.'

'Damn right,' he said, and looked annoyed.

'. . . goes down on you,' said Max.

'So you're getting married?'

47

I shrugged. 'God, no . . . I mean, I might, I haven't decided . . .'

'Hasn't he asked you?'

'That's not the point.'

'Are you going to force him into it against his will?' he smiled.

'Only if I really, really have to. And just with guns and dogs and things, nothing major.'

'I'm sure you won't have to. You should get married.'

'And what makes you the great authority?' I asked, panicking suddenly.

Why was I panicking? This was ridiculous. And anyway, he wasn't wearing a ring: I'd checked.

'I'm thinking about it.'

'Oh, yes? Who's the lucky girl? Haggis McBaggis, famous fisher lady of Aberdeen?'

'Hello,' said a beautiful dark-haired girl, suddenly appearing out of nowhere.

'Who's this?'

'Well, she fishes,' Clelland says, 'but only for compliments. This is Madeleine.'

'What are you saying about me?' the girl said. 'Ignore him, he's unbelievably rude.'

'See?' said Clelland.

'You are going to be in serious trouble later.' And she tickled him on the nose.

'Fantastic,' he said.

Who's this tart, I have to admit I was thinking.

'Are the first four years of all relationships the worst?' said the girl. 'Tell me they are. I don't think I could stand it any more.'

And Clelland put a strong arm around her and squeezed her to him.

'Well, it won't be like this when we get back to Africa,' she said.

* * *

Is it my fate, I wonder, to always end up at the fountain at parties? I had slipped out the door as soon as I decently could, even though I could hear my mother asking people for me in the querulous tone she gets when she's feeling upset. The twice-daily phonecalls were enough at the moment. I took my glass of champagne and wandered down the path. All wedding-focused country hotels have fountains. It comes with the brief.

I dallied my hand in the water again, and tried to think. Why – why did I feel like this? I was practically shivering. I felt suddenly as if my head was full of shame and fear, and just misery, and I didn't know why. What was the matter with me? I was having a near-violent reaction to something that happened every day. So I'd met someone who used to be special to me – it was sixteen years ago, for goodness' sake. It was as long a time since I'd last seen him as it was from when I was born and the time we first went out. God, that was grim. That whole summer was a period of my life I tried not to think about.

I certainly wasn't thinking like an adult now, a sorted, happy person. I sipped my champagne and felt that dull ache you get at the bottom of your heart like when you're a kid and you do something terribly, terribly wrong and you're going to be in for it later. It's hard to ignore your conscience. Sitting by that fountain, I knew. If I wasn't going to end up like my father: dissatisfied, always looking for the main chance; if I wasn't going to stultify myself, but, more importantly, if I wasn't going to harm a good, decent kind man, who loved me, then—

'Ah, there you are,' said Olly. 'I've been looking all over for you. I'm starving.'

He sat down, brushing sesame seeds off his waistcoat, bought to cover up his creeping paunch.

'Hi, there,' I said, nervousness bubbling up in my throat. I could taste it. Oh God. How could this have happened so quickly? We'd gone from happy couple, living together, and now I was on the brink of . . .

Well, we weren't that happy, were we? Or rather, me, with my selfish, adolescent mind, and my desire to see the grass as always greener, and my dreaming my life away: Olly hadn't a chance. God, I was a bitch.

Olly unsteadily started to bend down.

'What are you doing?' I said awkwardly.

It looked like – it couldn't be. Tell me he wasn't getting on one knee. TELL ME.

I stared at him in shock for a moment, and he picked up my shock in his own eyes, which suddenly looked a bit panicked.

'Look, I know we don't always get on so well . . .' he started (badly, I thought).

'FLORA!' screamed another voice.

* * *

It is a witness testament to my immaturity and stupidity that for a second I thought it might be Clelland arriving, having realised as soon as he'd seen me that he'd been stupid,

50

finally doing his last-minute dash to save me, save me from this life I had asked for but didn't want.

It wasn't, of course. It was my mother. They don't sound at all similar, but I was in a very highly strung emotional mood. Nevertheless, at that moment, I was glad to see her. She came down the hill, looking frail and confused. I wondered sometimes if she was getting early-onset Alzheimer's.

'Flora darling, where are you? We need you!' Her tone was querulous. 'They're cutting the cake.'

Olly stood up and pasted a big fake smile on his face.

'Hi there, Mummy!'

'Oh, hello, you two lovebirds. Wouldn't think you'd want to miss this bit. Also, darling, you want to see the cake. I'm sure Tashy could tell you where she got it. You never know, could be useful . . .'

And she linked her arm into both of ours as we exchanged glances – his rueful; mine, I suspect, terrified – and we marched back up the hill to the house.

* * *

The cake was indeed a teetering, rose-encrusted thing of wonder. Tashy was grinning in that slightly terrified way again, and Max looked like he was getting quite frustrated with her as he was trying to get her to put her hand underneath his, rather than on top.

I glanced over where Clelland and his lovely girlfriend were deep in smiling conversation. Of course they were. Probably planning the same thing. And only a spiteful person wouldn't wish them well. Everyone looking so happy.

I gulped. I was thirty-two years old. Suddenly it was as if I saw all round me people who were caught in a bubble of affection and love. And outside, unseen, there was me. My mother. My father. The spectres at the feast. The people who made the wrong choices. Who stuck with someone they didn't really love out of age. Or fear. No, it was worse – my mum and dad had at least loved each other once. It was only me, with a good man I couldn't love. I'd forgotten to sit down when the music stopped. Booby prize for me. I blinked back tears of utter, revolting, all encompassing self-pity.

'For Christ's sake, what's the matter with you?' said Olly. 'Are you trying to draw attention to yourself?'

Tashy and Max were lifting the knife.

'Darling? Darling, what is it?' My mother was tugging on my sleeve. 'Do you want one of my pills? I've got some in my bag. Shall we go outside?'

The tears were streaming now.

'For goodness' sake,' said Olly, hissing sharply. 'Pull yourself together. People are looking.'

I caught Clelland's eye. Well, maybe I was staring at him, wild-eyed and tearful. He opened his hands.

'What?' he mouthed. 'What is it?'

He didn't look pleased that I was on the brink of causing a scene. His girlfriend looked annoyed, as well she might. The happy couple were too far away to notice yet, but I couldn't stop the tears streaming down my Karen Millen and I was definitely causing a scene. But the lump in my throat wouldn't go away.

They brought the knife down.

'I wish,' I whispered, louder than I'd intended.

'What?' said Olly. 'This is not the time, Flora.'
I gulped.
'I wish I was sixteen again.'

Chapter Three

I groaned. God, I must have been pissed as a fart. I couldn't remember a damn thing. Jesus. A crack of light was creeping across the floor. Ow. Bugger it.

'Flora! Get up!'

I could hear my mother's voice. I panicked. Oh no. That must mean I'd got drunk and she'd had to bring me home!!! Oh no! She'd be sitting with Olly right now and they'd be having tea and agreeing with each other about what a handful I was, and how she doesn't know how he puts up with me. Later on I'll get lots of sniffy remarks from him about behaviour fitting a grown woman and taking responsibility. Oh fuck. It's like having my parents back together, those two sometimes. Except at least my dad can be fun.

I cringed as I remembered how mean I'd felt towards Olly. I hope nothing happened; I didn't go and throw a drink at Clelland's girlfriend . . . I didn't, did I? I probed my mind for any tender spots of excruciating embarrassment, but there weren't any there. Just a big black hole. That was peculiar. I don't usually have vast gaps in my memory. I can't—

'Flora!' Oh God. She sounds cross. Maybe I have done something really awful; my mother never gets cross at me nowadays. She's too afraid, in case I leave her, or stop picking up the phone. If anything it's the constant nervous entreaty that drives me so mad. This was almost better.

Suddenly I notice something. I'm in my old bed, at my parents' house. Oh God. Oliver must have dumped me here. Oh no. Something must be terribly wrong. Did he finally get up the guts to propose and . . .?

Now, surely I'd remember something like that. But there's nothing. Nothing there at all.

'Yeah? Mum, could you bring me a cup of tea?' I called out. Testing the water.

'You must be joking, young lady!' I could hear her starting up the stairs. 'If you're not up in two minutes, I'll get you up. In fact . . .'

Then she walked into my room and I jumped three feet in the air.

'What's the matter with you?'

But I couldn't speak. I couldn't do anything except point.

'Flora! Stop gawping like a fish and get ready.'

It was my mother – I can't dispute that. But here's the weird thing: she looked decades younger. Her skin was unlined, her hair brown and she seemed to have lost the hunch. Even her tone of voice was completely different. This was my mother how I remembered her from when I lived at home. I swallowed. I was half asleep, after all. She must have decided to sort her life out. Maybe after seeing Tashy's parents at the wedding. Maybe she'd started on HRT and it was just kicking in.

'God, Mum, you gave me a fright. You look great, by the way.'

She sat down on my bed. 'Look, Flora, I'm sorry your party didn't work out, but you can't mooch around for ever. You still have to get up and face everyone today.'

What the hell had gone on at Tashy's do?

Then she did something odd. As she turned to go she tutted and said something very strange under her breath.

'Teenagers!'

* * *

I couldn't quite have heard her as she said it. It just chimed in with the fact that something was very, very wrong. My room, for example, the room my mother had redecorated in beige as a guest room, even though the only guest she ever got was me, was covered in lots of pin-ups of R&B stars, and I don't even like R&B. There were clothes all over the floor that I didn't recognise. Had she got a lodger? Had I been unconscious for months? What the hell was going on?

I got out of bed – wearing, I noticed, a long flouncy nightie that I normally wouldn't be seen dead in – and stumbled down the hallway to the bathroom. I held on to the sink and looked at myself in the mirror. God, for someone who'd been so drunk she'd passed out and had to be taken to her mother's house to sleep it off, I looked great.

I blinked at the reflection again, then, like a complete idiot in a cartoon, rubbed my eyes to make sure.

You don't see yourself changing. Sure, you notice a wrinkle now and again, the odd half-stone that creeps on and off with annoying regularity. But it's still you. Your face. Your best *Zoolander* face in the mirror. The way you sometimes catch sight of yourself in a shop window, then hope nobody else saw you looking at yourself. When I was a teenager, I used to spend hours staring in the mirror, mooning at myself, wondering. Am I pretty? Will my curls ever straighten out? Is one eye bigger than the other? Will boys like me? If I sleep on alternate ears, will they stop sticking out? Who am I going to be?

And it was exactly this face that was staring back at me now. No straightening irons had been applied to this hair. No subtle blonde streaks. No serums. No carefully plucked brows.

I wasn't sure what was going on but had it pretty much figured for one of those extremely convincing dreams. Any moment, the Queen and a big hippopotamus were about to crash through the window and take me flying. Until then, I was going to make the best of it. I stared and stared. This looked like my face from at least ten years ago.

I had a crop of spots on my forehead. I moan about the occasional pimple now, but I'd forgotten what it was like when they used to grow in small fields. But apart from that, my skin was fresh, rosy . . . I turned round. I disappeared. I stretched out a long, white thin arm. Oh my God. How could I not have *known* this wouldn't stay for ever? How could I not have realised that years of pizza and red wine could have an effect on this? When I was really younger, I thought I had an enormous arse and spent my entire time covering it up. I turned round again. OK, it wasn't Kylie, but in absolutely nobody's world was this a big arse. Wow! I jumped up and down. Nothing wiggled at all. Look!

Look! Hip bones! Bones! Oh my God! OK, my hair was a
frizzy disaster, with what appeared to be pink bits dyed in,
but that's OK, I know about expensive haircare products.
I wished it wasn't a dream, because this could have been
so much fun. As if my body had turned into a Barbie doll,
I could dress up and parade around. This was the best
dream in the entire world.

'Get out of the bathroom! You're going to be late for
school!'

Now, this was too much. Oh my God. School. Tashy and
I sitting up the back of English, giggling our heads off.

No, I should just wake myself up before a monster came
or something. I'm always quite lucid when I dream anyway.
I always know that something won't happen. I'd probably
end up trapped in the bathroom, desperately knowing I was
late for school on a test day and . . .

I have never felt water flow over my hands in a dream. I
have never turned a tap on and got wet.

'Hurry up!'

The door was banging. And I had to realise: that wasn't
Ollie's voice. That was my dad's.

Bloody hell.

* * *

I stood in the shower for a long time, shaking, although I
turned the water up as hot as it could go. What the hell was
happening to me? It couldn't . . . this was impossible. What
was I doing standing, washing myself (with impossibly pert
breasts. Jesus, these were up by my neck!) in our old blue
bathroom suite?

I thought. What had happened yesterday? I had gone to

the wedding. I had met Clelland. I had fallen out with Oliver. I had made a wish over a wedding cake . . .

It couldn't be. It *couldn't*.

You know when something terrible happens and everyone says 'Don't panic'?

Now, I believed, was the time to panic.

* * *

Slowly, very slowly, I reached out of the shower and put a towel round my tiny waist.

I was back in my nightie, and my dad pushed past me into the bathroom. I barely caught sight of him. Jesus. Had I . . . travelled back in time? What was it, 1987? I caught my breath. So I could . . . what? Bet on general elections? Ooh, maybe go discover Take That! Maybe I could marry Robbie. He'd be older than me too. Was Jonathan Ross still free? He turned out to be a pretty good bet. Are the Backstreet Boys still children?

I stumbled back into my bedroom and leaned against the wall, my eyes closed, my heart racing a mile a minute.

Hang on, I should stop just planning on not-yet famous people I want to get off with; do something properly. 1987. Maybe I could save that baby who fell in a well! Oh my God! I have to save Princess Diana! Ooh, I can become the most successful medium there's ever been! I started to get feverishly excited. What could I invent? Did Dysons exist yet? Ooh, mobile phone stocks! I was going to be so rich!

I shook my head. This was nuts.

* * *

Opening my eyes, I took in a picture of – oh, for God's sake – Blue on my wall. And Darius, I noticed wryly. Oh shit. This couldn't be right.

I went and sat down in front of my old dressing table. Yes. Still incomprehensible, still from the eighties, still there. My old face. Right. *This* time, I was wearing sunscreen every day. Not a wrinkle to be found.

So. I tried to put it together in a brain that was dealing with sudden shocks equivalent to six bonfire nights and a bowlful of LSD. My parents were younger. And still together. But Darius was looking older than me.

I didn't want to come over all *Dr Who*, but, unbelievably, I was actually going to have to ask someone what year this was.

To postpone the inevitable, and try to calm my breathing, I tried to think about clothes. What age was I? The tits suggested nothing much under fifteen, anyway. Oh God.

I opened my wardrobe door tentatively. Yes, there it was, as if I'd never been away. That bottle-green skirt. The pale green shirt. The thick tights. Tashy and I had sworn blind we would never ever, ever put this damn school uniform on again. But what were my options at this point?

* * *

My dad, stroking his still-thick sideburns. I'd forgotten about those.

'Hey, love,' he said. 'Sleep well?'

I was too petrified to say anything, judging that this wouldn't exactly be an unusual response at the breakfast table from a teenager. Finally, 'Can I borrow your paper?' I stammered out.

60

'Nice to finally see you,' said my mother, and I sudd
felt a residual sense of annoyance that she was pleased
something I was doing.

'Tcch,' I tutted.

'Why do you want to see the paper?' asked my dad. 'I'll
read you your stars, if you like. Oh, here we are: Virgo.
"Today you are going to be late for school and are going out
dressed like a bin bag." Gosh, they're spot on, aren't they,
love?'

I fumbled my badly tied tie, hands shaking.

'Don't tease her,' said my mum crossly. 'For God's sake,
give her the bloody paper.'

'All right, all right,' said my dad. 'Here.' He handed it
to me. 'Happy now?' he said to my mother.

'I don't know. What time are you coming home tonight?'

He blew air out of his mouth. 'Well, I've got a few things
to drop off.'

My mother turned back to the kettle and said something
under her breath.

'What was that?' said my dad.

I buried my head in the paper. Oh my God. I'd forgotten
they'd been like this.

'If you've got something to say, just say it.'

My mother's thin ankles shook in their American tan tights
inside her horrid old carpet slippers that I could have sworn
I threw out years ago.

Fourth of September 2003, it said. Definitely. Completely.
The twenty-first century. Not the eighties. In fact, it was about
a month before the day I'd had yesterday, and Tashy's wedding.
WHAT? So – hang on. Me, Mum and Dad had gone back in
time, but they seemed completely fine with it?

Had I been in a coma? Had the rest of my life after now been a dream? Was I in an insane asylum and this was a brief moment of lucidity? Had I taken a dodgy pill and rendered the last sixteen years of my life a bad trip? Hang on, how many bad trips have you ever heard of that involved a regular visit to blood donors and a Nectar card?

'I've got to go,' I said suddenly.

'Walking are you, love?' said my dad, taking back the paper. 'Wonders will never cease. Might get some fresh air in those cheeks.' I stared at him in disbelief and dashed out the front door, pulling it shut behind me.

I stood outside and fumbled into my bag.

In real life, whatever the hell that is, my mobile is small silver and rather elegant-looking. This thing was pink, fluffy and had leopard skin on it. On the display there was a pixellated picture of a badger.

Chuffing hell.

There were fourteen text messages waiting for me, and I didn't understand a single one of them.

'RUOKWAN2CAPIC'

What was that?

I scrawled through to find Tashy's name. That's who I had to speak to. It wasn't there.

All the way on the train I couldn't think straight. I certainly couldn't consider – God – school. I just wanted to go home, go to sleep, wake up properly, and never take drugs again.

* * *

I bought my flat about six years ago, just before everything went crazily mad in the property market, although I didn't think that then: at the time I thought I was going crazy.

Although I spent most of my time at Olly's in Battersea now, I hadn't quite got round to getting rid of it ('No point. Don't you know anything about investments?' I recall Olly saying, at one point). It suited me: have somewhere to go for a bit of quiet time. It was a tiny studio, and the wall between the kitchen and the bathroom was purely for show, but it was in nice North London and I'd loved it; loved painting it different experimental colours to see if anything would make it look bigger; loved following the autumn sun round the room like a cat when I was reading the papers; strolling down and having an overpriced cappuccino on my own, and generally feeling like a grown-up. It was on the ground floor of a fussy Edwardian terrace, with the usual North London mix of inhabitants: a Persian couple, a teacher and a diffident trust-fund musician who owned the whole top floor, from which the smell of dope could permeate the entire building.

I was hurrying there now. The only thought in my mind was getting in there. OK, I didn't have my keys here, but I kept a spare set in the pots in the scrub at the bottom of the front garden. Once I was in I could sit down, take a few deep breaths, make a proper cup of coffee. I kept looking around suspiciously as I made my way up Embarke Gardens, but everything looked just as it normally did. The old blue car that never moved was still parked in the corner; Hendrix, the top flat owner's cat, was stalking carefully around on his neighbourhood watch patrol, as he did every day. I heaved a sigh of relief. Nearly home.

I crouched down and felt for the key. It wasn't there. That was odd. Mind you, Olly had probably gone nuts when I'd disappeared. He'd probably come round to find me. Might even be inside right now. Ooh. That wasn't something I particularly wanted to handle right at the moment. Also, he was one of those very rational thinkers. I didn't think he'd take my little jaunt into the unconscious too well.

Still, I had to get in. I rang the bell. No answer. Fuck. I rang the general bell to see if anyone would let me into the hall at least, but I couldn't get an answer from anyone. Shit. I took a look around the street. OK. This wasn't the first time I'd ever done this – this is where the key pot had come from – but I was going to have to climb in through the top of the window, which you could pull down if you had to.

I shinned up the badly done pointwork and found myself reaching up effortlessly. God, I was so lithe and limber! I could probably somersault in! La la la. I pulled the window down, and gracelessly collapsed on top of what should have been my favourite red squishy sofa.

Owwww.

Who the fuck put an enormous glass modernist coffee table with bumpy bits all over it into my flat?

I straightened up, clutching my back, and slowly looked around. And then again. Nope, it didn't matter how often I stared, there was no doubt that this remained, indubitably, somebody else's furniture, somebody else's books. No. No no no no no. I tore around the place, weirdly, looking for something – anything – that would prove that I used to live here, used to exist. No. My God. I couldn't. . .I couldn't not exist. That wasn't possible.

But then, if I was sixteen, it dawned on me pretty slowly . . . maybe I didn't own a flat in Maida Vale. After all, my wallet had disappeared.

No. This was awful. Even though I suppose if I'd thought

about it . . . no, that didn't help, of course. The more I thought about it, the worse it got.

Let me see. Oh my God. No flat meant . . . no money . . . no job . . . no . . .

It is, believe me, a profoundly shocking moment when you realise that the only person who may understand your predicament is David Icke.

Suddenly I heard a noise. Shit. Someone was coming in the front door. Please, please, please let it be the upstairs neighbour. Please.

The footsteps stopped, and I dived behind the black leather modern chair in the middle of the room – which looked rather good, I noticed. The door opened. For a heartbreaking second I thought I – or rather, my thirty-two-year-old self – was walking through the door.

* * *

It wasn't me, thank God, although the woman looked a lot like me. I guess she looked like how I used to look. I suppose I wasn't as unique as I'd always liked to think.

About my (old) age, quite slim, wearing a casual-looking trouser suit. I liked her face. She looked like the kind of person I'd like to be friends with. Nice, good-fun grown-up person. Who was going to have a screaming blue fit if she saw a sulky teenager wearing a cheap anorak hiding behind her sofa.

'Fuck!' she yelled. 'Where's my fucking keys!'

She started throwing pillows and papers around. Was London really this full of cross thirty-something women? Whoever this girl was, it was like watching a facsimile of my own self. Was I really this stressed out all the time? Did I get that frown line down the middle of my forehead?

'OK. If it's not bad enough that I'm already late for my fucking meeting with my fucking prick boss, I can't find a fucking thing in this overpriced shoebox.'

This was uncanny. She could be me. Closer up, I could see there was a crease in the middle of her forehead, a bloating around her hips – too many late nights staring at a computer screen, too many corporate lunches. No wedding ring. Flustered, snappy.

She wasn't me. But she was.

* * *

When she found her keys and slammed the door hard on the way out, I sat on the floor and started to cry. Properly cry too. Big, dripping tears that went down my nose and hurt my throat. I didn't make much noise, but they just kept coming. What was happening to me? What was I going to do? Had I been erased for everyone? But what about Mum and Dad? They seemed to know who I was. Where had I been? Where was I now?

I felt so sorry for myself. But no matter how much you feel like crying yourself sick, it can't last for ever. Eventually, I pulled myself up and left quietly this house that was no longer mine, wondering who I might be, and where I might be going.

Chapter Four

I walked. I walked and walked for hours. Every time I caught sight of myself in a shop window I nearly passed out. This couldn't be real. It was horrific. I didn't have any money, and I wasn't going to steal from that nice lady's flat. The first place I walked to was my office in the Strand, all the way from Maida Vale. I actually went into reception.

Hang on, hang on. This wasn't right at all. It was the same reception guard I'd seen every morning for the last eleven years. And he didn't look a day younger. So, it looked like whatever nightmare I was in, I was in it alone. Except with my parents. Which, of course, made it even more of a nightmare than it might have been otherwise. Oh Christ.

'Hey, Jimmy,' I said to the reception guard, exactly as I'd been doing for the last eleven years.

He looked at me suspiciously. 'Can I help you?'

Actually, I was hungry. I was starving. I had always skipped breakfast, but now I felt hungrier than I had in years. I wanted to ask him for a sandwich, but I had something else to do here.

'Can you put me through to the extension of Flora Scurrison, please?' I asked. Even my voice sounded ridiculously high-pitched and screeching.

'Who?' he said gruffly. I'd noticed this already. OK, I was scruffily dressed, but he was eyeing me warily, as if I was looking for trouble. Had they done this when I was really sixteen? I couldn't remember. Perhaps I'd been a tad wrapped up in myself.

'S-C-U-R-R-I-S-O-N.'

He shook his head. 'No one here by that name, love. Sure you've got the right address?'

On some level I had known that was going to happen, but it was a real slap in the face. On the way I'd tried going into the bank with my account details. That hadn't yielded anything either. But a big fear – of running into myself – didn't seem to be on the cards, not yet at least.

'Shouldn't you be in school?'

Jimmy, I suddenly remembered, had a daughter...er, my age.

'Probably,' I said, then turned to go. 'Say hi to Jinty for me.'

'What? Are you one of her friends?'

No. At the moment, as far as I could see, I literally didn't have a friend in the world. I had ceased to exist. I was no one. While everyone else, Jinty included, was still going strong.

As I turned to go, I nearly ran smack into my boss, Karl Dean, a sour, halitosis-ridden old man with a dour world view, as useful for accounting as it was miserable for his life

68

and for anyone else who ever came within three feet of him. He looked at me without blinking. There wasn't a second's worth of recognition. He didn't even look at me as if he thought I reminded him of someone but he couldn't quite place me.

Beside him there was someone who could have been me but was not me. It was the woman from the flat. She was looking nervous, and fiddling with her spectacles.

'I mean,' he was saying, 'you've got to care about getting it right. It's your responsibility. You're not just letting the company down, you're letting yourself down. You've got a long career ahead of you here, and you want to make a success of it.'

'Yes, sir,' said the woman. But just as she said it, for a split second she caught my eye, and I sensed I saw in her a desperate wish for flight. She looked at me, and for a moment I think she wished she was me, a teenager bumming around with nothing much to do. If only she knew.

* * *

Lunchtime came and went, after I found a pound in my coat, and was thankful teenagers in McDonald's weren't exactly a rarity. I'd spent the day tramping the London streets, my thoughts exhausted. I just didn't know what to do. I didn't want to go home. I didn't want to give in; to admit that I was trapped. Not only trapped, but trapped with people I didn't know, in a time that didn't belong to me. Sighing heavily, I found my tired feet heading down to Waterloo. To Tashy's office.

I was trying to get it straight in my head. There was only one me. I was . . . a bit different. But it was possible that

69

Tashy wouldn't be there either. Every time I'd had a problem, for most of our lives I'd always taken it to her. We'd laughed and talked about every single thing that had ever happened to each of us for practically as long as I can remember, and she'd made me feel better every single time. I was an only child, and Heather was a witch, and school was no picnic, so we were closer than sisters.

I went down outside the huge office, terrified she wouldn't be in this strange new world, and sat on a bench, sadly watching people pour out, looking cold, tired, defeated as they tried to raise their spirits enough to manage the long commute home.

My eyes were so blurred with tears, weariness and fear that at first I didn't notice her. Then I became aware of somebody sitting next to me. I turned, slowly, scarcely able to believe that somebody I knew so well was right there. And she would never know it was me. Not only that, but she was crying too.

Tashy sniffed loudly. I stared at her from out of the corner of my eye. My heart was thudding like a drum. It took every ounce of strength I had not to leap on her and smother her with kisses.

'Sorry to bother you,' I said, which sounded ridiculously weird. 'Are you alright?'

She turned round and, I swear to God, she nearly leaped straight up in the air.

'Oh my God,' she said, trying to catch her breath. I kept looking at her, feeling as miserable as I ever had in my life.

'I'm sorry, but you look just like a friend of mine. Sorry, it's the strangest thing.'

'What's your friend like?' I asked, my heart racing suddenly.

'Oh, it doesn't matter. You're much younger than her.'

'Is . . . what's her name?'

Tashy stood up, roughly rubbing her eyes. She was looking paler than of late – must be all the subsequent sunbed sessions. Her small solitaire ring glinted sadly.

'Why?'

I swallowed hard. 'Tashy.'

'How do you know my name?' she said, suddenly looking very frightened.

'Please . . .' I said. 'Flora . . .'

'What's going on here?' She looked around her, holding on very tightly to her handbag.

'When did you last see her?' I croaked. My heart was in my throat and I could hardly get the words out.

'What's going on?' Tashy peered at me. 'What have you done? The likeness is unbelievable.'

I heaved a big sigh. I couldn't believe somebody recognised me. Or, she didn't yet, but she would.

'Look. This is going to be really difficult to explain.'

'Are you a gang of fiendishly evil Eastern Europeans who have kidnapped her identity? Because if you are I'm telling the police.'

At that, I was tempted to tell her her PIN number, which I knew in case of emergencies but, I figured, best not.

'No,' I said. 'I swear on Dave Grohl's life.'

She shook her head, dazed.

'Tashy, remember when we were fourteen and we swore faithfully the only man we'd sleep with before marriage was Prince Edward?'

She stared at me.

'Remember when you got locked in a toilet with that boy

71

at McKaskill's party? You weren't really locked in, were you?'

She shook her head.

'Remember when we tried to drink your parents' crème de menthe and hurled all over the shagpile rug?'

'We were never going to tell anyone about that.'

'We never did. What about the time you . . .'

'OK, what? WHAT?!'

Her face was a picture of confusion and despair. I took a deep breath. She was staring at me, eyes and mouth wide.

I lowered my voice. 'A certain tampon withdrawal failure? Being discovered on the end of a certain man's . . .'

Her hands went to her face. 'OH MY GOD. OH MY GOD. It's you. WHAT HAPPENED?'

'I don't know.'

'It just – can't be.'

'I know.'

She came up to me and squinted right in my face. I tried to keep still.

'God,' she said. 'What the *hell* have you done now?'

'So, I couldn't get away with it just being a very good facelift and lots of healthy living?' I said glumly.

'Who would believe that of you anyway?' She was staring at my face in a quite unnerving manner, and put her hands up to touch it. 'My God . . .' she said.

'I know.'

'What . . . what happened?'

'I wish I knew,' I said.

'I saw you just a couple of days ago.'

'No! That's the thing. I just woke up this morning. Well, when I say "this morning" . . .' I paused. 'We really, really need a drink for this,' I said. 'Want to nip over to the Atlantic?'

She half sniggered. 'A teenager says what now?'

'What?'

We used to love the Atlantic. So expensive, but so pretty, and we could watch the mating rituals of the predatory scrawny English blonde, and merchant bankers and Eurotrash.

'Tash, it's me. It's ME ME ME ME. So can we go to the Atlantic or not?'

'Well, if we can get you in.'

* * *

We made it in by my taking off my school tie and whisking past the doorman when he was distracted.

'This is terrible,' said Tashy. 'Look at my hand shaking. I feel like your evil auntie. But that's OK, because in a second − ' she sipped her Mojito − 'you're going to tell me the secret of eternal youth. Or I'm going to wake up.'

'I've been waiting for that all day.'

'And it hasn't happened?'

'Not so far.'

This time Tashy took a gulp, closed her eyes firmly for five seconds, opened them again and stared at me.

'OK,' I said. 'This is going to sound crazy.'

'No shit.'

'We were at your wedding.'

'My WHAT?'

'We're attracting attention.'

'My wedding NEXT MONTH!'

'Shh. Yes.'

'Oh my God.' Tashy's eyes were darting around. 'What's it like? What's the weather like? How do I look? How's the food?'

73

'Um,' I said.

'Does everyone cry? Is there a fountain? Is Max all right or does he look a bit of a dick in his morning suit?'

'Um, Tash, I don't know if I should tell you.'

She was very red in the face. 'Oh. This is bullshit, isn't it? I'm out of my mind. OK, tell me: what have you done with my friend?'

'Max wears a bottle-green waistcoat,' I barked out suddenly. 'He looks like a prick to start with because he's embarrassed, but he relaxes into it and looks alright. And your Vera Wang is gorgeous.'

'Fuck a duck,' said Tashy, sitting back. 'Fuck a fucking duck.'

'I'm just. . .I mean maybe all this is weird enough. Maybe you're not supposed to know the future or something.'

'But what about. . .? I mean, you must know other things that happen.' She beckoned over another couple of drinks.

'Really not much,' I said. 'They elect a right-wing president in Europe, but there's not a lot we can do about that. And I know who wins *Big Brother*, but I doubt the odds are great.'

'If you're from the future you should really look older,' she said grumpily.

We sat there.

'How old are you?'

'Well, judging by the spread of my pubic hair, I'd say about sixteen.'

Tashy took a long draught of her drink. 'Fuck. I mean, how the hell?'

'You know when you cut the cake at your wedding . . .?'

'You didn't make another stupid wish?'

I nodded slowly.

'Your wish came true at my wedding?' she said slowly.

I nodded. There was a long pause.

'Well,' she said finally, 'that makes one of us.' I remembered her sniffling on the bench.

'Thing is,' I said, 'the only person who recognises me is you.'

'Oh no,' said Tashy.

'What?'

'Maybe you're a complete figment of my imagination, like that giant rabbit.' She examined the huge bill the waiter had put in front of her. 'Maybe not. So what are you going to do?'

'Fuck knows. My job is gone.'

'Really? I think Flora Scurrison, Teenage Accountant has something of a ring to it.'

'My flat too.'

'Oh, your little flat. I'm so sorry. Have you spoken to Olly?'

'God, no. I'm just so relieved somebody recognises me I hadn't thought about it.'

'Wow, he'll be thrilled to get some nubile little—'

'Don't be disgusting. And don't be stupid. If I'm going to be a nubile little teen I'm definitely going to be after Jamie Theakston or Gareth Gates or someone, anyway.'

'You're joking.' She stared at me suddenly. 'Yes, yes, of course.'

As she stared at me, Tashy's face started to crumble.

'Tash. Tash, what's the matter? What is it? Why were you on the bench?'

She let out a familiar Tashy wail. 'I don't knooow!'

'It's not Max, is it? Please, don't let it be Max.'

She looked up at me, tear-stained, as I beckoned over another couple of Mojitos.

'Maybe,' she said quietly. 'It's just nerves. I don't really want to talk about it.'

'I'm sorry,' I said. 'I promise I didn't bring about an inexplicable cosmic phenomenon just to bother you about your wedding.'

She studied my face for a bit. 'Is that an enormous spot you've got brewing on your forehead?' said Tashy.

I rubbed it crossly. 'Stop changing the subject.'

* * *

'So, what's the matter?'

Tashy shrugged. 'It's daft really. When you're younger, you think, oh yeah, I've got tons of friends, it'll last for ever. Then you grow up, and everybody's working and so busy and settling down, then tons of people move out of London to have babies and you never hear from them ever again. Ever. Like they've been eaten by polecats. So, then you wake up one day and you think, God, I've got a problem, who can I call. Then you realise that your partner, your life, the person you're meant to spend your life with – you can't talk to them.'

'You can talk to me,' I said gently.

'I have a teenage soulmate,' said Tashy. And she rubbed fiercely at her wandering mascara. Then she leaned forward. 'This time,' she pointed at me, 'don't marry someone just because they're nice to you when you're thirty-two.'

'Tashy, I just look younger, I'm not retarded. And there are worse things than marrying a nice man,' I said.

'I know. Oh, I know how lucky I am. I know. I know,' she said. Then, in a smaller voice: 'I don't know if I can watch him eat a boiled egg every morning for the next forty years.'

'Every morning?'

'He makes it perfectly. Then he lets out this ridiculous sigh through his teeth, like: "Ahh. Egg. Jolly good." Then he breaks the shell very carefully, and nibbles round the top bit with his teeth. Yeeugh. Like a little rat.'

'Hmm. Do you think just the riot squad, or are we going to have to call "S.W.A.T."?'

'Yes.'

'Tashy, that's nothing. You've just got wedding nerves. Everyone says the first year of marriage is by far the worst. You have to wrestle each other into submission, then after that it's completely fine.'

'Yeah, they say that, but they don't tell you what to do if you feel like kicking his head in when you see its bald top shining over the top of the *Telegraph*.'

'Look, I remember you,' I said. 'You were so bloody excited about getting married. You were ticking a box. There's nothing wrong with Max. OK, he's a little bit boring, but you were OK with that, you really were.'

I didn't remember Tash being this bad the first time round.

'Yes. And you were doing so much better with Olly. Now you'll probably run off with Jamie Theakston or something.' She let out a huge sigh. 'Every day you get older, there are fewer choices. That's what getting older is. A daily diminishment of options.'

I stood up to go to the toilet, but the room was swaying.

…l sick,' I said.

…hy?'

…Shit . . . I mean, I feel so pissed.'

'You've had two and a half cocktails.'

'Ohhh, Tash . . .'

'Fuck. I don't believe you have the drinking capacities of a teenager.' Tashy started to laugh.

'Oh, come to me, lovely fresh liver . . .' I started to sing.

'Shit.' She put her drink down. 'This really isn't funny.'

'Is everything alright here?' The smooth maître d' came over, pretending to be polite whilst fixing us with beady little eyes. 'Are you together?'

'We're just leaving,' said Tashy firmly, standing up and dragging me with her.

'Yeug-bleh,' I said.

Tashy took the hood of my anorak firmly and marched me to the door.

'Hff-nng mnay,' I dribbled at her, staggering up the stairs, which she eventually managed to correctly interpret as 'I don't have enough money for a taxi', and stuffed a couple of tenners into my pocket.

'Call me tomorrow,' she said. 'Don't worry, we'll work something out.'

'Blergff.'

'Take her home,' she said to the cabbie.

'Will she be sick?'

'No!' I said. I wanted to say, 'Actually, in no sense in my real life could I get inarticulate on two Mojitos, but clearly I have a very different body going on. It's all a misunderstanding I'm sure can be worked out by some practice.'

78

'Get her in then.' He looked disapprovingly at Tashy. 'Next time, leave your babysitting charges at home.'

* * *

Through the back window I watched Tashy staring at the retreating vehicle, then remembered nothing else until I woke up outside the front door of my parents' house. Not noticing all the other vehicles lined up outside, I blearily lurched inside, with the exaggerated gait of someone trying to pretend they're not pissed. My parents were standing, staring at me. Next to them were the next-door neighbours, other people from down the street, and two policemen.

'Oh my God!' screamed my mother. 'Oh my God!'

The policemen looked at each other.

'This,' one said to my dad, 'is why we don't come out to over fifteen-year-old cases till after twenty-four hours.'

But my dad was already rushing towards me.

'Where the hell . . .? You stupid, stupid little cow . . .'

He dragged me up and enfolded me in his big arms. My dad hadn't hugged me like this in – God, so long. It felt good. I nestled into him, smelled his familiar smell, of properly ironed shirts and bread, before he left and started to smell of aftershave and conditioner, if I got close enough to smell him at all.

'Jesus. The stink off you,' he said.

'Oh my God, is she drunk?' said my mother.

'A sixteen-year-old girl drunk,' said one of the policemen to another. 'What an extraordinary event. Shall we head off and see if we can find any pigeons in Trafalgar Square?'

'Perhaps there might be a bear in the woods who needs our assistance in a toiletry matter,' said the other.

'She was gone *all day*,' said my mother, tearfully trying to justify herself to the policemen. 'She didn't go to school. If something had happened you'd have had to read a poem at her funeral and get an OBE.'

'Yeah,' said the policemen thoughtfully.

One came over to me. 'You're too young to drink,' he said.

'Not in a restaurant,' I said, wobbling.

'Who took you to a restaurant?' barked my mother.

'Don't worry your mother,' the policeman told me. 'Do you hear? Be careful. There are lots of bad things out there. I know you think you're an adult, but I can assure you, you're not.'

'Except in the eyes of the law,' said his colleague. 'Oh, no, forget I said that.'

'Don't you have a phone?' he said.

'Yes,' I said, staring at the ground. I was definitely sobering up a bit. I had kept the phone switched off all day, terrified that someone I didn't know might call me and ask me something I was completely unaware of.

'Didn't it even cross your mind to phone your mum and dad to tell them where you were?'

Um, of course not.

'No,' I said. 'I'm sorry.'

'The young today,' said the second policeman, who looked about twenty-two. 'So selfish.'

'Forgetful, not selfish,' I said. 'It's not easy being sixteen. Growing a lot, you know. By the way, I am so hungry. Is there anything to eat, please?'

'Huh,' said my mother. 'Eat! It's a good crack round the ear you're needing.'

'Don't say that in front of a policeman, Mum.'

'This is serious, Flora Jane. Have you any idea how frightened we were? All those stories? Miss Syzlack phoned us after registration this morning. You didn't turn up the whole day. You never miss school.'

I must have done, surely. I couldn't remember. Was I really that much of a goody-goody? No wonder everyone had hated us.

'Your mother's been driving up and down the streets looking for you,' said my dad. 'We've had the whole neighbourhood out.'

I felt bad. They really were flipping their lids. Indeed, the people from the street were now hovering in the sitting room, looking awkward. Their promised evening of excitement was turning into a dull domestic.

'Now, you can talk to me, darling,' said my mum seriously. 'Have you just been to have an abortion?'

'Mum! There's nine people here!'

'You can tell us, you know. We'll support you.'

'That's nice to know, but trust me, if I needed an abortion, number one, I'd make my own decision, and number two I would never, ever tell you about it. And I certainly wouldn't be drinking alcohol afterwards. Or standing up, in fact.'

A complete and deadening silence fell over the room.

'Quick, Martin. Um . . . a burglar!' said one policeman to the other, and they left hurriedly, followed by the rest of the street.

* * *

'Go to your room,' said my mother. 'I can't even look at you at the moment.'

81

This was my mother? For a horrible, heart-stopping moment I felt like saying, 'Well, see if you want to look at me when he disappears with Superbitch Stephanie and it's your turn to beg for help.' But, oh goodness, she looked so fragile. Her arm was reaching out as if she wanted to lean on my dad for support, but couldn't bring herself to.

'OK,' I said contritely. 'Can I have some dinner?'

'You've been to a restaurant and now you want to eat?'

'Um, let's not concentrate too hard on the restaurant,' I said. 'Just an omelette? I'll make it myself.'

They both started laughing.

'God, that's the first smile I've had all day,' said my dad and, too late, I remembered I learned to cook when I went to university.

'I mean . . . a cheese sandwich of some kind.'

'Where were you?' said my mother, getting up with a sigh.

'I went into town to see a friend.'

'A male friend or a female friend?'

'A female friend.'

'What's her name?'

'Tashy.'

I watched them closely, hoping they'd say, 'Oh, Tashy', but they didn't. They had no idea who she was at all.

'And where did you meet her?'

I couldn't explain this. How could I? And I was very, very weary. I wondered if the teenage truculent secret weapon still worked, because I didn't know what more I could say.

'Are you going to run my life for ever?'

My dad came and stood over me. 'If you're going to go out with complete strangers and get pissed illegally, young lady, then yes, we are.'

'It was just a drink,' I said sulkily. 'I just wanted to see she was all right.'

My parents looked at each other.

'Well, if you won't tell us where you were...'

'I can't,' I said. There was no way I was going to start telling them anything. They'd have me committed. Hadn't they seen *Girl, Interrupted*?

'Fine. You're grounded,' said my dad.

I was what? 'Oh, for goodness' sake. Grounded? What is this, nineteen seventy-five?'

'And I'm taking you to school tomorrow to make sure you get there.'

'I think we've been far too relaxed with you,' said my mother. 'I think that's the problem.' She looked at me sincerely. 'We trusted you, Flora. And you let us down.'

I hated to see her face like that.

'I think you'll find it was Dad who did that,' I wanted to shout, but couldn't. Inside I was boiling at the unfairness of it all.

'Well, things are certainly going to change around here,' said my dad. I looked at him, panicking slightly. By my reckoning, they had about a month left together. A month. Things certainly were going to change around here.

I slouched up to bed, the sound of their bickering ringing in my ears, very unwelcome after all this time.

* * *

I woke up the following morning with a start. That was the weirdest dream of . . . no, shit, piss, bollocks. Here I was, still underneath a gingham duvet, trapped in a ridiculous prison for God knows why. Even more trapped now I was grounded. I cursed myself for not realising how stupid it would be to disappear for twelve hours. But being sixteen took a bit of getting used to. I squeezed my cellulite-free thigh for some reassurance, but it wasn't cheering me up properly at all. Then I thought of my lovely coffee maker. There's nothing that makes me feel grown up in the morning so much as grinding my own beans, then getting in the shower and letting the smell of fresh coffee permeate the flat. But in this house, as it had always been, it was Nescafé. For some reason it was the small details – the coffee; my wardrobe, full of nice suits and beautiful shoes; my Clarins products in the bathroom rather than own-brand mega jugs of supermarket shampoo – that I suddenly missed more than anything else. I sniffled away to myself.

'GET UP!' my mother was shouting again. 'Your dad's dropping you at school. Wants to see how your first hangover's going.'

I heard some muffled protest about this, and got up, nervous as . . . well, as a kid on the first day at school. Except this would be far, far worse, because it wasn't as if I didn't know anyone. If my mobile was anything to go by, I did. I just wouldn't be able to recognise anyone or know anything about them.

I hid my head under the duvet.

'I feel sick!' I shouted. Actually, I felt fine. I'd forgotten how quick hangovers passed when you were young. Nowadays I take two days to get over them. Or did, when I still had a 'nowadays'.

'That's how it works,' shouted my mum. God, was she always this assertive?

I tried to put a brave face on things as I got dressed in

my old school uniform, crying only once in a tie struggle. Dark green, grey, light green. I looked like a mildewed pond. Spice Girl-style loafers, which I couldn't have loathed more.

OK. I swallowed hard. I had hated school. But that was then. This time I was going to do much better. No one was going to call me Scurrilugs, and if they were, hell, I'd dealt with enough junior analysts and work-experience people to bother about that. And this time round I was going to be cool, cutting and smart, and nobody was going to get to me.

Likewise, I was *extremely* unlikely to get mega-crushes on any of the boys or teachers, seeing as that would be child abuse, and I certainly wasn't going to be insanely self-conscious, because I had a fabulous body and looked great. Hell, I peered into the mirror, where did that spot come from? Never mind. And I wasn't going to squeeze my spots this time round either. Though it looked so tempting . . .

And I was going to know everything. I'd seen three different productions of *Hamlet* now, so they could hardly catch me out on that, and anything sum-related should be pretty nifty too, what with the old accountancy degree. I was going to keep my head down, my mouth shut, and in a month's time I'd go back to Tash's wedding, and, well, and . . .

'FLORA!'

I was not nervous. I wasn't.

Fuck.

* * *

My dad seemed a bit off in the car too.

'I won't be able to pick you up tonight,' he said. 'Tell your mother.'

'Where are you going?' I asked, immediately suspicious. My mother had talked about how late he'd been for a year. Being so wrapped up in myself, of course, I hadn't noticed at the time.

'Just out, darling,' he said, looking surprised I'd asked.

'Where?'

'Nowhere you can go, that's for sure.'

'Dad,' I said, 'you should keep an eye on Mum, OK? She's not feeling so good just now.'

I watched him go slightly pink and grasp the steering wheel hard.

'Don't you worry about your mother and me,' he said.

'I can't help worrying, Dad,' I said. 'You know, in the next couple of years I'm going to leave the nest, and that's a real danger time for lots of marriages.'

He looked at me as if I was a changeling. 'What the hell do you know about it?'

'Nothing,' I said. 'Well, I've read a lot of the literature.'

His face crinkled up in disbelief. 'Right. OK. Well, why don't you just concentrate on getting your A levels?'

I suddenly felt a jump in my chest. How old was I? I was taking my GCSEs, surely, where you get points for spelling your own name right.

Crap, I realised. It was September. Back at school. Lower sixth. Tits.

Calm down, calm down. Breathe. Didn't they make them super easy these days so the government can pretend they can magically make stupid people cleverer?

Jesus Christ. Of all the years I could have picked I had to go for my sixteenth.

Chapter Five

When did kids get so big? This lot were, collectively, absolutely enormous. Huge, milk-reared giants. A lot of fat kids too. When I was in school there was one fat boy and one fat girl per class. It was like a government ration. Now, there were huge people everywhere. Everyone was either enormous – pink, ruddy, like somebody from *Trumpton* come to life – or skinny as a pick – mostly the girls – who, I was pleased to notice, were still rolling their skirts up. Not everything changes.

I stood at the school gates and took a deep breath. I hoped the teachers hadn't changed too much. I recognised Miss Syzlack, thank God. She'd been a brand-new junior English teacher when I'd been there, sixteen years ago. They'd given her all the shitty classes, and she had a reputation for running out of the class and crying. At the time I thought it was pathetic; now I thought if I was twenty-two and had fully grown boys shouting sexual abuse at me, I'd probably be out of there too. But she'd clearly stuck with it. A bit of me hated to think of her still there, and, by the sounds of things, not married either. Everyone knows that teachers always change their names the second they get married, because they realise their kids are completely unable to believe they have lives outside the classroom, and it adds (however slightly) to their disciplinary range if they sound a bit more grown up.

I could remember where the registration classroom was too, assuming it hadn't changed. Sixth form was a lot smaller than the rest of the school, and the two years shared a common room Tash and I were never cool enough to go to. But as to who the hell was who, I was fucked for that. I planned to hang around as long as possible and be the last person sitting down, so that I got the right desk.

* * *

It was the smell that hit me first. It hadn't changed at all. Gym kit, adolescent sweat, strange chemicals, poster paint, dust, formaldehyde, trainers and, overlaying it all, litres of sprayed-on cheap deodorant and aftershave, choking up the yellow hallways and sweaty plastic handrails.

This place hadn't changed an iota. I couldn't believe it. The tiles were cracked in exactly the same places they had been when I'd left. Who could go sixteen years and not think to replace a cracked tile? The grim pink linoleum hadn't changed. The supposedly soothing, prison-like shades of pale green and yellow still haunted the corridors, grubbied and coloured with years of Sellotape. Posters along the walls advertised the periodic table and how to say no to drugs (as usual, illustrated with a revolting shot of a needle going in to somebody's vein rather than, say, a really good relaxed party with everyone having a nice time, the point at which someone is actually going to have to make a choice).

I walked along in a kind of a wonder. For the first time, I really did feel transported. This was a world I hadn't been in for a long, long time. There was a stern exhortation not to run on the stairs. There was a cabinet containing skeletons of animals. A line of kings and queens that I think had been there since I was at school. Some toilets with a telltale whiff of smoke. The school's rather threadbare coat of arms, and its Latin motto for 'Let us do our work this day', 'Get your homework in on time', or whatever it meant. My head was spinning.

'Miss Scurrison!'

That was . . . I definitely recognised that voice. I turned round, conscious I was wearing that expression that people do when they listen to a 'blast from the past' on *This is Your Life*. I also suddenly felt my stomach seize up in a sort of panic.

'Don't you have a class to go to?'

It was Mr Rolf, evil geography teacher incarnate. This man had scared the living daylights out of every one of us. Tashy and I always reckoned it was a possibility that he was actually just sizing us up so he could choose what would be the best moment to pull out a big machine gun and kill us all. If someone answered correctly, they got the piss taken out of them. If someone answered wrongly, they got the piss taken out of them. Shouting was unexpected, detentions arbitrary and shockingly swift. I have a vague recollection of someone once getting three thousand two hundred lines. This was a man who regretted the loss of corporal punishment and told us so, repeatedly. He often lamented the lost legal right to bang children's heads against walls until they saw sense.

One's body's ability to hold sense memories is extraordinary. I straightened up and flashed a nervous smile.

'Good morning, Mr Rolf!'

Even as I said this, I couldn't help looking at him. The last decade and a half hadn't been kind to him. Always scruffy, he was now unkempt and grubby-looking, and the ever-present teacher's dandruff still covered his shoulders. I recalled that he wasn't married. At the time we'd scoffed that we weren't surprised. Now I was looking at a sad man, lonely and broken by years of butting up against people who simply would never be able to care about geography. It came out before I could help myself.

'Are you OK? You look tired.'

He stared at me for half a second.

'Fuck,' I said. Then I regretted that even more.

'INSOLENCE!' he shouted, in the off-key bark I suddenly remembered so well. 'DETENTION!'

What? I had my own secretary! I didn't get detention.

'I'm sorry, sir,' I said, blushing. I'd never got detention when I was at school. Jeez, and how long had it taken me this time round? Four seconds.

'I ask you again – why are you stalking the corridors looking for people to insult when you should be in class? Or have you been taken on as our new counsellor, hurr hurr?'

Ooh, teacher's sarcasm. There's something else I'd missed.

'I'm sorry.' I tried to look penitent and stared hard at the floor. I suddenly felt as if I was going to cry. Must be all those teenage hormones whooshing about my body.

'Honestly! And you're usually one of the better ones! Get out of my sight.'

I scuttled off down the hall.

'That's the wrong direction, Miss Scurrison.'

I scuttled back past him.

'Additives in orange juice,' he muttered obliquely, his sour breath hitting me square on as I passed.

* * *

The entire class looked up as I took a deep breath and stepped inside. Everyone seemed to glance at each other. Or was I just assuming this in my new hell dimension?

Miss Syzlack was recognisable, but, like Mr Rolf, looked tired. She was in the pits of fashion hell as usual. Her dingy cardigan and high-waisted floral skirt made her look like somebody's grandma, and it was with a shock I worked out she couldn't be more than thirty-seven or thirty-eight. I mean, God, Madonna had barely got started by that age.

'Sorry,' I said.

There were two empty seats in the room, and I followed her gaze to one of them. Next to it was a cheeky-looking dark-haired girl gesticulating under her desk. I rushed over and sat down.

'Where you been?' whispered the girl. She was very short, and had a long nose, black eyes and sharp, seesawing eyebrows. 'Are you OK? Last night – it was OK?'

I went to reply.

'No talking,' said Miss Syzlack, and started to read out the register.

'It happens, OK?' said this very familiar small person, sympathetically.

'Constanzia Di Ruggerio, are you chatting?'

The imp beside me tried to look contrite. 'No, miss.'

Constanzia Di Ruggerio? Cool. My friend had a really nice name. I shot her a smile, and she wiggled her eyebrows. From the back of the class someone did that thing where they pretend to cough but they're actually saying something.

'Lesbonerds.'

I was a lesbonerd?

The list of names through the register went on. Who were these people? And, more importantly, what the hell were they called? First time around, I had the most unusual name in the class, and nearly all of the girls were called Tracy, with or without an 'e', Claire, with or without an 'i', or Anne-Marie, in about one hundred different spelling combinations. All boys were called Mark, David, Kevin, Peter or Andrew, and quite right too.

But who were all these Courtneys and Hayleys, Jessicas and Ashleys? We appear to have been taken over by an American sitcom. Fallon? That rang a distant bell. Surely not. Yes, someone had been named after a *Dynasty* character they would probably never see.

I turned my head to see who Longworth, Fallon was, and caught sight of a tall, skinny dark-haired girl at the back of the class. Her long nails were painted silver, and she sneered when her name was called.

'Nice of you to make it today,' said Miss Syzlack.

Fallon merely sniffed her response. Then she caught sight of me, and gave me what I can only describe as a look.

I'd forgotten about 'looks'. In my life – my old life, my thirty-two-year-old life – if you have a problem with someone you sort it out, or, well, you don't really see problems with people, because you can choose your friends and you don't fall out with them, and if it's someone at work it doesn't matter and you can tell your boss and complain and . . . Oh no! She was talking to one of her friends and now they were both looking at me and giving me a look! Crap! Bollocks! Now she was mouthing something at me. I couldn't tell what it was, but it looked a lot like 'dyke-oh'.

'Scurrison, Flora?'

I whipped round when I heard my name being called, but was confused and not sure what to do.

Miss Syzlack looked at me too. Why did I used to remember her as nice? The years must have shrivelled her up, like fruit.

'Have you forgotten your name, Miss Scurrison?'

'No, Miss Syzlack.'

She rubbed one of her eyes. 'Stay behind and see me,' she said.

* * *

I wanted to crawl out of the door behind Constanzia, who shot me such a soulful and sympathetic look I wondered if there was maybe some truth in the lesbian stuff after all. For some reason, Fallon tutted loudly as she passed me. No no no no! I wanted to stop everything and say, 'Guys, that was yesterday. I may, perhaps, have been a lesbonerd. But now, today, I'm supercool! I can help you out! I bet I have the necessary nonchalance to buy stuff in an off-licence, and boy stuff. Come to me, I've done it all.'

'Flora,' said Miss Syzlack. She was sitting perched on her desk, in that nonchalant, 'mmkay?' way teachers do when they're trying to pretend they're down with the kids.

'Is everything all right? You had a lot of people very worried yesterday, you know.'

'Yeah, sorry about that,' I said. I'd have loved a confidante right now, but I hadn't quite come up with a way of telling my story that wouldn't end up with me in the secure unit, tied down on the bed next to the girl who makes the poltergeist appear, so I decided to keep my counsel.

'Well?'

I felt like saying, 'Miss, I don't want to come over all Trinny and Susannah here, but have you heard of highlights? Why don't I show you this really friendly women's gym? In fact, while I've got you here, why don't you give up this teaching thing you so clearly hate altogether and go off round the world?'

I shrugged. 'I suppose I just panicked,' I said. 'A levels and all that. Just had to blow off some steam. That's pretty typical for my age, isn't it? My hormone levels are all over the place. I'm surprised I don't have a crush on you.'

Oh, for fuck's sake.

'I mean, things change every second. I can't even keep up with my own bra size at the moment, never mind the social, academic, biological and cultural pressures teenagers are under.

'And it is absolutely not true that these are great years – anyone will agree with that. It's unfair also to show us advertisements showing teenagers having the times of their lives, as if it's good for anyone to end up like Britney Spears. They should really just say, "Keep your head down, your twenties will be fantastic." Look at these people. They haven't even got their personal hygiene sorted out and they're the number one demographic zone-in for advertisers, convincing everyone else in the world that being sixteen is fantastic. Well, it's not, I tell you. OK?'

The teacher looked at me, stunned.

'Um . . . yes. Perhaps, maybe you'd like to visit our educational psychologist.'

'For what? Plunking it for one day in my entire school career?'

'Don't talk to me like that, please, young lady.'

'Why not?'

'It's rude.'

'It's not rude! And you're the one who just suggested I go see a bloody psychologist!'

Miss Syzlack looked down at her desk. 'Well, I had hoped this session might help you. But instead I see no choice but to give you detention.'

'No choice? None at all?'

'For insolence and truancy.'

'Fine,' I said, raising my hands.

Miss Syzlack watched me, shaking her head. 'What's got into you, Flora?'

'Maybe I'm growing up,' I said.

* * *

I found the third class, thank God, and sat through a frankly baffling hour on community festivals, none of which I could hear or make any sense of. It was droned at us by a man I didn't recognise, and fortunately everyone else was staring just as much into space as I was. Finally, the bell rang, and it was – Jesus Christ – playtime.

I trailed out after Constanzia, who was still sitting next to me, my stomach hitting my stupid Spice Girl loafer shoes.

'Well?' she said, those crazy eyebrows of hers beetling up and down. 'You show them you are miserable, huh?'

'What?'

'Nobody comes to your birthday party – so fucking what, yes? But you plunk it without me?'

'My birthday party?' I just asked stupidly.

Oh no. Surely not. What unearthly fucking world had put me back in the WORST PERIOD OF MY LIFE.

'I just can't believe it,' said Constanzia, throwing her hands up. 'It's like the worst betrayal of all time. We have bad party, you don't come to school. I think I'm going to hang myself, like all those kids who go to Cambridge when they're twelve.' She looked at me, black eyes twinkling, clearly trying to pretend she was having a joke, but feeling bad all the same.

'Don't do that,' I said weakly.

'You wanted me to die? Is that why you did it?'

'No,' I said slowly.

'Well, if you wanted me to die, that's exactly what you should have done. Take a day off without me, your best friend.'

'You're not dead,' I said.

'Oh yes?' she said. 'You know when I am at school. What is it we say when we are not here?'

With a sinking feeling I started to think back to when it was me and Tash. If she wasn't there, I hated it, because I'd have to sit by myself in class, and vice versa. Fuck, fuck fuck. Why couldn't I have been a cool kid this time round? Was that really too much to ask? As well as being trapped in this hellhole with no way out in sight, I had to be a complete smeghead at the same time – not that any of the kids here would even remember the term 'smeghead', although I'm sure they had something equally pleasant.

'I'm sorry,' I said.

'I could have been dead. I was Dead Constanzia Walking.'

'Sorry.'

'I had lunch sitting in the stairwell. And for what? So you could go and become a drunk person in the West End. I am very happy for you.'

'It's a bit more complicated than that,' I said.

'Oh sure.' Constanzia kicked heavily at a piece of filthy, mud-encrusted grass, as we circled the grounds. Younger boys were running around and playing football, younger girls were touching each other's hair and whispering. So much for an extra sixteen years of gender studies.

'Oh, look, the gruesome twosome reunited, innit?' came a low, drawling voice. For some daft reason, though it wasn't posh, male or growly, it reminded me of Shere Khan in the film *Jungle Book*.

We turned round. It was Fallon, and two acolytes, one blonde, one brunette.

'Don't tell me – you were on your way to school and you got picked up by the animal pound,' said Fallon, looking straight at me. 'Your parents were going to let you get put down and then changed their minds at the last minute.'

Why couldn't I have been popular this time round? This wasn't in my plan. In fact, of course, in my plan, such as it should have been, I was on the way to Paris by now, surrounded by people who wanted to make me their muse.

Instead I had some witch trying to make my life hell. The first time round it had been Sheena. She'd ended up working on a supermarket counter, getting pregnant to a succession of guys then dropping off the radar all together. That was meant to happen to the bad girls.

But Fallon didn't look like Sheena. Sheena always looked vaguely fashionable, but it was always the cheap, Netto end. She didn't always smell fantastic and there were rumours of a horrible home life, which, in retrospect I'm sure were true. My mother was right: she did deserve sympathy more than fear, not that I could find it in me at the time.

Fallon was dressed more expensively than I did as a grown-up. You can always tell, can't you? You don't always care, but you can always tell. I was sensing Nicole Farhi, Ralph Lauren, all just for the very plain components that make up a school uniform. Her hair was glossy and carefully dried. This wasn't skeggy little schemie bully. This was big-time cheerleader style. Well, she wasn't going to intimidate me, jumped-up little brat. I'd let this happen to me too many times as a child and it wasn't going to bother me now. I swallowed my fear.

'Fuck off, boring person,' I said.

'Ooh!' went her almost as well-groomed acolytes.

'What's that? Are you telling me to – what?' said Fallon in seeming disbelief.

'Let's go. I'm very bored here,' I said to Constanzia.

'Oh, the little swot's bored?' Fallon's eyes were flashing. 'What's the matter? Not enough swotting around for you? Or – don't tell me – there are too many people talking. Makes you feel like you've got friends. Good party by the way?'

'I've got friends,' I said, shocked despite myself.

'I can't believe you invited us!'

I didn't. Mind you, I'd invited Sheena the first time round. For fuck's sake.

They giggled loudly.

'Anyway, it's party season – you must be going to Ethan's party tomorrow? After all, you invited him.'

She said this to Constanzia. Constanzia shook her head.

'Really? What a shame. Of course it would be too boring for you – they've got a swimming pool. And a wine cellar. Everyone else in the class has been invited. Never mind, you two.'

I couldn't believe this. I was feeling terrible about the fact that I wasn't invited to a party by someone I didn't know. Who cared?

'Just the two of you staying at home then? On your own? No, that'll be much more fun. Much less boring.'

And they strode off.

'Christ. Has she always been like that?'

Constanzia looked at me. 'Erm, remember when you got that scar?'

Sure enough, looking down on my arm I saw a scar that I hadn't noticed before.

'She pushed you off the climbing frame.'

'Witch.'

'Head witch,' Constanzia agreed. 'And you know, yesterday, you leave me to face the witch all alone. You do this if you want a friend dead, yes? There, see – go into the gingerbread house by yourself, stupid child.'

'I'm sorry,' I said.

'Buy me a Twix,' she said.

'No!'

'I'll share it.'

God, it'd been a long time since I'd eaten a Twix. Chunky Kit Kats are a much more adult snack, I believe.

'All right,' I said.

* * *

'Why are we so unpopular, Stanzi?' I said, as we sat on the wall and licked toffee off our fingers. For a second I forgot I was thirty-two, that I had a mortgage and a near-fiancé and had been chairman of our university leaving ball committee. I was just at school, sitting on the same wall near the science lab I always used to sit on, staring at the same sad windows and dripping brickwork, tasting chocolate and caramel on my tongue and utterly absorbed in the universe that was school.

Constanzia stared at the floor and ate her last piece of Twix. 'Because you're a swot and I'm the smallest minority in the whole school, remember? And I used to have a moustache. And you never have any tits.'

I looked at her. True, she did have a very heavy line of yellow hair on her top lip.

'And they just decide they didn't like us and that was that. Anyway, why is this worrying you now? It's always been like this.'

I swung my feet. 'I don't know. I'm just getting sick of the whole thing.'

'Don't worry. Just hold on for two years and we can go to college. Yay! Hooray! Sex and boys all night long.'

'You'll be surprised how quickly that gets old,' I said, and then did a double take. 'Two years?' What if I couldn't get out of here? No way was I staying two years.

'Well, you have to. You leave now, it's all over for you. "*Big Issue?*"'

'Look, I'm not going to leave school, OK?'

'"*Big Issue?*"'

'Stop that, it's not nice.'

The bell rang.

'I can't remember a thing. With this new timetable, the school has deliberately set out to destroy me.' Constanzia pulled out a crumpled piece of paper.

I pounced. 'Me neither. Let me see.'

'Why are you looking at mine?'

'Oh, yeah.'

'Yesterday, when you having such a great time without your best friend, you fall down? You get hit on the head?'

'Kind of.'

'Your Italian *e schifo*.'

'Is that good?'

She smiled at me. 'You have to go be maths idiot now, yes? Run along, *piccolo rana*.'

* * *

I'd managed to raise Tashy on the telephone, sneaking out at lunchtime and buying an incredibly expensive top-up card for my mobile.

'It was all a dream?'

'No.'

'Oh God. I can't believe it . . . I just can't. Oh God, Flora. What the hell are we going to do?'

'Look, look . . .' I almost laughed as I watched two boys in the middle distance have a fight. Everyone else immediately swarmed over and started screaming their heads off.

'Oh God,' I said. 'OK, I'm in hell.'

'Really? Hell exists? Is this what this is?'

'No, I mean. I'm back at school. On top of everything that's happened I'm back at school. It's like – after my terrible party.'

'Oh,' said Tashy in a small voice. 'So it's not any better this time round?'

For some reason, the kids watching the fight had started chanting the 'c' word very loudly. Mr Rolf had come out of the main school building, but even he looked in two minds at approaching the roaring throng. I hoped nobody had a gun.

'I wouldn't say that,' I said, and started to snivel.

'No, no, don't cry!' said soft-hearted Tash, diving in. 'I mean – you're in hell? Ha! I have six meetings double-booked for this afternoon, I can't get caterers to fold napkins into roses instead of swans – fucking swans – we have twenty-nine days to the wedding and you can still get into children's clothes and not pay any VAT on them. How can that be hell?'

'School's SHIT!' I said.

'Oh, petal, it must be easier this time round. Think of all the clever stuff you know.'

'I'm the most unpopular girl in the school!'

'No! Don't they still have those kids who have glasses stuck together with Elastoplast?'

'Don't think so,' I sniffed. 'And I have a suicidal mad best friend.'

'What do you mean?'

'My best friend. She's a bit . . .'

'I'm your best friend.'

'I know that,' I said slowly. 'I mean, in this new world.'

'Do you like her better than me?'

I cried harder.

'I mean, I know I've been very busy with the wedding and everything, but—'

'No no no no. Stop. Shut up. You're my best friend. This is just a weird creature who follows me about, OK?'

'Is she pretty?'

'She looks like a cat who has evil powers.'

'Yeah?'

'She has a voice like a fire in a pet shop.'

Tashy sounded less suspicious. 'OK. Look, sit tight, and I'll come and get you tonight, OK? Can you hold on till then?'

'I can't come out tonight.'

'Why not?'

'Tashy! I'm grounded. And I have detention.'

'Well, duh. Don't be stupid. Skip it.'

'They'll send me to borstal!'

'You know, you sound just like yourself on the phone,' said Tashy musingly.

'I am myself, OK? We have to get control of the situation. I am myself. I just can't do anything.'

'Were we really not allowed out when we were sixteen?'

'Yes, but only under laboratory conditions.'

'Can't you say you're staying at your new best friend's – whatever her name is?'

'Constanzia.'

'Con-what?'

'And anyway, no, because I don't know her phone number or where she lives. And I'm grounded.'

Tashy heaved a sigh. 'This is terrible.'

'It's hell,' I said. 'Are you *sure* I haven't actually died in

103

a terrible tragic accident and you're being too nice to tell me about it?'

'If this is what's at the other side, I bloody hope not.'

* * *

I'd never had detention first time around. Yes, I was one of those kids. And now, watching every other kid skip, laughing and screeching, down to the gates where the cars and buses clustered, I could see how it worked as a punishment.

Of course, most of those kids wanted to go home. And so did I. But my home didn't exist.

Sighing slightly in the mild September afternoon, I stomped off to where I did remember the bad boys hanging out the window in detention and whistling at the girls like men in prison (where, indeed, many of them now are).

Mr Rolf was patrolling up and down outside the room, which was filled with boyish shouts and retorts. He smiled, very unpleasantly, when he saw me coming and my teacher's sarcasm radar started bleeping urgently.

'Ah, Miss Scurrison. So glad you could make it on such a glamorous evening. I know you're a newcomer to our esteemed great social occasions of the top wits and charmers of the cultural élite that is Christchurch Secondary. I imagine you'll fit right in.'

I walked in, my heart filling with trepidation. All the boys here looked exactly like any group of lads you'd cross the road to avoid, full of the usual combustible mix of teenage fear, bravado, hormones and cider. Who'd be a teacher, I thought, not for the first time. At what point did that job get fun? Give me my boring, safe desk, computer, long lists of papers, any day. I can't believe I was getting nostalgic for strip lighting and quarterly VAT returns.

A collective 'wooah' went up from the room as I went in. Obviously they knew who I was and I doubted very much whether I'd been seen in here before. This was nuts. I couldn't believe a bunch of complete strangers with a shared IQ of about forty-five knew more about my life than I did.

'Hey, sexy baby. Wanna get some ed-u-cation?' said one pimple-faced giant, slouching next to me and carving 'FUCK' slowly and methodically on the desk.

'Yeah,' shouted another one. 'I'll make you stay late . . . very late . . .'

I raised my eyes. Soon they'd start boasting to each other about made-up sexual experiences and move on.

'Haven't seen you round here,' said one skinhead.

'Fresh meat!' yelled someone else from the back of the class, to general amusement. Unbelievably, fucking Rolf stood by and just watched this happen. If this had been the office, Olly would have slapped the whole damn lot of them with a sexual harassment suit within fifteen seconds.

I sat down. On the board, it said, 'Essay topic: the useful-ness of nothingness.'

'Hey, baby, now you're in with us, do you think you'll be . . . letting it all hang out a bit more, yeah?' whispered one sweaty voice behind me.

'Get fucked,' I said.

There was a definite wooh. My heart was beating really hard. This was horrible. I couldn't believe they would let people be so intimidating. It felt dangerous.

'Are you swearing, Miss Scurrison?'

Immediately I lost all the sympathy I had for this broken

man of a teacher and indulged a quick revenge fantasy that involved prison and limitless penance. And kicking.

'No, sir,' I said quickly, like a cowed dog.

'Yeah, she was, sir.'

'Do you want to pay a speedy return visit?'

'No, sir.'

He nodded and pointed to the board. 'Better get on with it, then.'

He left the room – the school had clearly deteriorated if they had to split detention in two. My face burned bright hot with fear and a sense of injustice; a whispering started up.

'We're going to get you, whore.'

Jesus.

Suddenly, there was a cracking noise. It sounded like somebody smacking somebody else hard on the knuckles with a ruler.

'Fuck,' said the same voice.

'Shut the fuck up,' said another, near-familiar one. 'Do you want to get done for sexual harassment, or just spend the rest of your life here?'

'Wot?'

'Just shut it, OK?'

I risked a look behind me, and nearly had a heart attack. When I'd come in I hadn't even raised my eyes from the floor and taken the first seat at the front. Which was why I hadn't noticed the boy currently holding another boy by the ear and threatening to swat him with a ruler.

'Fucking lanky bastard,' said the lout, but he returned quietly to his reading.

Justin Clelland's eyes met mine. He betrayed – of course – no knowledge of me, beyond me being some girl he'd seen around. There was no interest, no enquiry, suspicion or flirting. I, by contrast, knew I was gawping. This boy looked so like Clelland in his school uniform I wanted to throw up.

'Thanks,' I said.

He shrugged and retook his seat directly behind me.

'Flora,' I said, putting out my hand. He stared at it. Maybe handshaking doesn't start till later.

Eventually he took it. 'I know,' he said. 'You hang around with that dark-haired crazy girl.'

I nodded. 'And you're Justin.'

He nodded politely. Of course, he must be a year ahead of me. Oddly, and I guess perhaps it had something to do with my being a couple of inches shorter, he didn't look quite the droopy, grumpy teenager he had at Tashy's wedding. Compared to the rest of the greasy Neanderthals whose features hadn't dropped into place yet, he was tall, smooth-skinned, with soft, baby-fine curls, and calm grey eyes just like his brother's. On the whole, I suspected he was a bit of a school heart-throb.

'What are you in for?' I whispered.

'I protested against another year where they refused to order recycled textbooks. They didn't take it too well.'

Awww, Clelland II.

I decided to get a bit cunning.

'Don't you have a brother who's in Africa?'

He immediately looked frightened. Oh, crap. I'd just revealed myself to be one of those terrifying teenage stalkers who write names all over their textbooks and fill their diaries with 'I love you, John Bloggs, and we WILL be married', over and over again.

He coughed.

'Are you talking, Miss Scurrison?'

This bastard moved on oiled wheels of silence, I swear to God.

'No, sir.'

'You haven't got the hang of this at all, have you, Miss Scurrison?'

'No, sir.'

'I think that's why we'll be seeing you on Monday.'

At least this time I managed not to swear.

* * *

My parents looked like they were sitting shivah for me as I peered in the lighted windows through the oncoming twilight. They probably were: mourning the studious, well-behaved daughter who had woken up yesterday morning and would never be the same again.

'I was in detention,' I said, hanging my coat on the wall.

'We know,' said my dad. 'We asked for you to have it.'

'Thank you,' I said. 'I'm sure you'll be pleased to know that my essay on "Nothingness" was a great use of my time during my AS level year.'

My mother put dinner on the table in silence. Ooh! Nobody had made me a proper dinner since – well, she'd pretty much given up cooking for herself after Dad left. Just didn't care any more, I suppose. I had to make sure she was stocked up with Marks and Spencer's stuff, and that she knew how to heat it up.

That was a shame, because she was a great cook. I tucked into the sausages and mash with gusto. Olly and I usually went out or ordered in, and I'd forgotten how good a well-made onion gravy could be.

'This is really, really good. Isn't it, Dad?' I said enthusi-
astically.

They both looked at me.

'Um, yeah,' said Dad.

'Thanks for cooking, Mum.'

My mother looked amazed. 'Just the same old—' she
started.

'Yes. Thanks, Joyce,' said my dad, embarrassed, as if I'd
shown him up. My mother blinked and fluttered.

I stared at my plate and went back to eating in silence in
case I said anything else completely stupid. Then I remembered my mandate to get them back together and started
racking my brains to think of some nice friendly family
conversation. Which, looking back, I couldn't actually
remember much of from this part of my life first time around.

After a hundred years, my mother piped up, 'You're not
going round to Stanzi's tomorrow night.'

'We weren't going to do anything,' I said sourly, thinking
of the unknown Ethan's party.

'Well, you can go to work, and that's it.'

I nearly choked on a piece of mashed potato. Work? I had
a job? What kind of a job? I thought back to when I was
sixteen, at the Co-op. Endless boxes of biscuits. No, no, no.
Saturdays were for shopping, and pedicures with Tash. Please,
no. Whatever my job was, I didn't want to do it.

I swallowed slowly. 'Actually, you know . . . it's been such
a big week, here or there . . .'

My dad looked at me. I thought for a brief second he
could sense my inner confusion and turmoil.

'Don't think you're getting any money from us.'

'You don't want to lose that job, Flora,' my mother

109

reproached me. 'They're good people at the Co-op. And, Duncan, for Christ's sake, shut up. If she needs money we'll—'

'No, of course I don't,' I said hurriedly. Had they always spoken to each other in this way? I was a bit cheeky to Ol, but this was just awful. 'But, also, you know, I've got a ton of homework to do too and . . .'

I got up and left. My dad was glaring at my mother. He looked as if he was thinking something he'd never say aloud.

My first stop: I should just get fired from the Co-op. Tashy would give me the money, surely. She had plenty sloshing around that wedding fund of hers. And I could pay her back . . . I swallowed a big gulp of uncertainty. I would pay her back when I got out of this mess. Jeez. And hopefully, when that happened, nobody would remember I'd even been here at all. I had to believe that. I had to.

* * *

I paced around my bedroom, picking up unfamiliar things. I needed some space I couldn't trip myself up in, plus I'd already seen this week's episode of *Friends* and *Have I Got News for You* a month ago, and I didn't want to give away any possible psychic abilities. And I certainly couldn't relax. I mean, when I'd thought about being sixteen again, I'd thought about staying out late and having fun, not having detention and staying in on Friday nights, watching old *Have I Got News for You*s listening to my mum and dad rip each other to shreds. Which, when I thought back to it, I had done quite a lot of. Before Clelland had come along and . . . no, I wasn't going to think about that. Not only was it long ago, it was in a completely different world.

Plus, I couldn't have sat still even if I wanted to. I fidgety and antsy, and the atmosphere between my mum dad was too frosty for words. I wanted to run out the house and go find some friends and pretend none of this was happening, but I didn't want to see that look in my mum's eyes again. So I was a trapped animal. I looked around my blue-wallpapered bedroom.

I would have thought I was far too old for CDs by Gareth Gates, but clearly not. Oh well, I was the uncoolest girl in the school, so maybe that explained it. There was some old Steps, going back a couple of years, and lots of No Doubt, whom I clearly loved. Good. I put them in the woefully poor quality pink CD player that must have been a present. There were also plenty of other people I really hadn't heard of, which was a bit embarrassing. I thought I was a bit more up on music than this, but I had no idea who Jay-Z was, or who those seventeen pikey-looking boys in the poster on my wall were. I leafed idly through several copies of *Smash Hits*, and wondered if I could remember who was about to become number one, so I could put a bet on it. I wandered over to my white, faux Louis XIV desk, which was horrible, and had a framed picture of a tiger above it – I loved tigers. I opened the drawers, one after another: magazines, free lipsticks and endless, endless screeds of useless-looking homework dribbled out. Then I got to one that was locked. Ooh, locked drawer.

I felt perversely guilty and sneaky about this. I was sneaking on a teenager's privacy – the most precious thing to them. She would be horrified, totally horrified and mortified if she knew a complete stranger was going to look at her secret things. Even if the complete stranger was me.

111

I fiddled about at the bottom of the pink fluffy bag and, sure enough, there was a tiny key there. Feeling guilty, and with my heart thumping quite loudly, I turned the lock.

There was a miniature bottle of peach schnapps (which I drank immediately, of course, gagging slightly at the cloying sweetness), some cigarette papers, a couple of pictures of men with their shirts off – foxy – a copy of *Fanny Hill* (I smiled ironically to myself), and, oh God. Yes. What I had probably been subconsciously looking for all the time.

I drew it out. It was rather nice, actually, a plain, lined book with a silk cover that looked like a big investment of my Co-op money.

My Diary.

I had actually burned my own 1980s version of this little beauty some years before when I realised that, in fact, when I was an old lady sitting in a home I probably wouldn't be that fascinated by reading who had annoyed me particularly that week, and if I couldn't remember a person's name ten years after the event, I'd be very unlikely to do so in my brief periods of geriatric lucidity. There also seemed less and less point in hoarding it for grateful biographers from the British Library.

More than that, though, I didn't like seeing the lonely and confused little girl I was. I know all teenagers are lonely and confused, to greater or lesser extents, but surely a point of being an adult is that we get to dump that entire thing, like a snake shedding its skin, and escape into a world of lasting friendships, real fun, a lifting of the terrible, ever-lasting self-consciousness that weighs on your shoulders every single second of every single day. I didn't want to read about a girl who didn't know she could be happy. I didn't want to read about a girl who painted castles in the air, who didn't know what the world could bring, who planned the wedding that was currently driving Tashy crazy.

And everything did get better, of course it did. In the shape of a degree, and a nice little car, and a flat, and a nice boyfriend. She got all of these things. I'm just not sure that's what she meant, or thought that's how they would feel.

And here I was *again*. I lay down on my purple eiderdown and cringed. You know, I didn't think I'd changed so much. I looked at my soft, lily-white hands. That wasn't how I expected my hands to look. They wouldn't have chipped black polish on them, for a start. But as I forced myself to read the book, I forced myself to realise the truth, however weird it was.

This girl was me, all right. Unbearably, unreadably so at some points.

'Fallon is a big WITCH. She thinks she's so brilliant but I think she's probably a VERY UNHAPPY PERSON who thinks sending round notes about Somebody else's feelings is funny, which means she is probably SICK.'

Yeah. Oh, no, please, what was this?

'I think I'm in love with Ethan. I can hardly say it out loud, it makes me feel so strange. But I really do think I love him. I think this might be it. And he looked at me at least three times yesterday.'

Oh, fuck a doo, surely not. These bloody lads. In two years' time they'd be DROOLING over us at university, and at the moment they were too busy playing top trumps to even think of including someone . . . OK, I was not going to have my feelings hurt by someone I had never set eyes on. Let me see . . .

113

There was an incomprehensible scrawl that seemed to indicate Constanzia and I had drunk two bottles of her father's wine as an experiment and passed out. I had stopped dotting my i's with circles only a year before. And the more I flipped back and forth in the book for it, the more I realised the truth. It had been true then, and it was true now.

I was still a virgin. Of course I was. I'd just turned sixteen. It's just – at this I got a sudden twinge, I didn't know why. It was very peculiar. Being a virgin wasn't something I'd thought of as a state for so long, or at any rate as something to kick against as a prerequisite in women in geopolitical terms.

As soon as I left home – the increasingly sad, inward-looking place home had become after Dad's departure – I'd got rid of it as quick as was humanly possible. It was sore, fumbly, damp and embarrassing.

Things had gradually improved, of course, and it's rarely a romantic highspot for anyone, but I could feel the hopes and dreams tied up in this book, my blank slate, and hugged it thoughtfully to my tiny chest.

'You don't even know,' I whispered to it. 'Well, don't accept any invites to any college balls willy-nilly.'

'It was really nice kissing Felix at the s.p. We kissed for four hours and twenty-eight minutes.'

OK, this was from last year, but still, I was quite impressed by that. When had I last snogged for any time at all? I couldn't remember. I mean, Olly and I kissed, didn't we? Well, on the lips when we saw each other, which wasn't quite snogging, and in bed, I guess, but that wasn't quite snogging either.

But it's a teenage trait, really, isn't it? That's why they're always catching glandular fever.

'I hate working in the Co-op. Mrs Bentall is a complete b***h. It's so unfair. Stanzi just gets money off her mum and dad and a clothing allowance. It's not fair. If Dad was ever in I might get a clothing allowance.'

Oh, gosh, a whiner. I looked down at the grumpy life I was holding in my hands. This girl was on the same trajectory as I was.

My phone bleeped. I leaped on it. It was a text.

'World fucked up,' it said. Thank goodness Tashy had never learned text language either. 'Will pick up tomorrow for escape bid.'

Chapter Six

Thank God for Tash. I couldn't sleep. I eventually curled up in a ball in the bed when I heard the *Newsnight* music downstairs, and had jerked awake all night, clutching the stupid diary. I'd texted Tash at as near first light as I could manage, and met her round the corner, in traditional teenager sneaking-out way. I'd just have to resign from the Co-op; Mum never went there anyway. She thought it was the supermarket of communist Russia.

Tashy was sitting at the wheel of her little Audi. She raised her eyebrows at me and I realised that perhaps the miniskirt/striped jersey ensemble I'd pulled out the cupboard might be a bit much for a Saturday morning.

'What?' I said crossly, even though I was so relieved she was there I could have burst.

'Nothing,' she said as I got in. 'You're just so tiny. Let me fiddle with your upper arms a second.'

'LEAVE it.'

She pushed up the skin under my eyes with a finger.

'There you go, see. That's what you're going to look like in sixteen years' time. Fuck, you have so long.'

I studied myself in the car window as she reversed from the kerb. It's true, my skin, where it wasn't breaking out, had a definite bloom on it. But I also looked less like myself. You couldn't really tell from my appearance what I was like. A blank slate, of course. My face hadn't quite settled.

'You know, I've been eating nothing but bloody steamed fish for six months and I still look nothing like you.'

'You look great,' I said, with the reflex action you have with your best friends.

'So I bloody should,' she said dreamily. 'How do I look on the day?'

'Oh, one must not know one's own future,' I said. 'It is forbidden.'

'Is Max's speech funny?'

'Yes,' I lied. 'Um, how is Max?'

'Well,' she looked worried suddenly, 'I said, "You'll never believe what's happened to Flo."'

'Uh-huh?'

She concentrated on the road ahead. 'Well . . .' she said. '*What?*'

'Here's the thing, Flo. He's never heard of you.'

'He's never what?'

'He had no idea who I was talking about.'

The terrible crushing fear came back.

'Oh God,' I said. 'Oh God, I don't exist. In this world, or the old world, or the . . . what the *fuck* is going on? Who am I? I don't . . . how will I be able to do anything or get back or . . . I'm no one!' I started to hyperventilate.

She clutched my arm. 'You do.'

'But . . . not for Max, not for bloody old Karl Dean, not for Miss Syzlack, even though. . .I mean, she knows someone else altogether.'

'I'm sure there's a rational explanation.'

'LOOK at me!'

'OK maybe not rational exactly.'

I gulped suddenly. 'Oh my God, what about Olly?'

'I wondered when you were going to mention him,' said Tash quietly. 'He must be worried sick.'

'Well, where are we going now?'

'You'll see.'

'You've invented a person-ageing machine?'

'Yes, I call it "management accounting exams".'

'Ha-ha.'

We parked near the centre of town and walked up across Piccadilly, down the steps and over to beautiful St James's Park. It was a lovely autumn morning, not wet, just a faint mist rising off the lake and through the trees. Apart from the usual complement of manic joggers, there weren't many people around at all.

'Let's go feed the ducks,' said Tashy meaningfully, taking some bread out of her pockets.

'I'm sixteen, not six.'

'Come on.'

'You've set me up for MI6,' I said, suddenly panicking. 'You're going to sell me to the military, aren't you, so they can run all sorts of tests on me and work out how to use me as a weapon?'

'Yes, that's what friends do,' said Tash snidely.

'We're near Whitehall! Experiments! Don't do it, Tash. What if I get kidnapped by a cosmetics company?'

'Ssh. Ssh. Stop being paranoid,' said Tash, indicating a tall figure walking towards us through the trees.

'I have every fucking right to be paranoid.'

'It must be your hormones.'

'Hormones they're going to extract with an enormous probe! Oh shit.'

The figure resolved itself through the trees. It was Olly. He stopped dead still about six feet away from us.

'Jesus God,' he said, staring at me.

'He knows me!' I exclaimed. Why some people did and some people didn't, I hadn't the faintest idea. I hadn't realised the extent of my terror until then, and it had left me weak with relief and gratitude. 'You know me!'

Tash had already gone to meet him and was holding his arm.

'Sorry,' said Tashy. 'I didn't quite know how to explain it over the phone.'

'Clearly.' Olly sounded hoarse. 'What . . . *WHAT?*' His head hit his hands. 'I don't get it. What?'

I stared at him. He looked tired and – God, I admit it – after staring at myself in the mirror far too much over the last two days, I thought he looked old. He looked like my dad.

'He remembered you all right,' said Tashy to me, to cover the silence. Olly was shaking. 'Apparently your phone's been out of commission.'

'Yeah, in the netherworld,' I said.

'From Tashy's voice I thought you were pregnant,' said Olly incredulously, his voice cracking. 'Or you'd had a really traumatic haircut. What *happened* to you?' He came forward and stood in front of me. I looked into his eyes. He shook his head. 'Look at you,' he said quietly. Then he put out his hand and touched me in a curious prodding motion, as if I was a specimen in a laboratory.

'Well . . .' I began. Then I told him everything, excluding the bits about my worries about him, and meeting Clelland again, so it didn't take long.

Olly listened extremely carefully in complete silence, so he could bring his rational lawyer's mind fully to bear on it, but still occasionally shaking his head in incredulity. Then he stood in silence for a very long time, staring out on the water. He finally turned to me and looked straight into my eyes. He swallowed one last time. I rubbed my skinny limbs nervously.

'You . . . you wanted to wish your life away?'

'Or back.' I shrugged.

He hung his head. 'How unhappy with me *were* you?'

I hadn't expected that at all. I looked at his face and felt completely dreadful. We were, after all, only a month away from him going down on bended knee, and he must at least have been considering it. So I did the best thing I could think of under the circumstances. Lied.

'Don't be silly, darling. This wasn't about you. I was just idly speculating, that was all, and this crazy thing happened.' I tried to make it sound light and not so much of a problem.

'God, I can't . . . you have to see yourself say that, you really do. Do you know you have purple in your hair?'

I nodded.

'Anyway, I thought you said you wished out loud.'

'Hardly. It was just a passing thought . . .'

'Just as well you weren't thinking about big monsters,' said Tashy.

'No, that was *Ghostbusters*,' I said. 'I think this is more *Peggy Sue Got Married*.'

Olly couldn't stop staring at me. 'So, have you seen into the future too?'

'No, I've just lived it already. And only a month of it.'

He frowned. 'Do you remember how the market closes?'

'I can't even remember what was number one. I've tried this already.'

'We have,' said Tashy. 'But my wedding is on a nice day and I fit into my dress. Ooh, I think I can have a cake.' I loved her for trying to lift our spirits with a bit of jollity. And I hated what I was about to say.

'I'm not sure you can,' I said. 'I'm here now. That might change everything. But you recognise me, and Max doesn't, and my parents are all young and weird, and I don't know what the hell's going on and what I can change or not change. I don't understand it at all.'

'Oh,' Tashy looked defeated, 'OK. No cake then.'

Olly stepped up to me and took my shoulders. 'My God, you're shorter too,' he said sadly.

'I know,' I said. 'But, on the plus side, my tits are further off the ground.'

He looked at me, his eyes wary. 'Well, um, this is a shock. Shall we . . . shall we head for home?'

'Um,' I said.

'Oh God.' He jumped back. 'Are you even legal? Am I a paedophile? Fuck.'

'It's not that,' I said. Poor Olly, terrified of accidentally touching up his own girlfriend. What a mess. 'Anyway, I'm sixteen.'

'OK, good.' He thought for a second. 'Better than good, actually.'

'I can't,' I said. 'I have to stay at home with my parents. And they'll go nuts if I stay out all night.'

121

'Oh. Right. Can't you tell them you're staying at Tashy's?'

'It's amazing how quickly everyone remembers their teenage guile. Anyway, no, I can't, because Tashy's a big scary adult woman, and anyway, I'm grounded.'

'Really?' He started to laugh. 'You're grounded. This is fucking *nuts*.'

'It's not funny.'

'I know. It's nuts! Would you like me to buy you an ice cream to make up for it?'

'Do you fancy me more now?' I asked. Despite everything, insecurity was creeping in.

'Olly,' ordered Tashy. '*Never* answer that question.'

'OK.' Olly decided that, after all, we would have an ice cream. Ice cream was one of his major food groups. We followed him over to the van.

'And a flake for the little lady,' he was saying.

Tashy looked at me. 'I think he's taking it rather well.'

'Rather too well,' I said. 'I don't want him getting boners for teens.'

'Oh, come on. You watch TV. It trains them like beagles.'

'Hmm,' I said.

'I wasn't serious about Jamie Theakston. Were you?'

'Well, I find his dungeon proclivities a little overwhelming for my untouched body, but I'm not automatically ruling out any of the boy bands.'

'Be serious. What about when you get back?'

I didn't say anything.

Olly returned, bearing 99s.

'So,' he said, 'when are you going to get back to us?'

122

'Well, assuming I want to come back,' I said musingly.

I surprised even myself.

* * *

'Student grants,' Tashy was saying earnestly. We'd repaired to the ICA. 'Sweaters with big holes in the sleeves. Living off one pot of chilli for an entire week.'

'Finals,' said Olly.

'Sitting your driving test. Which, by the way, they've made much, much harder.'

'The Co-op.'

'Other idiotic young people all around you.'

'High hopes being dashed all over again.'

'Middle-class students exploring socialism over long boring conversations.'

'Trying to get on the London property ladder.'

'Middle-class students telling you all about how their gap year in India really changed their life.'

'Having to dance in public.'

'Smoking dope again.'

'A LEVELS!!!'

'OK, OK,' I said. 'Look, it just came out. A possibility. I know it would be awful.'

'Crazy awful.'

'It's just . . .' I said. 'I could . . . I could choose everything. Do things differently this time.'

'What's wrong with what we had?' said Olly, staring hard at his cappuccino.

'Nothing,' I said. 'Just . . . there's so many possibilities. I mean, what if I went to film school?'

'Flora, your favourite film is *Goldeneye*,' said Tashy.

'Mmm. He's so beautiful. Oh God – and, really, far far too old for me now.'

'I don't think they let you in to film school just for fancying movie stars.'

'They should,' I said. 'Then they'd stop casting Robin Williams in things.'

'Hmm.'

'Well, it doesn't have to be film school. Maybe I could be an illustrator, or a teacher . . . OK, maybe – no, make that definitely – not a teacher. Maybe I could go travelling for a bit. Ooh, join an ad agency. That always looked like fun. I could work as an intern. Maybe go into government. Be one of those clever wonks like in *The West Wing*. I bet there's billions of things I could do. And I know what they are. And I know how to network. And this way, I could choose my life, properly, based on the world as it is and not someone desperately trying to get their UCCA forms filled in on time.'

They both looked at me. Olly stopped playing around with a packet of sugar.

'I always thought we had a good life,' he said quietly.

I suddenly hated the fact that Tashy was here.

'We did,' I said as earnestly as I could.

'You say that. In the past tense, by the way. Of course. It sounds reasonable. But then. . .but then, you hated it enough to rent the fabric of space and time to get away from it. From us. From *me*.'

Suddenly, savagely, he threw down the sugar, which ripped and sprinkled over the top of the table like a tiny hailstorm. He stood up, put on his coat, and made to storm out. Then he realised he hadn't paid his share, paused, took out his wallet, threw some money on the table, and, finally, left.

* * *

'Don't look at me,' said Tashy. 'I didn't even know you two were having problems that bad.'

'Well, I didn't know you were having problems with Max till I found you weeping on a park bench.'

We both stared at our coffees.

'I—' We started at the same time.

'You go first,' said Tashy.

'I think . . . honestly, you haven't seen what happens at the wedding, but it's not pretty.'

'Why, *what* happens at the wedding?'

'I'm not sure I should say.'

'What?'

'Olly proposes.'

'Ohmigod! Congrat—'

There is a default setting for thirtysomething women, and Tashy hadn't quite learned how to switch it off.

'I mean, gosh, that puts a spanner in a few things.'

'I know.'

'Ooh, does he steal my thunder? Bad, attention-stealing friend.'

'Definitely not. In fact, he doesn't even get a chance to finish. Mum interrupts. In fact, we get interrupted just before your cake cutting.'

'Shit,' said Tashy. 'So you really did do it on purpose.'

* * *

125

We walked to the tube station together and were just about to go our separate ways, Tashy tutting when I bought a child's ticket when she knew for a fact we both used to do it until we were nineteen, when I heard a rapidly becoming familiar voice.

'Flora! Flora! What, so, now you go travelling without me, yes? Perhaps you'd be happier pretending I didn't exist, no? You run away from home, you run away from your job, you run away from your best friend – you've gone crazy? You're on drugs? Perhaps somebody gave you drugs in detention. So now you are up, in Trafalgar Square, working as a prostitute to earn more money for drugs? You're a crack whore now? That is why you are too ashamed to see your best friend? All the whoring, yes?'

Her accent seemed to get ridiculously strong when she was annoyed. Stanzi was wearing a hideous off-the-shoulder grey top with a pair of white combat trousers covered in ribbons, and little white ankle boots. To my eyes she looked like a crazed baby slut. She was clearly furious with me.

'Stanzi,' I said, trying to give Tashy a rueful smile but not quite managing it, 'this is Tashy.'

Constanzia looked at her with what I realised was a glazed expression she kept for grown-ups. 'Very nice to meet you,' she said cursorily. Then she leaned over to me and whispered, 'Is that your crack whore madam?'

'Ssh!'

Tashy gave the tight smile she normally reserved for traffic wardens and people who work in electrical appliance shops. 'Hello. Nice to meet you.'

'And what is your connection to Miss Scurrison,' said Stanzi in a ludicrously polite voice.

'Um . . . this is, er, an external guidance person my parents hired for me.'

Stanzi looked suspicious. 'Oh, how lovely!' she said, as if she had just been invited to a castle for tea.

'And this is Constanzia,' I said.

She was tugging on my arm again. 'You have a head shrink and don't tell me?'

'She's very boring,' I whispered back.

'Yes, Constanzia, I have the authority to have Flora sectioned if I want to,' said Tashy loudly.

'I have to talk to her in private for a second,' I said to Stanzi.

'She's insufferable!' said Tashy, as soon as we were in the corner alone.

'She's alright,' I said.

'Yeah, right.'

'I wish you were there with me.'

Tashy smiled. 'Look. I've got an appointment with the dressmaker this afternoon.'

'Yeah?'

'Well, I always wanted to ask you, but I never felt I could because you'd hate it so much. But now it's all so weird that I'm going to.'

'What?' I said.

'Would you like to be my bridesmaid?' She laughed as she heard herself say it.

I stared at her. 'But I might not still be . . .'

'Well, let's deal with that when it comes up, shall we?'

We hugged. 'Will you phone Olly for me?' I said. 'See how the land lies?'

'Of course,' she said. 'It was the first thing I was going

to do. And you take a good long think about a damn fine man.'

* * *

Stanzi wanted to talk, to ask me things about school, but it wasn't working. I felt numb. I was worrying about Olly, I was worrying about Tashy, and I was worrying about myself and what I was doing, and where.

'You don't listen to me any more,' complained Stanzi, as we sat in the bumpy carriage back to Highgate. 'You don't want to be my friend any more, is that it? You never chat. We never play Pogcode any more.'

Oh God, I doubted very much if there would be a time in all the histories of the world that I would understand whatever Pogcode was.

'You don't even want to try and crash Ethan's party?'

'Grounded.'

'Yes, so you wait till your dad goes out and talk your mum round, like always.'

'I'm not really in the mood for a party.'

She stared at me. 'Are you sick?'

'I haven't been feeling myself lately.'

Ha-ha.

'OK, what about we go and hang around outside his house again? You know you love doing that.'

'No I don't!'

Constanzia shrugged. 'Felt like you did all those other times we did it.'

Oh, for God's sake. I stared out of the carriage window.

Finally I felt a quiet push at my elbow.

'You still want to be my friend?'

'Of course I do,' I said. 'I'm sorry.'

'You shouldn't love Ethan any more.'

'I don't,' I said.

'Really?'

'Couldn't pick him out of a line-up.'

Stanzi smiled. 'And we're still in the We Hate Fallon club?'

'We invented that club.'

Then Stanzi did some kind of funny hand-punching motion towards me that I was clearly supposed to know how to reciprocate. I ducked, grinned and punched her on the shoulder.

* * *

My dad was in the sitting room, putting on his shoes. My mum was clattering out of sight in the kitchen. I checked my watch.

'Oof, work!' I said loudly, stretching. 'They said I was putting too much in, so they sent me home early.'

My mother leaned out of the kitchen to give me a searching look, but I did my best imitation of total innocence. My dad didn't look up at all.

'Going out?' I said.

'Yes, love.'

'Where?'

He looked at me, puzzled. 'Just down the club. You know. As usual. Couple of jars with Mike and Peter.'

I'd forgotten about them. His two best friends, from way, way back, when he was sales repping around the North East. His two best buds had covered for him on Saturday nights when he went off to see his bit. It was so ridiculously old-fashioned, it was just plain stupid. Him and his little gang of friends had conspired to make my mum so ill I sometimes wondered whether she'd be better off in hospital. And he could sit here, neatly tying his shoes and tell me that's what he was going to do.

'Mum,' I said, as she came in from the kitchen to see me.

'All right, love?' she said. 'How was work?'

'Yeah, yeah,' I said. 'Listen, why don't you go out with Dad tonight?'

My dad stiffened.

'It'd be nice if you had a night out. You might enjoy it.'

My mother clutched the dishtowel close to her stomach. 'Flora.'

'Give you a bit of a change.'

'Now I don't know about . . .' Dad started.

'Oh, Flora.' My mother came over to me and put her hand on my shoulder. 'Do you have a boyfriend? Is there someone you want to bring back here? Duncan, I know you'd like to put everything off till doomsday, but I think it's time we all had the talk.'

'No, no, that's not it at all,' I said in horror.

'Do we have to do this now?' said my dad. 'I'm late. Er, for the lads.'

My mother shot him a filthy look, then crouched down beside me. 'Now, Flora, we know you're old enough, legally now . . . and we know you've always been a good girl.'

'Christ,' said my dad. He got up heavily.

'Duncan! For Christ's sake, for once in your life take responsibility for your own child. Sit down. This is important.'

'So. Have you met someone?'

My insides twisted in six different types of agony. I wanted to cover my ears, then say: 'No, but why not have this little chat with Dad?'

'We just have to say,' she glanced hard at my dad, who was staring at the floor, 'now you're sixteen, we don't mind if you want to go on the pill. But we'd be much happier if – ahem – you wanted to use those, er, condom thingies.'

I shut my eyes tight.

'And you will understand, won't you, if we say that you can't stay under the same roof?'

My mother was blushing heavily. We stood in silence, the only sound, some drivel coming from the television set.

There was a very long pause while I tried to work out what to say and how to handle it without coming across like an overexperienced tart. Finally, I decided on the mature approach that would make them proud of me and raise my grounding, so I could go and get pissed at Tashy's. I summoned up all the agony columns I'd ever read.

'Mum. Dad. Thanks. Thanks for feeling free to have such an adult conversation with me. That makes me very proud. I just want to say that I'm not having sex – ' I had a sudden flash of Ol, sitting by himself at home, and felt terribly sad – 'nor am I likely to in the near future. If I do, you can rest assured I won't be going on the pill, as I don't want to be infertile by the time I'm thirty-four, particularly with the way fertility's going in males.' Christ, I hadn't thought of that. What if I stayed here, then by the time I got to twenty-five, the entire male race did actually go extinct after all, as promised by Germaine Greer? 'And I do know how to use a condom. Um, they teach you in school.' Well, maybe they do now. 'But it doesn't matter anyway, because studies show that sixteen is actually emotionally very young to have sex, and many people who do lose their virginity at an early stage regret it later, not waiting for someone important.' That'd be me then.

My parents stared at me.

'Oh God,' said my dad.

'You have met someone, haven't you?' said Mum.

'No!'

'I can't believe she's thought it through,' said my dad, shaking his head. 'My own little girl.'

'What! I'm just being really mature about this!'

My mother gave me a cuddle. 'Oh, darling. And it seems like yesterday you were just our innocent baby!'

'I'm not doing anything!'

'I have to go,' said my dad.

I stood up and looked him in the eye. 'Don't you do anything either, Dad!' I pretended to make it sound jolly. And, I hate to say it, but as he scurried out the door I was pleased.

'Come on, Mum,' I said. 'Remember how we used to bake together?'

'When you were seven, we used to bake together,' she said, confused.

'Well, let's try that again.' I took her arm and we went into the kitchen.

'Oh, no, it's not a teacher, is it? Please, let it not be a teacher,' she said.

Chapter Seven

For a teenager, with supposedly very few responsibilities beyond school and my own good time, I couldn't believe how unbelievably tired I was. I had thought I would be full of youthful energy, forgetting that teenagers sleep even more than students, amazingly. The situation was worse in my case because I felt I was constantly performing in a play without cues. I got through most of the following week under house arrest from my parents. They were watching me very carefully, and whispering to one another in corners, which I was going to have to take as a good sign, because last time round, they hardly spoke to each other at all.

Then there was school. How the hell did I ever do any of this? I was doing English, maths, chemistry, and general studies A levels. Again. In fact, this was the first problem. I had long regretted – well, accountancy, obviously. One of the things I'd always wondered was, if, instead of doing business studies at university – dry as dust but, as my dad had pointed out before I went, 'very useful'; obviously he was already predicting who was going to have to be the main provider in our little family – I'd done something I'd always fancied – history of art, say. Long hours of cultural discussion in libraries. Ooh, maybe I could go to St Andrews and see if I couldn't get a crack at Prince William. Or even go for the big boys, Oxford or Cambridge. Nothing wrong with Birmingham, of course, it was a great laugh. But it hadn't taken me long in life to realise that yes, going to one of the really snobby places really did open doors for you.

On the next day back at school I picked up the first book out of my book bag. The folded-over corner was on a chapter entitled 'Reagents and Conditions for One-Stop Conversions'. It was full of Greek characters. I didn't have a scooby about a single bit of it. And even if I read it and read it and managed to convince myself I did, what was the one thing I'd already worked out in my head? What was the one thing I knew for definite I did not want to be doing in whatever bollocks-up of a future I might be in for this time round?

It wasn't going to be accountancy, that was for effing sure.

* * *

Miss Syzlack smiled sympathetically when I walked in. Honestly, when did the diktat come down that teachers were allowed – nay, expected – to dress like they'd had to run out of Oxfam when it was on fire and everything melted to their skin? Then I realised that perhaps looking sharp and sexy wasn't the kind of thing you necessarily wanted to encourage standing in front of a roomful of fifteen-year-old boys.

'Hello.'

'Hello, Flora Jane,' she smiled, sympathetically but a bit warily.

'Can I sit down?'

'Of course.'

I really, really could not remember school etiquette.

'It's about my A levels,' I said. 'I think I'm doing the wrong ones.'

She consulted the register sheet. 'Maths, English, chemistry. You could do anything with those, surely?'

'That's the point, erm, miss. You can do anything with anything, unless I wanted to be a research chemist. And I can assure you, I'm not going to be one of those.'

'Yes, your chemistry teacher agrees with you.'

'See! Really?'

We both leaned back at the same time, eyeing each other up. She cracked first.

'Well, what were you thinking of taking?'

'I'm going to swap maths for history, and chemistry for art,' I announced grandly, based on a decision I'd made fourteen minutes before.

'That's quite a big change. What do your parents say?'

'Erm . . . I haven't mentioned it to them yet. But I'm sure they'll be fine.'

'Hmm. Flora, you don't even have GCSE art. In fact, if the doodles in your English textbook are anything to go by, I'd say it's really not the right direction to be heading in.'

'I want to do history of art at university,' I blurted. 'I don't want to end up doing . . . business studies in Birmingham, or something like that. I want to go to art school, or the London Film School. Or Notre Dame. Or

Harvard. Or St Martin's College of Art and Design.' I said it with all the purpose of a successful professional, but as it came out I knew I sounded like a caricature of an over-hormonal teenager.

Miss Syzlack laughed. 'OK, OK, calm down. We are going through a bit of a phase, aren't we?'

'It's *not* a phase.'

God, I could go on a murder rampage right now and still be 'going through a phase'.

'That's exactly what someone going through a phase always says.'

'Can I just change my subjects? I'm going to be late for my next class,' I said.

'Look,' said Miss Syzlack. 'Changing your A levels is a big deal. It's a really big decision.'

'It's not!' I said. 'What A levels did you do? I bet you can hardly remember. I bet once you were in university you never ever remembered them ever again.'

'We're not talking about me, Flora.' She came and perched on the front of the desk again.

'Look, I know at the moment, growing up seems scary. It all looks very confusing. There are so many choices and options out there.'

Yuh-huh.

'People your age — I mean, there's so much pressure on you: to look right, to choose the right things, the right courses, the coolest friends . . . but it won't be as hard as you think, I promise.'

'I know that!' I said. 'That's why I want to make sure I do something I like.'

'You know, a lot of people want to go and do creative

things,' she said. 'I wanted to be a photographer.' She smiled, looking slightly embarrassed. 'But life doesn't always work out like that.'

'Well, it certainly won't work out if I take chemistry,' I said. 'Look, miss, you know I'm right on this. If it all goes tits up, then I can go join the civil service or something. In the end, it won't matter. It's never too late to sit your accountancy exams. But it will mean a lot to me now. At least I won't regret having a shot.'

She looked at me.

'I'm sixteen years old. I have years and years and years to fill in with mistakes of all kinds. There are loads of stupid things I have absolutely no doubt I am going to do. But putting myself through two years of maths and chemistry hell isn't one of them.' (And neither is sleeping with one of my lecturers again I harshly repeated to myself.)

Miss Syzlack shook her head. 'You'll have to catch up.'

'Trust me, I can.'

She rummaged among the folders on her desk. 'Well, here's the form. Your parents have to sign it.'

'My parents get to decide what I have to spend two years doing?'

'Take it to the European Court of Human Rights, Flora,' she said wryly. Then she gave me a close look. 'Are you sure you're OK?'

'I'm fine. Please stop asking.'

'You definitely don't want to see the educational psychologist?'

'Honestly, I'm fine. I've just realised that I don't have to do three years of a business degree and join a city firm. How could I not be fine?'

She looked at me, and shook her head. 'Off you go.'

I glanced out the window. Stanzi was there, waiting for me. Fallon was standing near by, obviously talking about her. Stanzi was trying to look as if she didn't care.

'You know, I think getting through secondary school may well prove to be the hardest thing I'll ever have to do,' I said.

'Imagine what it's like if you never leave,' said Miss Syzlack. Then she realised what she'd said. 'Right. Out! I have marking!'

* * *

Stanzi was sitting, doing her best nonchalant act, on the low wall outside.

'Hey,' I said. I felt bad for confusing this nice person, who hadn't asked for her girlfriend to have been turned into a thirty-two-year-old overnight. 'How's it going?'

'If we were boys,' Stanzi looked speculative, 'we wouldn't have to fall out with anyone. If they're cross, they just have a fight, then the next day they all go and play football together.'

'I know,' I said. 'Why do you think they grow up to be such emotional retards? They never talk anything through.'

'Or bitch anyone up enough.'

Fallon walked over.

'Sorry, Stanzi, but I couldn't help but wonder – are your shoes Prada or Gucci? It's hard to tell at this distance.'

Amazing. I turned to Stanzi and, without thinking, said, 'Oh my God. Is she like this all the time? I mean, really every day?'

Stanzi looked at me, shocked at the outburst. Her big eyes were a mute plea for me to shut up, not to make the situation any worse than it already was.

'Who the fuck are you talking about?'

Fallon turned to face me. Her face had that heart-shaped prettiness that does well at school then often grows up rather odd, like Anthea Turner, with the grim set of a jaw not afraid of confrontation.

She laughed, evilly. 'I almost forgot. Ethan asked me to tell you to stop sending him poetry. He thinks it's hilarious, and read it out to all his friends, but he wants you to stop bugging him.'

'Poems!' said one of Fallon's equally expensively dressed but not quite so pretty henchgirls. They all started squealing with laughter, and I felt my ears beginning to burn.

I had no idea what I'd been up to in this version of events. I knew I hadn't just sent any poetry, but, once, long ago, I had. To a tall, skinny gothman who liked to read Sartre at parties. I had long since repressed what the poems had said, but I could take a bit of a stab in the dark.

'In fact, I have one here.'

Oh no. No no no no.

'I told him I'd get rid of it for him.'

This woman was going to end up Prime Minister.

A couple of other girls, whom I recognised dimly from my registration class, wandered over.

'Hayley! Paris! Come over and listen to this.'

You know, if I'd been standing there naked, this would have perfectly corresponded with my worst nightmare of all time.

The girls gathered round and, as they did, other people followed them. Schoolkids. Unbelievable. Sheep, every last one of them.

'Baaa!' I said under my breath.

'What was that?' said Fallon, homing in. 'You want me to read out your poem?'

A shocked hush went through the crowd. They knew they were on to something good.

'OK then!' She turned and cleared her throat. '"Be of Me, My Love" by Flora Scurrison.'

Somebody tittered. My fight-or-flight responses were up to full mast. Inside, I felt like I had heavy menstrual cramps.

'My nights are heavy, like the days
That settle on your glorious ways.'

Oh, fucking hell. This was going to be even worse than I'd imagined. Next time I saw Tashy I could tell her I was going back to being thirty-two alright if I got half a chance to influence anything, for sure. Wrinkles, crow's-feet, missed opportunities – bring 'em on! Anything was better than this.

Fallon, of course, was using her most dramatic tone, but speaking slowly, so that nobody missed a word. In her head she was probably auditioning for Lady Macbeth with Heath Ledger.

'Your walk, unbidden, golden goes,
From all the beauty yet unknown.'

Oh God, teenagers write terrible poetry. Mute with horror, Stanzi was trembling.

I closed my eyes and muttered, 'I wish I was . . . um, twenty-six,' but, nothing.

'And I, so alone, so different stay
And yearn, alone, for one fine day.'

140

Stab me in the heart already. The cruel laughter from the other girls had stopped being merely complimentary to Fallon and was becoming genuine, twisted embarrassment. No doubt they probably all had something similar under the bed at home. And, let's face it, if it had been somebody else, I'd probably have been laughing too.

I suddenly realised why Stanzi was pinching me so hard. Approaching were two boys. One, with that face as strange and familiar as walking past a restaurant and getting a sudden smell of your mother's cooking, was Justin. Next to him was a tall boy with blond hair, very pretty in a Greek god-ish kind of a way. They were wandering over.

'When we can come, together all . . .'

'Ooh, they're going to come together!' shouted one wag. 'Didn't know he was that good in bed.'

'Neither does she!' shouted somebody else.

'When we both so in love do fall.'

My worst suspicions were realised when somebody called out his name.

'Ethan!'

'Girls, girls,' he said, coming over. 'What's this, a fan convention?'

'I just thought a certain poem deserved a public reading,' said Fallon, lowering her head and lifting her eyes in the patented technique of bitches through the ages.

'Oh God, yeah. Did you hear about this?' he asked Justin.

Justin looked at me and, from my burning face, instantly

realised what was going on. 'Come on. Don't fart about with this shit,' he said to Ethan.

'No, no, I want to hear.'

I lifted my head – I'd reverted to staring at the ground – in amazement.

Ethan was handsome, alright, there was no doubt about that, with his blond hair, a long forehead and a lovely patrician nose.

'Oh, Ethan, you're going to love it,' said Fallon, her voice instantly softening and her head dipping in that annoying Princess Diana style.

'Tempt me,' he said.

Surely not. Well, we were young, after all. But it looked to me as if Fallon, and every other woman in the world, was going to be very disappointed by young Ethan indeed.

The idiocy of what I was doing – standing, letting myself be completely humiliated – suddenly dawned on me. I grabbed on to the last remnants of my adult brain.

'Come on, Stanz.'

'Oh, don't you want to stay?' said Ethan.

'You could ask her out if you like,' said Fallon.

'No thanks,' said Ethan.

I'm a grown-up. This is a child. A very camp child, I reckoned. Whom I have never even met. How can this possibly make me so embarrassed?

'This is fucking lame,' I said.

'This is fucking lame,' said Fallon. Ah, imitation: world's easiest way to be completely annoying.

I finally de-rooted my feet from the paving stones and walked off.

'I think you've broken her heart,' I heard Fallon crow as I went, cheeks flaming. I was even close to tears.

'It's hormones,' I told myself. 'Just teenage hormones. You are better than this. You are so much bigger than this.'

But I still had a little sniffle in the toilets by myself.

* * *

It was almost a relief to slip into detention, which wasn't full of people from my class who knew everything that had happened at break time and were sniggering and pointing throughout the afternoon. It always amazed me, first time round, that teachers wouldn't be aware of the simmering tensions and ongoing sieges in any class situation. As an adult, of course, all teenagers look the same to me. Until they're at eye level.

I took the same seat as last time and started in on today's hot topic, five hundred words on 'Why Detention Works'. Justin came in late, and I barely glanced at him. OK, I deliberately made a huge point of not looking up. I didn't want his interest and, more importantly, I didn't want his pity. It would remind me a little too much of somebody else who was kinder than Ethan, but probably hadn't liked the poems much either.

'Hey,' he said.

'Hey,' I said, writing furiously, 'Detention may only be regarded as superior when compared to the method of repeatedly beating children's skin with birch.'

He shrugged. 'Sorry about . . . you know, that, today.'

'Honestly,' I said, 'in the scheme of things, it doesn't matter.'

'That's a good attitude,' he said. 'I know girls can be pretty rough to one another.'

'It works out for the best later,' I said. 'Apparently.'

'Really? Huh.'

I bent my head back to my page and wrote, 'It also starts to look pretty good compared to the whip, and steady and repeated buggering.' I wondered if Mr Rolf would let me get away with that one. Probably not. I have to say, there was a tiny bit of fun still to be had in a world where one wrote with pencil. I rubbed it out.

'You know, I shouldn't worry too much about Ethan.'

I lifted my head again.

'What do you mean?'

'Well . . . you know, he never really has a girlfriend.'

'Justin, he's queer as a coot.'

'Miss Scurrison! Quiet, please.'

The look on Justin's face was absolutely something to see. I'd forgotten just how unthinkingly bigoted and homo-phobic teenage boys were. Everything was batty to them, and homosexuality hugely amusing and terrifying at once. I almost felt sorry for them; with their penises bobbing up and down at the slightest provocation, probably male and female, they were panicking at being marked out from the pack. God, poor Ethan. He probably hated being a teenager even more than I did. I wanted to tell him not to worry, he'd be very popular when he grew up.

'He's not,' whispered Justin fiercely. 'He just doesn't have a girlfriend.'

'Because he loves the world of men,' I said, in a mock news announcer's voice.

'Just because he doesn't fancy you, he's a poof?'

'Well, yes, partly that, obviously. Tempered only by the obvious fact that he's gay. Give your friend a bit of support, won't you?'

He stared at me while I wrote, 'Detention is also to be preferred to the sacrifice of teenagers to Inca gods, widely practised at one time in South America.'

He was still staring at me, in that gauche way young boys have. I stuck my tongue out at him.

'You,' he said finally, 'are not at all what I thought you'd be like.'

'Amazing,' I said. 'Person in not-pathetic-victim shocker.'

He smiled.

'Clelland! Scurrison! Do you really want to stay another day?'

'Sure,' said Justin. And he winked at me. And for the first time since I'd arrived, I felt rather pleased.

* * *

As we came out of the building, Justin self-consciously moved over to walk beside me. It was getting dark.

All of a sudden we heard, 'Oi! Little Britches.'

It was a familiar voice and I stopped dead in my tracks.

'Oh, for fuck's sake . . .' said Justin. 'It's my brother. He thinks it's hilarious to call me that.'

'Your brother's picking you up? Here?'

'He just got back from Africa and won't leave me alone. Some bonding bollocks,' said Justin. 'Here he comes now,' as the familiar shape loomed out of the dusk.

FUCK!

* * *

Clelland stopped about five feet away, stock-still, his face as white as a sheet, just staring at me.

It would appear that he recognised me, but that he thought he was seeing a ghost.

'Hey, retard!'

It was Justin. He sauntered up to Clelland and hit him on the arm. I remember how he used to pad after him as a baby and concluded that, underneath it all, Justin still worshipped his brother.

Clelland continued staring at me. I tried not to meet his eyes.

'Spazmo,' said Justin, when he couldn't get a word out of him.

'Sorry, I . . .' Clelland blinked and looked at me again. 'You look like . . .'

'I have to go,' I said. 'Bye, Justin.'

And I ran like the wind, tie and schoolbag flying behind me, all the way home.

Chapter Eight

It was the following evening and I was huddled on my single bed; my new, prominent rib bones made me so thin I was cold all the time. I was on the phone, my parents were downstairs having a fight about a frying pan. The frying pan so far hadn't come into play, but I had a horrible suspicion it was just a matter of time.

'Tashy, we have to—'

'I know. Don't worry.'

'What?'

'I've already spoken to John Clelland. I have never heard a man panic so much in my entire life.'

'He called you about me?'

'No, he called Ghostbusters. Yes, of course he called me. Or rather he called my mum and left a very frantic message. He thought he was cracking up.'

'Wow. He remembered me.'

I think to have met Clelland again and then been wiped

from his memory circuits for ever would have been more than I could have borne.

'After all this time. You know, he hasn't seen me yet, not till the wedding. And he still recognised me! That's amazing.'

'Yes, yes, my wedding, the wedding, blah blah blah. Anyway, he called. Apparently when Justin told him your name he started to gibber. He wondered if you'd died recently. Do you know, I'm getting quite nonchalant at explaining it now.'

'How did he take it?'

'He suggested we both required medication. And he wants to see you.'

My heart leaped. 'I may . . . Um, maybe I should go see him to explain things.'

There was a pause.

'To explain things?' Tashy sounded suspicious. 'Are you going to wear a Britney Spears top that shows off your perfectly flat tummy?'

'It depends on whether I feel the situation requires it.'

'Flora.'

'Uh-huh?'

'There is someone you really have to see, and it's not Clelland.'

I knew that. It was stupid, stupid, stupid. I was in a ridiculous situation, and pining after someone from a long time ago wasn't going to help anything.

'I know,' I said.

'Call him. Sort it out. Then decide what you're going to do. Then sort your life out. Then make everything right again. Then make sure everything is good for my wedding. *Then* you're allowed to worry about John Clelland.'

The noise of a frying pan hitting the wall came up the stairs.

* * *

I tentatively crept downstairs; I needed to use the house phone. I couldn't afford to keep my mobile in minutes. My parents immediately jumped apart, then arranged their faces into ghastly intimations of being pleased to see me.

'Aren't you getting ready, darling?' said my mother. 'I thought you'd have been more excited.'

'Excited about what?' I said.

'Oh, you teenagers!' said my mother, as we all ignored a big dented frying pan in the middle of the kitchen floor. 'Ha-ha.'

The doorbell rang. My mum answered it, and Constanzia burst in in a whirl of black curls with a tiny shredded fishnet lace top thing on.

'Did your mother let you out the house like that?' said my mother.

'No, Mrs S.' Stanzi held up a bag. 'I've got a jumper in here. That's what I was wearing when I left.'

'Well, you'll need it. You'll catch your death.'

Stanzi looked at me in horror. 'You not ready? You want, what? A white dressing room with lilies, like Jennifer Lopez?'

'Yeah,' I said, desperately stalling for time. What on earth was she talking about? I already had too much in my head. God, I had to see Ol. 'Want to come and help me get ready?'

'But we've got to get there early! To get down the front!' Stanzi's face was a picture of frustration.

'I know. I'll be quick, I promise.'

'Mrs S, can you make her hurry up?'

149

'I'm afraid I thought the fact that Darvel was waiting for you would be enough.'

'Darius, Mrs S,' she tutted. 'It's Persian. He's descended from a long line of kings. And doctors. It's a very good combination.'

'We're going to see Darius?' I exclaimed, before I could help myself.

'Well, yeeaahhh,' said Stanzi. 'I thought for a moment you'd forgotten.'

* * *

I was swept up in Stanzi world and I let myself get carried along. Music was easier, at the moment, than thinking about anything else.

I'd forgotten what gigs were like, I really had. A gig to me is somewhere, probably seated, melodic folk rock. You turn up late, miss the support, get yourself a gin and tonic and settle back for some mellow enjoyment and try not to let your boyfriend tapping out of tune annoy you so much.

That's not gigging. This was gigging. I larded on Sophie Ellis Bextor-style makeup ('Wow, you've got really good at putting on makeup,' said Stanzi), and wore a push-up bra (my breasts really were still practically nonexistent) and a little pink tanktop with a slashed V at the top, then a little denim miniskirt. I twirled in the mirror. I looked like my fantasy self, my best-looking self, the one I had to scrunch up my face to see. Why, then, was my diary full of complaints and moans?

'You think you are very beautiful, huh?' said Stanzi.

'Yup,' I said.

'You going to get off with Darius?'

'I'm going to turn him down.'

We both giggled.

'Are you lovely ladies finished in there?' came my dad's voice. 'Because there's a pop star who won't stop calling the house and begging you two to come to his concert.'

'It's not a concert, Mr S,' said Stanzi, opening the door. 'It's a gig.'

My dad laughed.

'He'll only be bloody miming, won't he? It's not even a show. Maybe you should just stay home and watch the video.'

Stanzi's face was suddenly aflame.

'That is NOT TRUE. Darius sings and writes all his own songs. And we're going to be his fans for ever.'

'He's only teasing you,' I said, hitting her lightly on the shoulder. 'And it doesn't really matter. As long as we like him, that's all that counts.'

'Good God, Joyce, our Flora just said something sensible.' He looked at my mother with a 'can-we-make-up?' expression, comically scratching his head. My mother looked through him as if he hadn't said anything. I wanted to shout at her: 'MUM! You don't know what he's going to do.'

'*Please*, Joyce' he said. 'Could you cut it? Just for tonight? It's the girls' big night.'

Stanzi and I looked at each other and shuffled our feet.

'Yeah, stop it, you two,' I said.

'OK, OK,' said my mum. 'Have fun, everyone.'

'Stop it, everyone!' commanded Stanzi. 'If we don't go now I'm going to DIE.'

* * *

Any thoughts I might have had about being a tad under-dressed were dispelled when we got to Earls Court. There had to be five thousand teenage minxes there, milling about inside. In fact, we were verging on the oldest. Lots were there with their parents, dragging baby sisters in tow, giving the thing the weird aura of a monster creche. Pink fuzzy Deely-boppers appeared to be back, I noticed.

We, however, quickly dumped my dad at the front gate so he didn't have to come in with us and we could make it look as if we'd travelled over on our own. 'I'll just wait for you,' said my dad, taking out his *Evening Standard*.

'Dad, it'll be hours. Why don't you go home . . . surprise Mum and take her a fish supper or something?'

He looked at me. 'Your mother never eats chips.'

'She loves chips, though. She'd really like it. Please, Dad. Go on.'

He thought it over for a minute. 'She always did love chips, your mum.'

'Go on. It'll be good.'

He sighed. 'All right, then. But if she gets annoyed at me, I'm blaming you.'

'She won't,' I said, fervently hoping this was true.

'OK. I'm picking you up here. And here . . .' He held out his hand. In it was a tenner and – bliss – a top-up card for my phone.

'I'll be outside,' he said gruffly. 'Be careful. Don't take any drugs.'

'Darius says no to drugs,' said Stanzi.

'Good for him. And I'll see you right here at ten thirty.'

I sneaked a look at my Swatch. It was six p.m. The support acts, of whom there appeared to be about nine hundred, started at seven thirty. The man himself didn't appear to be turning up for about three hours. Christ, half of this lot would be asleep by then.

'This is great,' said Stanzi.

'I can't believe people are queuing three hours early.'

'You're joking, aren't you? I wanted to come down at four, but Mama wouldn't let me. Cow.'

We passed one of the many stands dedicated to branding all things. Stanzi was in bliss.

'Look at this!'

'Who would pay twenty-five pounds for a T-shirt?' I asked, being a sixteen-year-old version of my mother, without thinking. 'Oh. You.'

'I work hard Saturdays,' said Stanzi. Then she picked up the baggy, cheaply made shirt. 'Mind you – I don't know. Do you think he's really going to like me better in a big T-shirt than in my Zara fishnet lace tops?'

'No, definitely not,' I said. 'And it's going to make it harder for you to play it cool. You know, with his name and face printed on your front. Almost makes you look a bit easy to get.'

'By having his picture on my front?'

'Yes.'

'My big baggy front.'

'Yes.'

She thought about this and concurred.

'Come on,' I said, as the queue inched forward infinitesimally. 'I'll try and scam you a beer.'

'Beer is horrid.'

I took a mad stab in the dark from remembering my own sweet tastes. 'A Snowball, then.'

'Voddy Red Bull more like.'

'Oh yes. Yum.'

From inside the booming arena came a muffled thudding.

'Ohmigod! It's starting!' wailed Stanzi, grabbing me hard on the arm.

'I don't think so,' I said. 'It'll just be the PA. They'll be putting on some music just to cheer everything up.'

'How do you know, smartie pants?'

She was right, I thought. I might as well just get in the scheme of things.

'I'm making it up to make myself look clever.'

'It's not working!'

I stuck my tongue out at her and marched through the doors.

We passed two girls even smaller than us, wearing Atomic Kitten-style white cheap synthetic tops and matching cowboy hats. They were carrying a big sign that said, 'Darius – MARRY US!'

'Sluts,' said Stanzi.

'Stanzi!'

'Well, they look like sluts.'

'So do we!'

'We do not. We look like sexy, legal women of the world.'

One of the girls turned round. 'What did you say?'

'Nothing,' I said hastily.

'God, look at those sluts,' said the other cowboy-hatted girl.

I grinned and wandered on.

Stanzi was hopping from foot to foot, looking at the line snaking on round corners we couldn't even see.

'There's too many people here! We'll never get to the front.'

'We're bigger than most of them. I'm sure we will. Smack 'em with their own lightsticks.'

'Yeah!' said Stanzi, looking as if she was up for it.

The vast cavern of Earls Court looked massive, partly, of course, because everyone was so small. But I hadn't been to anything on this scale for a very long time.

The air was heavy, weakening, with the smell of hairspray and something I couldn't quite place. Then . . . yes, there it was. I didn't know they hadn't changed it. If anything could make me feel sixteen again, the smell of Impulse would certainly do it. I inhaled deeply, suddenly thrilled. Impulse, source of exotic dreams from the ages of fourteen to fourteen and a half, when my dad said if I didn't stop smelling like a seraglio he was going to stop taking me to school.

'Bunch of BO babies,' said Stanzi sourly. 'Look at them all. What did you do, sleep here last night?'

'Don't worry,' I said. 'I'll get us up the front.'

Stanzi mutely followed me as I did my time-honoured push-to-front-of-bar, head-held-high strut. She looked at me with, I thought, new respect as I pushed my way through layers of disgruntled tweenies without a backward glance.

'Are you just going to cut up the side?' she whispered, following my path.

'Absolutely,' I said, batting some tinsel off a girl's head. 'The trick is to pretend you did it by accident. Oh, sorry . . .'

'Ow!' I heard from some luckless girl who'd just got in Stanzi's way.

'There we are!' Finally we were at the front, just – right up there, but watching from the side. 'Now, all we have to do is not go to the toilet.'

'Can we go on the floor?'

'No, if you really need to go, borrow one of the smaller girls' plastic handbags.'

She giggled, and I looked around, feeling like David Attenborough, examining the tight flesh and suspicious looks from the girls around us. Even the flabbiest had a tummy-bearing top on, which I rather approved of. Why should fashion belong only to the Britneys of this world, goddamit? It was for all, no matter how many Big Macs you felt like eating.

Nobody looked at us in the least bit strangely – well, why should they? And when the PA started playing 'Follow the leader, leader, leader', it suddenly seemed completely normal to hop to the right and hop to the left with sixty thousand similarly overtartrazined girls.

I tried to buy Smirnoff Ices with my dad's tenner, but despite my air of studied nonchalance, nobody but nobody was getting served here without some kind of special wrist-band, which obviously came with a credit card address, so I bought the most colourful, additives-filled soft drinks I could and two enormous hot dogs, which took most of my tenner, and I remembered I only had the one. Stanzi, however, insisted on counting out every penny of exactly half of the cost and I remembered how that worked.

The girls behind us asked us to keep their places while they went to the toilet, and when they'd gone we giggled our heads off about the vileness of them and what happens when you get fifteen Portaloos and seventy thousand girls just starting to conquer the many vagaries of puberty.

The noise was absolutely deafening, and it was pointless to do anything else except jump up and down, especially when the ponderous space music started.

Suddenly the lights went down — way down; we were warned to go out and buy some merchandise or else, there was an enormous drum roll, the lights came up from the front very, very slowly, and suddenly a big, lanky, just about popstar walked to the front of the stage.

I have never heard anything like the screaming that ensued. Well, I must have, but I just don't remember Howard Jones being this popular. These girls could have solved the world's energy crisis, if there was only a way to harness sixteen million decibels of pure raw screechpower.

'Jesus fuck,' I said.

'AAAAAAAAAAAH!' said Stanzi.

It was a great gig. We screamed, we cried, we watched scores and scores of people get hauled off by the St John Ambulance, we divided into two halves of the audience and really tried to get our half to win, we believed him when he told us he loved London audiences second (after Scotland, of course, we understood), we booed the names Gareth and Will loudly and indiscriminately, we yelled, 'MARRY US, DARIUS!'

Then came the slow number. The lights came way down and he kneeled down and peered around the audience exaggeratedly slowly. A massive 'ooohhh' went up, to counterpoint the screaming, which continued.

'Ah'm just looking for a special lovely lady tonight,' he said. It was cheese at its pongiest, but we lapped it up. Girls were bursting their arms out of their sockets.

'MEEEEE! MEEEEEE!'

'Will it be this side?' He went stage right, the opposite end from us. 'The middle?'

'THE MIDDLE!' screamed a thousand tiny voices, in

justifiable anger, seeing as they were the ones who had queued longest.

'Or here?' he said. And suddenly he was standing right over us, just a few feet away over the barrier.

I laughed in spontaneous pleasure. 'Hey!' I said.

He caught my eye and smiled back.

Then he beckoned me up on stage.

I nearly gagged. Stanzi was clinging on to my arm with a vice-like intensity. Two enormous Rock Steady bouncers were already heading over towards me.

'Thank you,' I mouthed, then indicated Stanzi to my right. 'This one.'

I really think it's one of the most mature things I've ever done in my entire life.

* * *

I have to say, seeing Stanzi up on stage being the object of a crooned love song was one of the funniest things I have ever seen, even though despite being someone who enjoyed sneering at the T-shirt prices, I was really beginning to regret not taking the opportunity.

On stage, surrounded by exploding lights and rapturous noise, the tiny fireball I thought I was getting to know had been entirely replaced by a bone-free rag doll, who swayed so alarmingly she practically had to be held up. Fortunately he's a big bloke, not like most pop stars, so she couldn't fall over completely. She stared into his eyes like Mowgli being hypnotised by Kaa, and swayed gently to the (very slow) song, mouthing along, slack-jawed, with the words, as the rest of the auditorium pretended to cheer (to show Darius how nice they were) whilst secretly wishing Stanzi killed in a million different ways. Didn't he know he was meant to pick the fat girl, for goodness' sake, so they could all feel he was only doing it for pity and would much rather be with them? But it wasn't, ha-ha-ha, it was my friend and it could have been *me*! Ha-ha!

I remembered suddenly, as I was waving along (I could somehow remember all the words) how jealous of Courtney Cox I was when she gets pulled out in that Bruce Springsteen video and wondering a little wistfully if I was the only person in this whole auditorium who could remember that. Not even Darius could. But I wasn't that person any more.

'She's rubbish,' said a girl wearing fairy wings next to me.

'Yeah, I bet he's really regretting it,' said her friend. 'Oh no! I've pulled a minger!'

'That's my friend you're talking about,' I said, trying to look taller than five foot four.

'Really?' said the first one quickly. 'Does she know him then? Can she get us backstage?'

I wasn't to find this out right away, as, when the song ended, and Stanzi received a big, sweaty hug and a kiss, which she seemed disinclined to let go of, she wasn't sent back into the crowd with me, presumably in case she got torn limb from limb by twenty thousand ravaging teenage beasts. They sent her off sideways, presumably smuggling her through a side exit, and I had to watch the rest of the gig on my own.

I didn't care, though. In fact — ooh, it suddenly occurred to me that if someone from school were there we might even get some cool points for this. Yeah, then we could start changing things around here; that would be great! I jumped up and down to 'Colourblind' in the encore with everyone else, excited.

I was sixteen all evening. And it was great.

* * *

I didn't really come down – and I didn't think Stanzi was coming down, ever. Hyperventilation was clearly going to be a way of life from now on. No backstage passes for us, alas, but she did get her Darius T-shirt – for free – and a big cuddle and kiss from the man himself, which is really quite a lot better than sex when you're a virgin teenager in love with a pop star, and she was jumping like a pogo stick when Dad and I found her round the side. Full-fat Coke at Pizza Express didn't help.

'It's love,' I said.

'I can't eat,' declared Stanzi dramatically. 'I will never eat again. I will fade away to nothing and die for love because nothing in my life can ever again be as glorious as tonight.'

'Can I have your doughballs then?'

'No!'

We had to drop her off when she became too incoherent to talk straight and I had to promise to Dad a million times we hadn't been drinking or taking anything we shouldn't.

* * *

I had an odd feeling when I woke up the next day. An absence of complete and utter dread. In fact, I felt almost . . . jolly. The sun was shining, my thighs were slim, pop stars loved us, what could be as bad as Monday? I almost had a spring in my step as I kissed my dad goodbye outside school.

'Oof,' he said. 'Been a while since you've done that.'

'Well, as long as you're on your best behaviour, you'll get another one,' I said, cheekily, enjoying his surprised face as I hopped out of the car. I'd decided to go for levity. If someone was making nice in our family, maybe the rest of them wouldn't be so horrible. I didn't put much hope in my theory, but at the moment it was the only thing I had; I had thought the fish and chips might have helped, but the stony breakfast silence hadn't changed at all.

Then I noticed someone at the school gates, and stood still. Looking the picture of agonised misery, slouching around trying not to be too obvious, straight ahead of me was Olly.

Crap. Crap. I should have called last night. How could I just leave him on his own to stew like this? I felt terrible.

'Ol,' I said. 'Ol.'

'I can't believe you'd make me do this, Flora,' he said, hands deep in his jacket pockets.

'Can't you pretend you're a supply teacher or something,' I said unhappily.

'Yeah. Well, unfortunately all my clothes match.'

'We can't stay here,' I said. 'I'll get in trouble.'

'I've got the car,' he said.

'Yeah, I'm going to get into an adult stranger's car outside the school gates. That's what I'm going to do now.'

'I really wish you were enjoying all this a little less,' he said.

'What, being tagged like a young offender. I can assure you I am not.' I gestured at him to walk and steered him into the dodgy little grocer's that appear to be close to most schools and still sell single cigarettes and chocolates without any chocolate in them.

Tiredly, he looked at me over the penny chews display.

'Is it over?' he said starkly. I don't know what I'd been expecting, but Ol is a very good lawyer. I swallowed abruptly.

'Tell me what happens in a month,' he said, 'at the wedding. There must be something.'

161

I shook my head.

'Tell me.'

'I can't.'

He picked up a fistful of lollipops, impotently, and put them down again.

'Well, I suppose that means we're through then.'

The fat old lady behind the counter, whose entire life had clearly insisted on a total 'don't ask, don't tell' policy, deigned to look up from the *Daily Star* at this.

'Ol,' I said. 'Olly, I've changed.'

'Oh, for fuck's sake,' said Olly, hitting the nearest box of Walkers. 'I can't believe you'd trot out that hoary chestnut.'

The fat old lady looked on the brink of phoning the police.

I took a deep breath. This was it. I was going to do my first chucking, destroying a four-year relationship, throwing away a pretty much guaranteed shot at marriage, a family, a life that I'd expected; at some stage wanted. I was going to break Olly's heart, and wreck his dreams as well as my own. And I was going to do it in a school uniform. Avril Lavigne has nothing on me.

'Olly.'

'Are you two going to buy anything?' said the fat lady.

Olly glared at me.

'Erm . . . flying saucers?' I said, panicking.

He tutted and put a handful on the counter. The woman eyed him up suspiciously and waited, arms folded, until we left the shop, me beadily checking up and down the road to see if anyone was looking out for us. Then I thought, sod it. This isn't fair. And I went up to Olly and I took his arm. I had to lean up on my tiptoes to get to him.

'I'm so sorry,' I whispered into his ear.

One hand went to his head, and with the other he pushed me away.

'Oh God, Flora.'

'It's impossible.'

'You won't be like that for ever. Will you?'

'Who knows?' I said. 'I didn't get a manual.'

'Well, maybe when you come back, we can see again then.' His voice cracked a little.

I shook my head. 'I don't know.'

He held me at arm's length. 'Do you know, I was thinking about—'

'I know,' I said.

He turned away. 'I knew it,' he said. 'I *knew* it. That's what made you do it, isn't it? That's what brought on this whole bloody . . . JESUS!'

'I'm sorry.'

'Counselling? No. Telling me what was the fucking matter? No, too tired. A holiday? No, I think I'll just go for the full body time travel.'

'Olly, maybe I wasn't that happy.'

'We were happy enough.'

'Maybe that wasn't enough.'

He stared at me. 'I know why you've gone back to being sixteen.'

'Because I never left it?'

'Because . . . yes. That's exactly what I was going to say.'

We were both quiet now, staring at the ground.

'I even thought . . .' He coughed, after a false start. 'I thought it would be cute. You know, if you were thirty and I would be forty-eight. And you would call me "old man", and play with the children, and run around, and we could do everything differently, and you wouldn't have to work if you didn't feel like it. You could potter, or go to art school, or . . .' He trailed off, and blinked hard.

I swallowed a lump in my throat. 'I'm sorry.'

'You're not,' he said, straightening up. 'I think you're too selfish to be sorry. You've bent the whole fucking world to your will, Flora. Enjoy it on your own.'

And he walked off, his herringbone overcoat flapping in the suddenly chill breeze.

Chapter Nine

I just about held myself together through history – by not saying anything, and keeping a very straight face. Beside me, Stanzi was too busy writing Mrs Constanzia Danesh very carefully on the cover of her exercise book and basking in the admiring murmurings of the other girls to notice.

At break, I almost ran out of the classroom, I was so desperate to avoid speaking to anyone I didn't have to. Stanzi, at any rate, was being mobbed, and was hardly going to miss me.

As far as I remembered, round the back there was a stairwell, close to the staff room – too close for the smokers and snoggers to hang around, but still not a place teachers were likely to go if there were free biscuits on offer upstairs. It was practically always deserted. Tashy and I used to come here to hide and play cards and keep out of the way of bullies. I finally let myself sit down and cry. I felt as if I'd cut the line tethering me to the mainland of my old life. Maybe I had. Maybe I'd just condemned myself for ever.

This was it now. I wasn't going to be heading home at night for one of Olly's famous shepherd's pies, which made him rosy-cheeked, like a stout farmer. Or taking his first corporate credit card and immediately getting drunk on it (Olly paid it all back, of course). Or that time we had in Morocco . . . or when he used to bring me the papers on a Sunday, then read all the good bits first. All the times I'd looked at him and thought, of this funny, gentle man, yes, this is it. This will do.

No love affair ever lasted that started with 'this will do'.

I fiercely rubbed my still heavily mascaraed eyes from last night (which is absurd, because if you're going to start living your life over again, you really should clear your bad habits, such as not taking your eye makeup off properly) on the side of my sleeve, and sniffed loudly, a proper, snot-filled trumpeting, luxuriating in, for once, being on my own.

'Jesus Christ, this sounds like the elephant house at the zoo.'

Justin was standing at the bottom of the stairs, looking at me in a half-amused, half-concerned way.

I did that awful, painful choking thing you do when caught crying and are desperately trying to calm yourself down. That didn't sound too attractive either.

'Are you all right?' he said, coming out of the shade, and presumably noticing the ruination of my face. 'I had to go to the staff room.'

'Actually I'm practising for a play,' I said quickly.

'A tragedy?'

'Yes.'

'Oh. You're good.' He moved towards me gingerly. 'What's up?'

'I split up from my boyfriend,' I said, staring at the floor. 'I might have ruined my life.'

'Oh.'

For a moment he looked slightly disappointed that it was a girly emotional problem, as if he'd hoped I was going to say 'my dad just got eaten by a tiger', which is the kind of thing boys like, and his cute face looked suddenly extremely young.

'I didn't know you had a boyfriend.'

'You wouldn't know him,' I said, still hiccuping a bit and hoping my face wasn't as dirty as my fingers were from where I'd been rubbing at my mascara.

'I might. What school's he at?'

'He's not at school.'

'Why did he dump you?'

'He didn't,' I said. 'I dumped him.'

This was clearly confusing. Let's face it, the least popular girl in school was hardly likely to be chucking boys old enough not to be in school. If it wasn't for the fact that I was hiding in here for my cry, rather than storming about the playground in floods, engulfed in a coterie of secretly jubilant other girls, in time-honoured fashion, I think he might not have believed me at all. Instead, he gruffly patted me on the shoulder.

'Why are you upset then?'

'Because you don't just wave goodbye to four years, which nobody around you has the faintest possibility of giving a shit about, without feeling anything at all.' I hiccuped again. 'No, I have to sit and have dinner with my parents, and casually never ever mention the man, who my mother thought was the best thing ever to happen to me, and the fact that he was about to propose. Jesus.' I realised I was crying again.

Justin sat. 'Calm down,' he said, clearly astonished.

'You have a bloody long-term relationship finish at my age and tell me to calm down!'

He was quiet after that.

'My brother was asking after you,' he said finally. 'Do you have some kind of unbelievable effect on old guys that the rest of us can't see?'

'Your brother isn't old!' I said, still snuffly and not quite right in the head.

'Do you know him?'

'Um, no. But he didn't look that old.'

'He's ancient! He's sixteen years older than me.'

I swallowed hard. 'Oh. Oh God, really? Maybe I didn't see him properly.'

'Well, he was certainly looking at you. He asked if you were still working in the Co-op.'

'Just gave it up,' I said.

'You know, you aren't at all the kind of person I thought you would be,' said Justin. 'You've quite the secret mystery life.'

I had to choke back a hysterical gasp of laughter. 'You have no idea.'

'Do you know where to get drugs and stuff?'

'Yes. But I'm not telling you.'

'Oh,' he said.

'They make you very boring,' I said.

'Well, I'm very bored, so I'd take a chance.'

The bell rang. I couldn't get used to the bells at all; I instinctively ignored them. Justin, however, moved like a well-trained dog.

'Are you sure you're OK?'

'Much better, thanks. Sorry. It's been a tough old day.'

'Yeah, breaking up with someone's hard. I broke up with Sonya Heeley, and that was really bad.'

'How long did you date Sonya Heeley?'

'Two weeks,' he pouted. 'But that's not what matters, is it?'

'No,' I said slowly, getting to my feet. 'No, it isn't.' I headed for the top of the stairs.

'Um, I'm kind of having a party on Saturday night,' Justin said suddenly, embarrassed and staring at the ground. 'You can come if you like.'

'Um, yeah, alright,' I said, without thinking. If I was here, I was here. 'Can I bring Stanzi?'

'Who?'

'The—'

'The nutty Italian you hang out with.'

'She's not nutty.'

'She looks nutty.'

'OK, she's nutty. Can she come or not?'

'Sure,' he said. 'Just . . . you know. You're not allowed to bring any of those boy grown-ups you know.'

'That won't be a problem,' I said, blinking hard.

* * *

My dad's face was like thunder. I didn't even notice when I got back, completely distracted with my own predicament. I walked straight past him.

'Flora Jane Scurrison!'

I slowly turned round. He was furious.

'We are talking NOW! Your mother's in there, crying her eyes out.'

Mum came to the door. 'Flora, darling. What have you been doing?'

'Nothing, Mum.'

My mother was looking at me, quivering. Her face was white. 'Flora, we know you're not a baby any more, but we really need to have a serious talk about your behaviour. Dad saw that man this morning.'

Oh, for Christ's sake. So much for our sweetshop subterfuge.

'Yes, yes,' I said. 'Does it have to be now? Please? Can we have it, but just in a couple of days? Please?'

'Sit down!' said my dad. 'This family is going to have a chat together once and for all!'

Suddenly my crappy day and my anger caught fire. 'That's rich coming from you!' I screamed.

There was silence. There was a distinct power imbalance in the room.

'What's his name?' my dad went on.

My mother was wearing that unhappy, downtrodden face that I was to get to know so well over the next sixteen years and I couldn't bear it for one minute longer. Nothing could be worse than that. Puce-faced and entirely het up with rage and upset, I let it out.

'I'm amazed you even noticed,' I spat. 'You're never here. How would you know? All you do is shout at Mum. Or ignore her. Or go out. Don't think I don't see what's going on. Don't ask what's his name. What's *hers*?'

There was a huge silence. My mother went even paler, if that were possible.

My dad was glaring at me. Within two milliseconds, it became too late for him to splutter out a knee-jerk denial of something that wasn't true. I noticed his fingers were shaking. I didn't want to make my father's hand shake. Oh God. Was there anything today I couldn't fuck up absolutely completely? We stood in a frozen triangle, staring at each other. I took the only path I could remember. I marched out and slammed the door. As soon as I hit the cooling autumn night, I realised how stupid that was. Red-faced I stuck my head back round the door.

'I'm going out,' I said. 'I'm not going to do anything bad, so don't call the police. I'm not going to see a boy, so don't panic.'

And I set off into the night.

* * *

A passing car hooted at me as I walked down the road towards Tashy's flat. Oh, thank you, Britney, for making everyone in a uniform fair sexual game. I kicked ferociously at every pile of leaves in my path. Bugger this and bugger everything. Well, I'd pissed on my chips in every conceivable direction. What was left for me – single, aged sixteen, having dumped a man who was prepared to marry me whatever age I was, and off to see my girlfriend preparing for a marriage I'd provoked severe doubts about, whilst watching my parents go through another civil war? One I'd just chucked a bomb into.

How on earth was I going to live in an Audrey Hepburn apartment in New York? Not now. Not ever, probably. I wasn't going to be anyone's muse in Paris.

I tried again to snarl at the moon. It came out as a kind of small growl.

'Grrrr!' I shouted. Quietly.

171

Just because my age was different. It wasn't going to change a damn thing.

'GRRR!'

Nobody was on the street. Nobody turned round.

'AAAAARRRRRGGGGGGGGGGHHHHHHHHHHH!' I yelled suddenly.

'Bloody teenagers,' said a woman loudly, passing by with a very large dog and a very small man. 'Probably high on drugs.'

'YYYYYYEEEEEEEAAAAAAAAAAAAAR-RRRRRRGGGGGGGGGGGGGHHHHHHHHH!'

That was better. I could feel my lungs opening up. I was in the world's most ridiculous position. I was hurting pretty much all over. But I could still make a very loud noise.

'AARRROOOOOOOOOOOOOOOOOOOOO!'

Tashy came running down the garden path. 'Is that you making all that noise?'

'NOOOOOOOOOOOOOOOOOOOOOOOOOO!'

'For goodness' sake, be quiet.'

'You're sounding more and more like my evil elder sister every day.'

'Ooh, get you, Avril Lavigne. What are you shouting for?'

''Cos everything's fucked up.'

She looked to the side. 'Are you on drugs?'

'Do we ever take drugs?'

'No.'

'So why would I be taking drugs now as someone who would get immediately caught, killed, arrested or laughed at if I attempted to get my hands on anything?'

'Well, you know what they say about schools these days.'

'That's right, Tashy, and if you don't let me into the house

172

right now I'm going to kill you with my Uzi, which I bought from a big kid at the gates with my lunch money, in order to get off my tits on drugs.'

She didn't immediately stand aside to let me pass, though.

'What?' I said. 'Are you not talking to me? Have we officially fallen out somehow? Please say that's not true. Something awful's just happened at home, and—'

'It's not that.'

I could hear voices from inside the house.

'You've got people over?'

She shrugged.

'It's OK,' I said, raising my eyes to heaven. 'I understand if you don't want to invite a very precocious teenager to your dinner parties.'

'It's not that. It's just. . . we were having a bit of a summit.'

I looked up, and there, behind her, his hair messy and his shirt crumpled, looking tired, was Olly.

'That man,' I said, still a bit exhilarated from screeching my head off, 'has an amazing habit of creeping up silently almost anywhere.'

'Don't let her in, would you, Tash?' said Olly unhappily.

'No. I'm sorry,' I said, and, instantly, I was. 'Please, let me in. Please, Tashy. I have nowhere else to go. My parents are fighting, and all I've done all day is drive everyone nuts. And I haven't had the chance to apologise properly, to you, Olly. I'm so sorry. Please let me stay. Please.'

Tashy looked at me. 'You know, it's not fair to make very small girl's puppy eyes.'

'It really fucking isn't,' came Olly's voice behind her.

'It's either this or buying some chips and hanging around the bus stop,' I said. 'I might get carried away by all that

White Lightning cider, and who knows what might happen?'

'You come in, sit down, shut up and behave,' said Tashy, standing aside. 'We're not happy with you.'

'Yes, Brown Owl,' I said meekly, and slipped inside.

* * *

Olly and Tash hovered in the sitting room.

'Can I have a beer?' I said.

'No!' they said.

'I think if you're discussing me behind my back the Geneva Convention says I'm allowed a beer.'

'Has she always been such a spoiled brat?' asked Tashy to Ol.

'Yes, I think so,' said Oliver. 'I just didn't notice with all the wrinkles.'

I let out a great big teenager's sigh.

Max came in to the room and stared at me.

'Who are you?'

He was looking tired and grumpy, and he thought his IT reputation meant he didn't have to polish his social skills.

'Hi, Max!' I said cheerily.

He turned on Tash. 'What is this? Who is this? I can't believe you're still trying to—'

'Max, it's me. Flora. Don't you remember? That time I lost your car keys, and the time I broke the glass and you stood in it, and . . .'

He shook his head. 'Tash, this is a crappy bloody joke.'

'It's not a joke,' said Tash.

'It's not,' said Olly, going to stand beside her.

Max looked at us. 'I don't know what the hell you're up

174

to,' he said, 'but it's really fucking unamusing.' He stormed out.

'Well, what should I tell him?' said Tash.

Olly patted her on the shoulder. 'I don't know. I'm sorry.'

'What are we going to do with you?' said Tashy to me.

'I'm not a child!'

'No, we know that. Technically. But there are lots of childish prohibitions on what you can and can't do.'

'I'm running away to New York and/or Paris,' I said. To myself.

'Don't be sullen,' said Tashy.

'Why are you telling off that child?' said Max. He'd paused at the door and was leaning on the radiator.

'I'm not fucking telling her off, and if you'd listen to me for five seconds, you'd realise that.'

'Do you have to swear quite so much when we have people in the house?'

'Why not? It doesn't seem to bother you when you're shouting at Cherie Blair on the television.'

'I believe in God, and the only thing that scares me is Cherie Blair.'

'Do you hate all working women, Max, or just successful ones?'

I looked at Olly. Christ, we were never this bad. He could clearly read what I was thinking, because he put his arms apart in an 'I know!' gesture.

'Erm, there's only three beers, Tashy . . . and . . . sorry, I've forgotten your name.'

The black curly-haired head peering round the door was talking to Olly.

'Oliver.'

'Of course. Sorry,' said Clelland. Then he caught sight of me and gasped.

'Oh Christ.' He took a step back. 'It's the wolverine.'

'Wolverine!' I said. 'Apart from the other day, I haven't seen you in sixteen years and one reverse month, and you call me a wolverine!'

Clelland moved cautiously into the room. Oliver was watching him closely. Clell moved over to me.

'Oliver told me you were a wolverine. Also, I thought that by ridiculing you, you'd go back into the fiery pits of hell from whence you came,' he said, trying to shoot me an apologetic grin and only succeeding in looking nervous. 'I mean, what the fu—'

'Does Clelland understand I didn't die?' I asked Tashy, who was still glowering at Max.

'I can't convince him,' she said. 'I can't convince anyone of anything.'

Max let out a long low sigh and disappeared.

'Tell Clelland I'm not a wolverine,' I ordered Olly.

'Grrr,' said Olly.

Well, if Clelland was allowed to stare at me, I could stare back at him. His dark eyes were still as hooded and interesting as ever, even as obviously confused as he was now.

'How's Madeleine?' I asked.

He jumped backwards. 'So you are a ghost,' he said.

Nobody said anything for a minute.

'Erm, she's fine,' he said then. 'Wants us to move to Africa permanently. Kind of missionary thing.'

'Position?'

'Job.'

'OK,' said Tashy. 'Shall we sit down?'

Everyone sat down carefully, except for me. I sat down cross-legged on the floor. Then I jumped up again, angry with myself.

'OK,' said Tashy. 'We were just going to meet to discuss what's happening in our – ahem – friend's life. And also, in ours because of it.'

'Without me here?'

Olly looked at me. 'Yes. You know, amazingly, we thought you might interrupt and be very intrusive.'

'I thought you never wanted to speak to me again,' I said. 'Luckily that lasted almost nine hours.'

'So,' Tashy addressed me, 'your mum and dad are younger than they were.'

'Yes.'

'But they're the only people who went back with you?'

'Yes.'

'And they don't recognise you as ever having been any older?'

'Nope.'

'And neither do the teachers at school?'

'Nope.'

'But we do.'

'Yup.'

'But nobody else?'

'Yup.'

'I asked my mum about her,' said Olly. 'She'd never heard of her.'

'She never liked me,' I said.

'No, I mean – well, that's true, she never liked you, but she really had no knowledge of your existence. Apparently I've never had a girlfriend called Flora.'

'Why didn't she like me?'

'She thought you took me for granted. Anyway, that's not the point. The point is, I think we're the only people who know about you.'

'That's stupid,' said Clelland. 'I haven't even seen her in . . . well, a long time.'

'That's because you've been off being a goody-goody in Africa,' I said.

'Ghost! Psychic ghost!'

'I have a theory,' said Tash. She took a deep breath and looked around sincerely. 'OK. We've all known Flora for years, right?'

There was a mutter of assent from Clelland and a deep groan from Olly. I remembered, again, meeting him that night in that noisy bar next to the law courts, when he was the only man gentlemanly enough to help me with my coat and buy me drinks. I'd thought he was so charming. He was. I looked at him, and he caught my eye, and I could tell he knew what I was thinking. He looked away. Pity was futile. Tash was still talking.

'Well. OK, I'm not looking forward to saying this out loud. But it seems to me that the only people who can "see" Flora are the ones who've known her the best. For the longest. The people who love her. Her true friends, if you like.' She gave a little laugh, embarrassed at having to use the expression 'true friends'.

I, though, was looking at Olly and Clelland, the two dearest men to me in the whole world, and Tash, my best friend.

'What the hell am I doing in this picture?' said Olly bitterly.

Tash shrugged.

'Hang on – is it right that I only have three true friends in the entire world, one of whom I've just dum— broken up with, and one I haven't seen for a decade and a half because he's been trying to find water for starving nations?'

'Surely it's much more sensible if we just assume she's a ghost,' said Clelland.

'I mean—'

'OK, OK, I'm sure that's not it,' said Tashy, looking at my downcast face. 'It can't be.'

'Three!'

'I'm sure that's not it at all,' said Tash. 'If anything, maybe we're the people you like the least.'

'Yeah, I'll go for that,' said Ol.

'No! That's worse!'

Everyone was looking at me.

'Have you tried anyone else in your address book?' said Tash.

'No,' I said. 'It doesn't exist and never has.'

'OK, we'll have to assume it's just us then.'

There was a pause while we all struggled to take this in.

'Ignoring the pointlessness of that just for a moment,' said Olly, 'what are we going to do? I mean, there's no point in taking you to a research base – nobody's going to believe us.'

'So, no living autopsy for me,' I said. 'Disappointed?'

'Yes.'

'Unless you could prove something that would happen in the future,' said Tash.

'As a lucky guess for two and a half weeks, mostly centring around highly predictable Big Brother evictions,' I said.

Clelland snapped his fingers. 'OK,' he said. 'I'm going to take some photos.'

'That's right,' Tashy said. 'Because in the history of magazines, nobody's ever done anything to a photograph to make anyone in it look younger.'

'And I won't be in it,' said Olly. 'Or if I have to be, I'm not smiling.'

'You're right – stupid idea. Hmm.' He shrugged. '*Okele Manoto*,' he said suddenly.

'What?' said Tashy.

He looked embarrassed. 'Sorry,' he said. 'That came out prickish. It's an African expression you hear a lot where I've been working. It means "take it as a gift".'

'It means what?' said Olly.

'Take it as a gift. Just let it happen and try and get the best from it. Well, I think that's what it means. It might just mean: "crap, we've been shafted by international colluding governments again".'

'What do you think I should do?' I asked Clelland, looking into his dark face. His features, now I could examine them again, were a lot more pronounced. He looked great as a man, much better than he had as a skinny boy.

'Take it as a gift,' he said. 'I just said. Weren't you listening?'

'Oh,' I said.

'I'm teasing,' he said. 'Doesn't anyone take the piss out of teenagers any more?'

'Everyone does,' I said. 'We're the scorned element of society.'

'Poor little you,' said Olly.

'OK,' said Clelland. 'Here's what I mean. You have the chance to do some things again, right?'

I nodded.

'And we think – well, this is what we were discussing before you came in . . .'

'Uh-huh.'

'. . . that you might be caught in some sort of a loop. Because you've gone back in time. That when we get back to Tashy and Max's wedding, something is going to have to happen there.'

'I might meet myself,' I said.

'There's that.'

'There might be a collision of matter and anti-matter and you might die,' said Olly.

Tashy went over and put a hand on his shoulder. 'Ssh,' she said.

'I'm just saying,' he complained. 'It's a possibility.'

'Don't frighten her.'

'OK then. The wolverine might disappear and I might get the old Flora back,' said Ol. 'And I'll get to chuck her. You're right. I like that much better.'

'Well, what I mean is . . .' Clelland was tentative, and he must have known what I might be thinking of, however much he seemed to be pretending, in his new role as grown-up, that I was merely a paranormal phenomenon. '. . . if there are some things you didn't do first time round, some fun you didn't have; do some good things you could have enjoyed.'

I couldn't say it. I couldn't say: what, all the things I missed when you went to Aberdeen?

'Well, maybe this is the time to do them,' Clelland finished. 'You may only have a month.'

He looked at me with his big grey eyes and I felt all funny inside. I noticed Olly darting him, and then me, suspicious glances.

'Enjoy the fact that there's no tomorrow, that's what I mean. Because you've done this already. You've done the hard work. You've built a life. This is a holiday. Take it.'

I noticed Tashy looking at Olly. She was patting him on the hand. She was a good friend to us.

Chapter Ten

The breakfast table was quiet. Too quiet. My mother and father were silently eating toast as I tentatively sat down. There was a long pause. Then my father coughed a little and cleared his throat.

'Flora Jane,' he said. If there's anything more indicative of trouble ahead than your parents using your full name, I don't know what it is.

'I'm sorry,' I said immediately. 'I'm a mouthy teenager with no impulse control. I'm really, really sorry. Mum, I really am. I only went to a friend's. I just needed to get out.'

My mother didn't even look up. Which was more like the mother I knew.

'We've been talking about you,' my dad said, which is hardly a surprise, as that's all parents ever do. 'And, we've decided . . . well, I think perhaps this family needs to do more as a family together.'

The seething hypocrite! This family needed to do a little less secretary banging, all told.

'So, erm, from now, I think we all have to make more of an effort. I'll try and be home earlier.'

Ooh, good.

'And we'll try and do more things as a family.'

Ooh, not so good.

'Flora Jane, I want to see more of an effort around here and I don't want you out gallivanting at all hours of the day and night.'

Getting seriously to the state of extremely ungood gallivanting was pretty much all I had left. And if Clelland was right about the time loop, I had rather a lot to fit into quite a small space of time.

'And we'll all help your mother a lot more. OK. Speech over.'

* * *

'What would you do,' I said, trying to sound jolly as Stanzi and I surreptitiously shared a Twix bar in Miss Syzlack's class, 'if you thought you might be scheduled to disappear or, um, die three weeks on Saturday?'

I'd been thinking a lot about what Clelland had said: it made my brain want to jump out of my ears. The idea, though, of either bumping into myself or spontaneously combusting had a curiously unreal quality to it. Frankly, I was more depressed at the possibility of seeing my thirty-two-year-old self from the back than ceasing to exist, and, even, bringing the entire universe to an end in some kind of anti-matter paradox calamity.

'I'd eat nothing but shortbread and offer myself up to Ethan,' whispered Stanzi.

'That's quite useful,' I said. 'Thanks.'

'Why? What is matter with you?'

'Is there anything you two are saying that's more important than *Middlemarch*?' said Miss Syzlack.

'Flora thinks she's going to die, miss,' said Stanzi helpfully.

With typical school compassion, the rest of the class started pissing itself.

'Die of what?' said Miss Syzlack. 'Too much talking, or too much detention?'

'I'm sorry,' I said. 'I was just speculating. Like, er . . .' It was years since I'd read *Middlemarch*. '. . . That character that can't have sex, ma'am.'

'That's enough,' said Miss Syzlack, going pink.

'Well, it's true,' I said sulkily.

'It's also not the way we talk about literature in this class.'

'What, the true way?' I said, half under my breath.

'Flora Scurrison, when I want you to answer me back I'll ask a question.'

'Ooh, Flora's going over to the dark side!' came a voice I identified as Fallon's from the back of the class.

'Eyes down, everyone.'

'What – Fallon cheeks me and it's OK, but I say one true thing about this book and it's serious trouble?'

'Drop it,' said Miss Syzlack. 'Please, just drop it,' and I looked at her face. Tired, weary; worn out from too many people that didn't want to learn. She was so brave, she really was. And I felt so sorry for her. I felt so sorry for grownups. You never believed for a second it was tougher going as a grown-up, but there were times when it bloody was.

* * *

'I have to nip out at lunchtime,' I said. 'And maybe longer. I have a free period after lunch and I need to do something in town.'

'To kill yourself,' said Stanzi immediately. 'No!'

'No,' I said. 'To make some mischief.'

'Can I come?'

Let me see. I could do with a partner in crime.

'Yeah, alright.'

'Hooray!' said Stanzi. 'That's almost as good as being invited to Justin's party.'

'Oh yes, I forgot to say. We're invited to Justin's party.'

No wonder Darius looked tired. I was nearly swept away as a tide of tiny Italian gave me a lurcher-style running hug.

* * *

'What are we doing?'

I could see Stanzi was slightly worried about the imposing building we were standing in.

'It doesn't matter,' I said. 'Consider yourself a special operative, working undercover.'

'We're wearing the uniform of our school.'

'Trust me, adults can't tell the difference between different school uniforms.'

'Really?'

'It's true,' I said.

'Huh . . .' said Stanzi, looking confused.

'OK, are you ready?'

We leaned over the plant-filled atrium we'd sneaked in to when I knew Jimmy, the reception guard, was off watching the *Matthew Wright Show*. As usual, grey faces were streaming in and out of the doors. When did someone tell all men they had to wear checked blue shirts and purple ties? It wasn't as cheering an effect as you'd think. And the man who runs Pret à Manger must have more money than God. But there was one bald pate . . . one odious, arrogant, unpleasant head I was waiting for more than anyone else's . . .

'Fire!'

We dropped the water-filled balloons solidly on Mr Dean's head.

'That,' I said, under my breath, 'is for when you made me make the coffee for those clients.'

Perfectly, both balloons hit their target: one on his dandruff-flecked suit, one right on his bald bonce.

'Ohmigod!' screeched Stanzi in surprise, as I dragged her into the tiny store cupboard I happened to know was up there, because Mr Dean had tried to drag me into it when he'd had a few too many at the 1998 Christmas party.

We waited till we heard the cross noises die down, then emerged from under the butler's sink in the cupboard.

'Who now?'

I hushed Stanzi as I rapidly took off my tie and my blazer.

'What are you doing?'

'I have to pass for staff,' I said. 'Just for a minute.'

'I'd get rid of the satchel,' said Stanzi.

'OK.'

She took her tie off too.

'No,' I said. 'This is a solo mission.'

'So I just have to hide here and panic while you do something naughty? How is that fair? What if I get caught? I'll have to give them your name under torture.'

'Don't worry about it,' I said. 'It's going to be fine.'

I snuck out of the cupboard, clutching the maths folder

I'd removed from my bag. It should look like work. Then I spotted someone I recognised: Mike, a bearded timeserver who never knew what anyone was up to.

'Mike!' I shouted jovially, head up. 'It's Rachel from M&A. We must have a word about the Phillips case.'

Mike looked bemused, but, as I hoped he would, immediately panicked that this was something he hadn't done and, without pausing, started to nod and stutter and automatically waved his security pass at the door.

'Are you new?' he asked finally.

'Work experience,' I said. 'I'm hoping to shake up the whole place.'

'OK . . .' He looked worried, as if a teenager might be able to do his job better than he could. Which was true, and not just this teenager either.

'I'll call Margo later, set up a meeting,' I said, worryingly.

'Um, yes, very busy, but . . .'

I peeled off to the left. The door to Mr Dean's office was open.

'It's just so disrespectful,' he was saying to his long-suffering PA, shaking down his jacket. 'I just don't understand it.'

I knocked on the door. 'I'm sorry . . . Mr Dean?'

'Yes?' he said abruptly, trying to hide what he was doing.

'I'm Rachel – John's new work-experience person in Mergers and Acquisitions.'

'Yes?'

I looked at the ground. 'I'm really sorry, sir. I don't quite know . . . he sent me up to tell you . . .'

'Yes? What?'

'That someone's tipped paint on your car, sir.'

'WHAT!?'

Dean grabbed his soaking wet jacket and tried to put it on. The material twisted and grabbed onto his neck, and he was a ridiculous sight, trying to force himself into something that clearly wouldn't go.

'Shit, bugger. What the hell is happening to the world?' he grumbled, face red and sweaty with exertion. As he struggled, I could smell some familiar BO from his damp shirt. His PA was trying to hide her giggles.

'Sorry,' I said, leaving, as he half tripped, half ran out of the office. Now the coast was clear.

* * *

My desk was almost exactly the same as I'd left it. No, it was tidier, that was for sure. Instead of a model of Bart Simpson looking annoyed, there was a model of Calvin and Hobbes looking annoyed. The picture of Tashy and Max and me and Olly, on holiday in Italy, had gone, of course, replaced by one of two couples who looked remarkably similar.

My doppelgänger was looking at her computer screen but, with the skill of long practice, I could tell she wasn't working. Her hand clicked at her mouse occasionally. Every so often she'd click on something, lean back and look at the screen. That must be her latest spreadsheet. She was probably doing what I'd used to do at work: know what had to be done, but be staring at it in incomprehensibility that she actually had to, good salary or no good salary.

She let out a quiet sigh. I didn't have long until Dean came back. I walked up to her desk and stood in front of her.

'Hello?' she said, not unpleasantly, very quickly switching applications, I noticed. 'Can I help you?'

I looked straight at her. 'You wouldn't believe me,' I said, 'if I told you who I really was.'

She looked to the side. Fair enough, I did sound completely dopey, and not in a good way.

'I'm a ghost of the future. I'm here to tell you you hate your job and you should go and do something else.'

'What?'

'But I knew you wouldn't believe that.'

'I don't hate my—'

'And I'd think very seriously about that boyfriend of yours.'

'I'm sorry, I think . . . who are you?'

The politeness of the English when confronted with insanity had emboldened me. 'I told you,' I said cheerfully. 'A warning from your future. Or past, I'm not sure.'

Her brow lowered.

'Yes, and I'm Johnny Vegas. Can you excuse me, please?' She turned back to her work. I didn't move. 'Or I'll have to call security.'

'I knew you wouldn't believe me,' I said. 'So I thought the best thing I could do would be to give you a day off.' And I picked up my specially secreted bottle of Tippex and poured it into the vents on her computer.

'What the *hell* are you doing?' she screeched, standing up suddenly.

But I was away. I'd never done anything even slightly bad before, and the pounding feeling of adrenalin was kicking me into gears I didn't know I had. At the door, I could see Dean steaming up the stairs looking furious. I couldn't go out that way – it would have to be the fire exit. And on that note . . .

I hit the glass window as hard as I could. Ow! This was why they had tiny hammers, damn it!

The woman was encroaching on me now, pointing me out to the secretaries, who were shaking their heads. Dean was behind me, his face puce with fury. I found the hammer and banged as hard as I could against the glass.

'DDDDDRRRRRRRRRRRRRRRRRRRRRR . . .'

The noise shocked even me, and caused everyone to pause. I paused for less time, though, as I'd been expecting it, and I had the reaction times of a peak-fitness teenager. I sprinted across to the fire exit and bombed it down the stairs like a wet cat, as the hubbub of an unexpected time off at lunchtime came rising up behind me.

I banged out the doors at the back of the building, and heaved round to hide behind the bushes to see if Stanzi would make it out in time. She did, heavily camouflaged in the careful meander of bodies, as people tried to pretend that if it was a real fire they were being completely brave and unconcerned about it all. I used some of my precious phone card to call her over.

She giggled. 'We do this? Is an initiation?'

'Something like that,' I muttered. 'Let's get back.'

Dammit, if I was going to cease to exist, I wanted to have done some good in the world.

Chapter Eleven

I had a problem. Well, of course, I had many, many, many problems in the scheme of things, and proper ones too, not those along the lines of worrying about picking the right time in the London housing market, or being unable to hire the right cleaning lady or the kind of guff that I used to hear at dinner parties all the time in my old life.

So this, for me, was more of a mini problem. It was Saturday, and I had simultaneously promised to go shopping for a bridesmaid's dress with Tashy, to go shopping for something hot to wear to Justin's party that night with Stanzi, and to go bonding shopping with my mum and dad as part of some ropy 'keeping the family together' session. I hadn't meant to mix it all up, but if I (possibly) only had three weeks on this earth, I wanted to make the most of it and see as many people as I could. Plus, it was shopping times three. We'd decided to go to Kingston; Mum couldn't cope with the West End, and Tashy didn't mind.

'Hurry up, Flora!' said my mother. Normally Olly chivvied

me along with my breakfast too. Clearly I had some sort of breakfast speed disorder.

'Yeah, yeah,' I said, spooning my cornflakes round their bowl in what I best remembered as a sullen teenage manner. Oh no, hang on, I used that one with Olly too.

My dad looked a bit mournful, smoothing down his polo shirt in front of the mirror.

'You all right, Dad?' I said.

'Yes . . . yes, of course I am. I'm taking my favourite girls out, aren't I?'

I felt sorry for him, eyeing himself up in the mirror. I knew how much more weight he was going to put on than that too. He was probably wondering if he'd ever get good sex again . . . well, I couldn't think about that.

'You look great, Dad,' I said as warmly as I could.

He looked at me out of the corner of his eye. 'If you think that means I'm going to buy you lots of tarty outfits, you can forget it.'

'Just a little bit tarty?'

'Absolutely not.'

'What about sluttish?'

He smiled. 'No.'

'Forward?'

'Flora Jane, please don't make me have this conversation.'

'I'm a good girl really, Dad,' I said, with a stain-free conscience.

He half smiled.

'Well, I try,' I said, guiltily thinking about the previous week's activities. In addition to work-related mischief I had also eaten sixteen cartons of Pringles, worn odd socks and snuck out all night to go dancing at the local nightclub, even though it was rubbish and I got hit on all night by the same stupid tossers I remembered from Mr Dean's office.

* * *

Kingston High Street was mobbed. It wasn't nearly as much fun coming here without a credit card. Tashy had subbed me again, but I wasn't entirely sure how much fun that was for her. Still, it would probably be enough, seeing as my parents insisted on constantly steering towards Marks and Spencer's and Bhs. I kept sneaking glances around. Then I realised that I was actually surreptitiously checking to see if Clelland might happen past and see me out shopping with my parents. Curse these blasted hormones! I caught sight of my reflection in a shop window and shook my head in disbelief at my knobbly knees and baby pout. But I couldn't help but wonder where Clelland was. Probably buying muesli and planning a baby with Madeleine.

'Can't we at least go to Gap?' I said. 'They're not sluttish.'

'Gap,' said my mother, tutting. 'Totally overpriced . . .'

I remembered why I told my mother everything I bought cost a tenner in the sale.

'. . . and nothing I couldn't make at home.'

'You don't sew at home,' I said crossly.

'I know, but I could. Just as well as they do at Gap.'

I let this go and followed them inside dutifully, as my mother fingered racks of elastic-waisted slacks and tried to tempt me into the plainest pair of jeans (which she called denims) she could find, to show she wasn't completely not down with the kids.

Stanzi and I had a dimly formulated plan to bump into

194

each other in Bentalls at noon or so, and try and encourage our parents to go and have coffee together. Apparently they all got on very well, although, of course, this was completely news to me.

However, as I struggled in and out of different shirt and cardigan combinations I started to doubt the wisdom of this plan.

'You're being very well behaved,' observed my mother. 'Usually by this stage you're swearing blue murder and insisting on those combination trousers.'

Combination trousers? Had I missed something monumental in alternate universe fashion?

'Like those ugly things,' said my mum, pointing to a girl my age with a full Christina Aguilera going on – dreads, parts of which were blue, pierced nose, shredded top exposing navel, and short combat trousers.

'The worst thing you think about that girl is her trousers?' I said. 'Whatever.' I'd heard Charlotte Church say this, so I reckoned it was down with the sixteen-year-old lingo.

'Quite right,' said my mother. 'Try on this nice poloneck.'

As I was struggling to get my head through the very small hole at the top of the poloneck, I heard a familiar shrieking.

'Mrs Scurrison! Mr Scurrison! Hello! What a surprise!' screeched Stanzi, in possibly the worst reading of a line requiring 'surprise' in the history of the universe.

I finally popped my head through and looked over. With Stanzi were two chubby parents, to whom she was clearly related.

'*Bella, buon giorno!*' said her dad, engulfing me in a huge and somewhat sweaty hug. '*Come stai?*'

Everyone looked at me as if I was required to say something

at this point, which was a little awkward as I didn't speak a single word of Italian.

'Ah . . . *sì*,' I said

'Sì? Sì? Oh, your daughter,' he said to my mum and dad. 'She no play any more, no? She grow up so, she think?'

My mother nodded. 'Well, you know how it is, Gianni. They're always going through one of those phases.'

'I know. My daughter, she is marrying a pop star now, yes?'

'Da-ad,' squealed Stanzi.

'They too old to be teased by their daddies? Never!'

And he pinched my cheek hard, which made me wince, particularly as everyone was looking at me as if I'd done something terribly rude, even Stanzi.

'Just joking,' I said brightly, and quickly moved the conversation on before anyone could enquire what that meant. 'Coffee?'

'Oh, coffee,' said Stanzi's dad. 'They say "coffee"; they mean "old parents please sit down out of the way and let us buy things with your hard-earned money", yes?'

Stanzi grinned. '*Prego, Papa.*' And she stuck her hand round his waist and pulled out his wallet.

* * *

'Do you always act like a nine-year-old round your dad?' I asked her when we were safely away.

'It always works, doesn't it?'

'Yes, but that's not—'

'I didn't see you complain before . . .'

True enough, as I looked down I reminded myself that I was holding an enormous ice-cream cone.

'What about this?' she said. We were in Topshop – of course! In fact, I know Kylie Minogue and Davina and other cool-looking thirtysomethings are always saying they shop there, but personally I can't handle it. It may say size twelve, but it certainly never looks it. Plus, all the teenage girls swanking about, looking groovy in the communal changing rooms . . . too depressing. Shopping with people younger and slimmer than you, no matter how much time you may spend thinking: ah, but you'll end up a lumpy-thighed accountant too, is just not fun.

'Let's try on one of everything,' I said.

* * *

OK, it was Topshop, not a Rodeo Drive boutique, and OK, I had pocket money, not Richard Gere's credit card. But I have never felt more like Julia Roberts in *Pretty Woman* than I did then – a movie, I was almost unsurprised to learn, that Stanzi was only dimly aware of, it having been released when we were both three years old.

I could wear *everything*. Well, not those Atomic Kitten white catsuits, because nobody can wear those, whatever Stanzi thought she was doing.

'It's a school party, not an invitation for the whole room to get you pregnant,' I hissed to her, when she came out wearing the full white waistcoat and camel-foot pants.

'Stop trying on ballgowns,' she retorted. 'You look retarded.'

'I look fabulous,' I said. 'Shut up.'

Stanzi raised her eyebrows. 'Me, I look terrible,' she sighed, staring at her limpid petite reflection. 'I am fat greaseball covered in steel wool.'

'You're gorgeous,' I said. 'You look fabulous. Here.'

I handed her a shocking-red top, which made her boobs look enormous and her hair stand out like Catherine Zeta-Jones's.

'Whore's clothes,' she said. 'Good.'

I slipped on a completely unforgiving ivory sheath with a metallic strap. The material was cheap, but when you are almost entirely hip free that simply doesn't matter.

'What, you are twenty-five-year-old going to get married? You look ancient.'

Crap, that reminded me. Tashy. I checked my Swatch. It was OK, I had half an hour or so to try on:

- teensy denim miniskirt that made my legs look skinny
- obscenely low-cut jeans I could normally only get one leg in
- sixties-style minidress with no waist, thus unwearable by anyone with curves
- huge gypsy-style Laura Ashley-type seventies dress (in sale), still hideous
- leggings (which hadn't worked for me at the right size first time round and weren't improving by much)
- innumerable Sharon Stone-style satin evening gowns, with gloves on my long slender arms, in which I took to parading round the dressing room as I looked so lovely. In no way did I need an evening gown, but, oof, I looked like one of those Hollywood starlets in them.

Stanzi was looking at me queerly.

'We should go,' she said.

'Ten minutes,' I said.

'Normally you always say you are ugly when you are shopping.'

'Oh yes,' I said, admiring my reflection in a yellow dress like Renée Zellweger wore to the Oscars. 'I look like a piece of shit.'

'Me too,' yelled Stanzi, obviously glad to be back in the game. 'I look like a pig in a dress!'

'You look gorgeous! I look like a wombat in tights.'

'No, you are beautiful. I am like a slavering space Martian who has been sent down to Earth to discover what makes Earth males vomit!'

'Why am I in this shop when the shop I need is the shop making outsize paper bags?'

We were giggling with each other as we made our final choices. Stanzi took the red top, which looked great on her, but insisted on wearing it with black trousers, which gave her a fat bum and made the combination subliminally resemble some kind of deadly spider. I'd kept the cute denim miniskirt – fake tan ahoy – and was teeming it with a cute off-the-shoulder stripy top, which was a bit eighties-fashion-back-again, but I figured if anyone had earned the right, it was me. We popped in to change back happily (sharing a changing room, which I'd forgotten was *de rigueur*), but both of us stiffened when we heard a familiar voice.

'Georgia! For goodness' sake, Georgia, can't you even get me the right size? A six, for fuck's sake. Only losers take eights.'

Fallon. Clearly slumming it in Topshop, like Kylie did.

'Crap,' I said.

'*Porca miseria,*' agreed Stanzi.

'We really look like lesbonerds,' I whispered. Stanzi

nodded. In honour of my 'bringing my family together' goal, I was wearing a Mum-approved long peasant skirt and gypsy top. I shouldn't have been nervous but any kind of confrontation gets my heart rate up and I couldn't help it.

'And I want one in every colour,' shouted Fallon. 'Chop chop!'

I glanced at my watch. Ten minutes to meet Tashy, and I had to misdirect my mum and dad, using some brilliant plan that hadn't quite occurred to me yet.

I stared at the floor. No way could I wriggle under that.

'You go,' whispered Stanzi. 'Explain. No. Explain something. I follow later.'

My eyebrows raised in gratitude at this self-sacrifice. 'Thank you!' I said.

'Shh! Go now!'

I squeezed her on the arm and walked out boldly. Fallon was gazing angrily at herself in the mirror, even though she looked absolutely great. Her head whisked round as she clocked me. There was a short pause.

Then, 'God. Can't go anywhere these days,' she sniffed. 'Wouldn't you be better off in New Look?'

'Just back from claw-sharpening class?' I said, and walked past her.

'I'm getting ready for a party,' she said. 'It's a thing popular people do at the weekend. You wouldn't like it.'

'I'll see you there,' I said.

She whirled round in shock, and stomped towards me, wearing killer heels and a tiny black dress.

'You're really not going to embarrass yourself by turning up?' she hissed.

'You're really not going to embarrass yourself by wearing that dress, you skanky ho?'

I couldn't believe I was actually saying these things. Obviously the possibility of being vaporised really concentrated the mind.

Her face twisted up. 'Who's the ho?'

'Um, no one, skanky ho.'

Oh God, what was I trying to do, get myself killed?

She gave me an absolute top-class filthy look. 'We'll see,' she said. And turned away. And I scarpered.

* * *

My heart was pounding and my face flushed as I reached where the Di Ruggerios and the Scurrisons were sitting in the food mall.

'Hello, my dear,' said my mother. 'Get anything nice?'

'Where's my daughter?' said Stanzi's dad, making faces at the coffee. 'You leave her for dead?'

'She's just coming,' I said. 'She's gone to the bathroom.'

Everyone stood up. 'Well, I think we're about to head off,' said my mother. 'Time's getting on.'

'And miss the football?' I said.

'There you are!' came a loud and familiar voice. 'I keep forgetting you're smaller now. And that you have purple hair.'

Tashy had completely forgotten the potential of parental punishment; it had been too long since she experienced what it was like when your mum and dad make your life seriously difficult. She wanted a sticky beak, and she was doing this on purpose.

'Mr and Mrs Scurrison!' she said. And even the haute-gushiness of her voice couldn't quite conceal her genuine astonishment. 'You're looking so *well*!'

My parents looked at each other. Who was this elegant older person? She certainly didn't belong to their circles.

Tashy stretched out her hand to be shaken, manfully ignoring the fierce kicking on the ankle she was getting from me.

'I'm Flora's new guidance counsellor.'

I raised my eyes as everyone else made those 'Ooohh' noises.

'Flora didn't tell us anything about you,' said my dad, unfairly directing a cross glance to me. Mind you, she wasn't a stranger, of course. My dad was giving Tashy throws in the swimming baths long before it became illegal for men to do that, and my mother let her sleep over whenever she wanted, although we only did it so I could stay at hers, with the constant television and fashion magazines.

'Really?' said Tash, having a fabulous time. 'That's very bad of her indeed. I've been at Christchurch since the start of term. I've been working very closely with Miss Syzlack.'

'Is this because of the truancy?' said my mother, panicked.

'Well, we just wanted to keep an eye on her. Don't worry, she's not in any trouble.'

'She'd better not be,' said my dad.

'I'm not!' I said.

'We worried. . .' my mother lowered her voice, even though there were clearly at least five people actually listening to the conversation, '. . . if there might be some kind of a man involved.'

Oh crap.

'I can tell you,' said Tashy, in her best 'getting on with grown-ups' voice, 'because I know she wouldn't want to blow her own trumpet.'

'Yes?' said my mother.

202

'There was an older man who did ask Flora out.'

'Oh God, I knew it,' said my mother. 'Please, tell me it wasn't a teacher.'

'No, it wasn't. But you'll be glad to know that Flora turned him down.'

'Thank Christ,' said my mother, colour flooding into her face.

Tash gave me a look and I tried to convey my intense gratitude.

My mum came and gave me an enormous hug in the middle of the arcade.

'Mu-um!' I grumbled.

'You're not grounded any more,' said my dad gruffly, which was good because it meant I could stop creeping out.

'Thank you,' said my mother, going up to Tashy and clasping her by the hand. 'I mean, you must know how hard it is to get teenagers to open up and . . . you do a wonderful, wonderful job . . .' She looked as if she was about to choke up. For heaven's sake.

Tashy patted my mother on the arm. 'There there,' she said. 'Listen, why don't I take Flora off for a cola?'

'Oh, that would be so kind of you,' said my mother. 'So kind. On your day off too.'

'You're allowing me to go off with a stranger?' I said. 'Just like that?'

'You should be a bit more grateful to Miss . . . ?'

'Miss Blythe,' said Tasha, grandly.

'Can I give you some money for cola?' said my dad to Tash.

'No, not at all.'

'Come on, I know what you teachers get paid.' And to

203

my mortification and Tashy's obvious delight he pulled out a fiver and gave it to her. 'I can't thank you enough for keeping our daughter on the straight and narrow,' he said.

'She's a one!' said Tashy. 'But we'll keep working with her. You know, as parents I think you're doing a great job.'

My parents gazed at Tashy like they'd fallen in love.

Stanzi came skidding towards us.

'That beetch, she is in there so long I think I am going to die of suffocation!'

She clocked Tashy. 'Her again! She is everywhere!'

Mr Di Ruggerio wasted no time. He gently cuffed Stanzi round the ear.

'You give your teachers more respect than that, huh? She help your friend; I think we need to get her to help you, yes? Huh?'

And, wildly protesting, Stanzi was borne away with the rest of the party.

'See you tonight then!' I yelled.

* * *

'I am brilliant,' said Tashy as we were left alone.

'You most certainly are not,' I said.

'I'm a genius. And now you must call me Miss Blythe. *And* we have a fiver to spend. Woo!'

'That could have gone really wrong,' I said.

'What plan did you have?'

'I was going to sneak away.'

'Ooh, sneak away. How very sixteen of you.'

'It could have gone wrong,' I repeated.

'But instead I got you off the hook and off being grounded.'

'Yeah.'

'And, in fact, any time you want to thank me for dispelling the fact that you've been seen out and about with a thirty-five-year-old man, go ahead.'

'Thirty-four,' I grimaced.

'OK then.'

'I'm going to call you Mum the rest of the day.'

'You jolly well are not.'

'Thanks, Mum.'

* * *

'Oh bugger.' Tashy was back to grumpiness and wasn't enjoying watching me try on size eight bridesmaid's dresses. 'Why didn't I get married when I was seventeen?'

'Because you'd have been a dejuiced neurotic old crone with four kids and on to number three out-of-work mechanic husband by now.'

'But I would have looked so fabulous.'

'No you wouldn't. You'd have chosen an exact replica of the Princess Di dress, complete with humongous flouncy sleeves and you'd have looked like one of those dolls people used to use to cover their spare rolls of toilet paper in the guest bathroom.'

Tashy was getting a fitting at the same time. She looked fabulous in her ivory sheath column, but she was sighing nonetheless.

'Tash, if it makes you feel any better, I have pimples all the way up the yazoo.'

'Really? Your actual yazoo?'

'No, my breastbone, but they're still pretty gross.'

'Huh.'

'And, like I keep telling you,' I took her hand, 'you look beautiful. Beautiful, beautiful, beautiful.'

'Really?'

I gestured at an enormous meringue in the window, which was corseted with crisscross gold thread, so it looked like some kind of wiring network. It had sleeves like hot-air balloons.

'Try this one on just in case!'

* * *

'I'd better get out of this dress,' I said eventually, when we'd gazed.

'Oh, I know, I know. It's just – actually, I think it's depressing me more than anything else.'

'I thought we were having fun,' I said. 'And, you know, fun is a really rare quality for me these days.'

'I'm just not . . .' She collapsed in a heap of tulle. 'I mean, I'm not even sure I want to have sex with him for the rest of my life. Or even one more time!'

'But, Tash, you've always seemed so happy; so suited.'

'I know.'

'I mean, before I came back . . .'

'You too also seemed so happy, so suited.'

We looked at the ground.

'Why do we do this to ourselves?' said Tashy sadly.

'Because it's the grown-up thing to do?' I said unhappily.

'Because this is all there is?'

'Because family is the answer?'

'Because Max was too cheap to buy wedding insurance?'

I stood up.

'Your dress is perfect,' Tash said, grinning through the tears. 'We'll take it. And now I have to go.'

'Where?' I said. 'What if I'm in need of some guidance?'

'But I'm seeing Olly,' she said, 'and he expressly said, and I quote, "If at all possible, could we meet without your juvenile delinquent?".'

'It's a step up from wolverine,' I said.

'No, when I said "I quote", I actually meant "I paraphrase without all the swearing". Right, I'm going to try it.'

'What?'

She stood up and closed her eyes. 'I wish I was sixteen again!' she said, quite loudly.

'Oh, that's a *great* idea!' I jumped up too. 'Come back too. We'll have a brilliant time! You can come to Justin's party!'

She half opened one eye. 'Tell me you're not going to a teenage party?'

'Er, no.'

'You bitch.' She pinched her thighs. 'This isn't working, is it?'

'Dunno,' I said.

She opened her eyes. 'Can I come to the party anyway?'

'Do you remember that Canadian school teacher who got sent to prison for cavorting with her charges?'

'Bugger, bugger, bugger.'

'Good luck with the happiest day of your life,' said the shop assistant as we both slouched out into the street.

* * *

Stanzi and I were being overexcited in my parents' kitchen. We had got ready together in the bathroom, and I'd introduced her to the delights of Nik Kershaw, which I'd discovered in my parents' record collection, shamefully enough. Stanzi had blue mascara on one eye and green on the other,

I was wondering how low I could get away with pulling my stripy top.

'Do you think I can show a bra strap?'

Stanzi snorted loudly, rubbing extra blush over her round cheeks. 'I've never heard of anyone who minded having a bra strap show.'

I guessed not. We danced around until we both looked fantastic (for trannies) and, leaving a trail of destruction across the bathroom – hey, if I wasn't a little thoughtless now and again surely they'd suspect something – we teetered downstairs.

'Erm . . . lovely,' said my dad, screwing up one eye. 'Are you sure, Joyce?'

My mother raised her eyes. 'You tell them.'

'I don't think this is a battle I want to fight today,' said my dad.

I beamed at him and pulled my sweater down a little just for badness.

'Now,' my dad said. I noticed suddenly he was covering my mother's hand with his, and she was smiling bravely, backing him up as he gave us his little pep talk. Well, this was something.

'I know there's no point in saying "don't drink", but I just want you to be responsible.'

We nodded vigorously, hopping from foot to foot.

'And DON'T let your glass out of sight.'

'I don't think there'll be that much Rohypnol at the Clellands' party,' I said.

'You never know, Miss Smart-aleck.'

'We're going to stick to alcopops,' said Stanzi bravely. 'Don't worry, Mr Scurrison, it's only two doors down.'

'Don't worry about you two slugging alcopops all night until you pass out. I'll try,' said my dad, shaking his head and looking at my mother.

'Now, I know you're both sensible,' began my mother, 'but think of the harm that could happen if you go too far with the boys.'

'Yeah – you might end up married at thirty-two,' I said, but quietly.

'It's not we don't want you to have any fun,' added my dad. 'We just want you to think: safe, responsible fun.'

'That doesn't sound like fun at all.'

'I'll come and pick you up at one o'clock.'

'Dad, it's only next door but one!'

'That's why you'd better be home by then. If you don't want me stalking into your party. In my pyjamas. With the fly open.'

'OK,' I said.

He smiled.

* * *

I wanted to walk around the block a few times, so that we weren't insanely early, but Stanzi was having none of it.

'You want my makeup destroyed so I get no boys? Is that your masterplan?'

'No, I just don't want us to be sitting like dorks in the living room, waiting for his parents to leave.'

'No! Let's go now! Go now! Go now! Then we can chat to Ethan first! He will be early too.'

'I don't think you should get your hopes up too much about Ethan, Stanzi.'

'Why not, huh?'

'I just . . . you know, I think he might be gay.'

I watched Stanzi's face as it struggled to come to terms with the unlikeliness of this.

'But . . . but he is so pretty!'

I nodded.

'And so clean and neat!'

I nodded again.

She grimaced. 'This is all Will Young's fault,' she said darkly.

'I'm sure it's not,' I said.

'Now I'm going to have to end up with Kendall.'

Kendall was a sweet-looking boy with spots and glasses, who sat behind us in English and looked longingly at Stanzi all the time. I thought he was going to be lovely when he grew up, but he equalled us for nerdiness at the moment.

'There's nothing wrong with Kendall.'

'He's a dweeb.'

'No he's not. He's a superhunk in waiting, and he still doesn't deserve you.'

We were at the gate. Inside, we could see lights glowing red, and heavy rap was distinct. A couple of uninvited ratboys were hanging around, looking pissed off.

I swallowed hard. I looked at Stanzi and she was just as nervous as me. This was stupid. I could happily go to scary client meetings, large corporate parties, strange weddings, and get along at all of them fine. Everyone was always nervous at big events, and it was easy to break the ice and find someone to chat to.

But this was different. This was a jungle; a completely alien civilisation with rules I had never understood. School at least had a veneer of adult control; this was full-on social warfare. In a world where everyone knew both the rules and everyone else. Except for me. Goddamn, I was nervous.

'Well, there's nothing quite as good as having fun, is there?' I said to Stanzi, who looked absolutely terrified, as if she was facing a lion's den. Which we were.

'Maybe we walk around the block,' said Stanzi quickly.

'Look,' I said, 'this is going to be fine.' I nodded, trying to convince myself. 'Think of it as kicking off our life of party-going, and they will get more and more fun after this, I promise. Then you'll get to a point when they stop being so much fun any more and they deteriorate and everyone talks about house prices and au pairs. But you can worry about that later.'

'Yeah?' said Stanzi.

'Come on,' I said. 'Let's go.'

And just as I said it, we opened the gate, and the door of the main house opened up to let us in and the smoke and the heat and the noise were almost welcoming.

Chapter Twelve

The first thing I saw was a couple pressed up against the wall, snogging. Well, looked like I hadn't had to worry so much about the niceties of timekeeping. Kids were everywhere; hanging over banisters, dancing in the sitting room. It was a long time since I'd been here, but Clelland's parents' place hadn't changed at all. There was . . . oh my God, a picture of Clelland that I recognised and had always loved. He's eighteen, and he's holding a squirming toddler in his arms. He looks sulky and embarrassed, but completely thrilled at the same time. It was very strange to see it yellowing in a frame: I remember the day we picked it up from Boots. The house was still full of the ornaments and mementoes that we had found so hilariously bourgeois at the time, but now I found them reassuring, and it was more than a little peculiar to be seeing them again after all this time.

Stanzi was clinging on to my coat, and I patted her on the hand to make sure she was OK. An older boy I didn't recognise – though I guess that didn't matter much – came up to me.

'Hi, Flora. Glad you could make it!' he said. 'You look cute.'

Well, well, well! Inside my heart leaped with the praise. Maybe this wasn't going to be such an ordeal after all.

'Hey!' said a couple of the other guys. 'Looking good, chica.'

I smiled broadly at them and headed to the kitchen. Someone wolf-whistled loudly as we went past.

Stanzi caught up with me in the kitchen.

'Something is wrong,' she said suspiciously, as I swigged my first alcopop and tried not to gag on all the sugar.

'What do you mean?' I said. 'Once you get everyone out of school they're really nice.'

A gawky boy with a couple of pimples pinched me on the arse.

'Don't be cheeky,' I said coquettishly.

'Hmm,' said Stanzi. She leaned over. 'Are you sure everything is quite OK?'

'Come on!' I said. 'Lighten up.'

And I swigged my alcopop, and this time it tasted better. Stanzi didn't stop eyeing me up, though.

Maybe because I'd had nearly two weeks of constant stress; maybe because the world might be going to end for me very shortly; maybe because I was young and crazy and foolish and I could do these things; maybe because I didn't want to be the wallflower any more. I can't say what it was. But I drank, and danced, and flirted, and was flirted with, and talked to everyone, and was loud, and waved to Justin, who waved back, looking slightly uncomfortable, and I decided to have a fabulous time. He couldn't possibly be embarrassed about asking us, I thought, when we were being the life and soul. Well, I was being the life and soul. I kept losing track of Stanzi; mostly because every time she came up and sensibly suggested we have a bit of a sit down, I waved her away.

The last party Ol and I went to was a dinner party. Two of his work friends had just had a baby, and kept being incredibly ostentatious about it, like it was a real achievement on their part. They kept getting up to phone the babysitter and, for fuck's sake, *express milk*. Why would you even tell people that's what you were about to do? It was absolutely crap. I wanted to get drunk but Ol wouldn't let me in case two of the other people at the table wanted to become clients of his (they certainly spent the entire evening asking for his advice free of charge). I'd called Tash halfway through and she was at Max's parents, and we fantasised about stealing the boys' credit cards and doing a speedy Thelma and Louise.

The music here was loud and fantastic. After all, it was indeed Saturday night, and the air was getting hot like a baby! I remembered this from first time round! I loved alcopops, especially the blue ones, and all these boys from school; they were just lovely, even if they had to keep reminding me of their names all the time. They thought this was terribly funny, and so did I. 'I can't even remember your names!' I was bawling, in absolute hysterics. Why had I ever thought everyone was horrible? Everyone was great! It was great here! Life was cool. I whirled in delirium, letting the sleeves of my jersey roll down to reveal my bra straps; dancing as sexily as I knew how. Everyone wanted to dance with me, it was fantastic. Time was passing in the blink of an eye. Suddenly I knew what I must do. I reached over and clambered up on the highly polished wooden dinner table that I used to make polite conversation with Clelland's parents round on alternate Sundays, and which had now been pushed to the wall, and started dancing fit to bust.

'Wooo!' shouted the boys. They could see up my skirt. I didn't care. The music came louder and louder and I was whirling and whirling and . . .

'FLORA?'

The voice cut across the noise of the sitting room like a whipcrack. Everyone stopped and turned round. Clelland, and his horribly gorgeous girlfriend, were standing, staring at me from the other side of the room. Next to them was Stanzi, gesticulating wildly at me.

'Get down from there at once.'

'Make me!' I said, suddenly feeling drunk, powerful and defiant.

'We'll all make you, Flora', said another voice, and there was grubby male laughter.

Clelland didn't take his gaze off me.

'What – if I don't get off your table you'll go to Aberdeen?'

He looked around. The music was still playing, but everyone was watching the drama.

'What's she talking about?' hissed his girlfriend. She was looking distinctly pissed off. Mind you, I wouldn't be that thrilled to have to give up my Saturday night to patrol a kiddy party.

'Please, Flora?'

I held up my skirt saucily. 'Make me.'

There was a mass wooing at this.

'Goddamit, Flo, stop titting about.'

I stuck my tongue out at him, and danced around.

'Were you always this annoying?'

'Were you always this boring?'

'Goddamit . . .' At that Clelland bit his lip and lost his patience. As all the other people in the room watched, he came up to the table, lifted me up and threw me over his shoulder in a fireman's hold.

There was a massive round of applause. Someone shouted, 'She's up for it, man!' and someone else shouted, 'Upside down for it, man!' and my face went very red as I was, in fact, upside down on Clelland's back and I knew my knickers were showing. Which didn't seem as hilarious an idea as I'd thought a couple of minutes ago. I felt sick and embarrassed and stupid and patronised. At the same time, there was a strange sense of familiarity in being pressed to Clelland's shirt, with his smell taking me straight back to our time together. Nothing can punch you back into the past as quickly as that.

Suddenly, there in front of me (or behind me I guess, as Clelland marched me out the door) was Fallon. She and three of her henchmates, dressed up to the nines in little bikini tops and tight trousers. They were laughing their heads off.

'Oh Jesus, did you see her!' Fallon was gasping, practically wiping the tears from her eyes. Then she looked at me and gave me the most malicious grin.

'Oh, John, is Flora alright? Would you like us to look after her for you?'

Clelland just grunted, passed through the door and deposited me on the third step of the stairs.

'Just what the hell do you think you're doing?' he asked gruffly.

'Having crazy teenage fun,' I replied, aware that my face was so red it must be scorching the walls.

'You're supposedly a grown woman, for fuck's sake. What was that: pole dancing?'

'Table dancing?' I said in a small voice.

He stared at me. 'You're losing it.'

I sank down to the stair and wrapped my arms around my knees. 'No I'm not,' I said. I realised how woozy I was feeling. Then I realised I'd been dancing like a slut on Clelland's parents' table.

'Yikes, I'm sorry,' I said suddenly.

'Your tolerance is way down,' he said. 'Quick, drink some . . .'

But Stanzi had already rushed up with a full pint glass of water. She was practically gibbering.

'Flora, you have to listen, you have to . . .'

'Could you give us a second?' said Clelland, not unkindly.

'Noooo! It cannot wait or I explode.'

'Well, if you're going to explode . . .'

I looked up. 'What is it?' I said. I seemed to be sobering up rapidly into a very bad mood.

'Fallon started a rumour! She said you were wanting to lose your virginity tonight! She told all the boys this was your first and last party and you would definitely, definitely have sex! Kendall told me.'

I sat bolt upright. 'Oh my God. That bitch!'

Clelland looked at me. Oh no. Bloody hormones again. I felt suddenly incredibly ashamed – almost like I might start crying.

'So that's why everyone was being so nice . . . all those boys I don't really know. I thought maybe underneath they were just shy, and . . . oh GOD, I'm such a fucking idiot.' My voice was a bit wobbly.

Clelland looked amused. 'You mean . . . please don't tell me you were showing off so the boys would like you?'

'It's not funny,' I said. 'It was a horribly cruel thing to do. It can scar people for life.'

I gulped down more water.

'Maybe I just wanted it to be different than the first time round. And it was. It was worse!'

He was still suddenly. 'What was so wrong about the first time round?'

'I threw it away on you, remember.' I'd meant to sound flippant but it came out as though I was bitter.

Clelland blinked slowly.

Suddenly all I wanted – *all* I wanted – was to be back in my own little flat, with a bubble bath, a magazine and the phone off the hook.

'I want to go home,' I said suddenly.

Stanzi nodded.

'You want me to walk you?' said Clelland.

'OK,' I nodded my head. 'Thank you.'

'OK.'

* * *

Our coats and bags had disappeared. I had a shrewd idea of where they might be – stashed away by any number of those so friendly and charming boys who might plan to help me go look for them later, in a dark recess of a dark bedroom.

As I mounted the stairs I heard Madeleine saying to Clelland, 'Really, they're awful at that age, aren't they?'

I made a face above her head.

'They're just kids,' said Clelland, in an amused tone.

'Well, I certainly didn't behave like that when I was a kid.'

I bet you didn't, I thought.

'I bet you didn't,' Clelland said. 'Another drink?'

'No thanks, darling.'

I don't like you, I thought. I hoped that would trigger Clelland to say the same thing again, but it didn't.

* * *

My bag wasn't in the first two rooms I looked in, although there were plenty of other suspects entwined in gruelling balls of spit and the occasional expostulated, 'No, not there.' In one room, the school hippy kid was lighting a joint, surrounded by wide-eyed acolytes desperately pretending they were really cool about this but actually looking like five-year-olds waiting in line to see Santa Claus. I was wandering up the corridor, feeling like some horrible tart – the elastic in my top had almost totally gone now, and I was holding it up with both hands – when I came across Justin, barring a doorway and looking completely miserable. His face lightened when he saw me.

'Oh, Flora, can you help?'

'What, give blow jobs to the whole football team? No, Justin, that was Fallon's little lie.'

He looked confused for a second. 'What are you talking about? Is this one of these bitchy girl things?'

'Yeah,' I said.

'Oh, I never listen to those anyway. Listen, we need help. And I think. . . well, I think you might be the only one who can understand.'

Fantastic. What was this, some kid was late filing his tax return?

'What is it?' I said

'You'd better come in,' said Justin. I walked in. This was the room at the back of the house that used to be Clelland's. In his day it was covered in Sisters of Mercy posters, with shelves lined with dog-eared orange Penguin originals and a black-and-white-striped duvet, and small pieces of cruci-fixion jewellery hanging around. Now there was a bright green iMac, a basketball hoop, several pairs of trainers lying around and a rather smart Paul Smith striped duvet. The room had clearly been tidied up specially for the occasion. I wondered who Justin had his eye on as the lucky lady who was going to share his bed at his party.

At any rate that was immaterial at the moment, because sitting on the bed crying his eyes out was Ethan.

'You've come out,' I said immediately.

Ethan and Justin looked at each other dumbfounded.

'I told you people would understand,' said Justin eventually.

Ethan sniffed and eyed me suspiciously. 'Why were you writing me all that love poetry then if you knew?'

'Often gay people are more sensitive and love the poetic arts,' I said on the spur of the moment. 'Of course, that's a terrible overgeneralisation. You can be whatever you want to be.'

I seemed to be handling this about as well as the Mmkay guidance counsellor on *South Park*.

'Look,' I said, 'I promise it really doesn't matter.'

'Scared the life out of him,' said Ethan sullenly.

'Hey, man, it was a shock, OK?' Justin looked guilty.

'Justin, if you go through life thinking every gay man you meet is going to fancy you, you're going to be pretty bored,' I said. 'Now, are you going to tell your parents?'

Ethan shook his head. 'What's the point?'

I nodded. 'I think,' I said, 'you shouldn't tell anyone until you're a bit older.'

Justin raised his eyebrows.

'They'll all know,' wailed Ethan.

'Well, that's OK. Here's the thing. School is notoriously homophobic, right?'

He nodded.

'But you're going to university, right?'

He nodded again.

'Next year?'

'Uh-huh.'

'I'd keep shtoom until then. People at university – they *love* gay people. There'll be competitions to see who can be your best friend.'

'Really?'

'Absolutely. Being gay at university is very, very fashionable.'

'That can't be true,' said Justin.

'It's true.'

'How do you know?'

'Oh, everyone knows,' I said with the kind of bored sigh guaranteed to buy the instant agreement of a teenager who's afraid of seeming as if he doesn't know very much.

'But, you know, I've accepted my true nature.'

'You can accept all those kickings too,' I said. 'I'm just telling you what I'd do under the circumstances. And tell your parents just before you go to college – maybe as you're walking out the door – otherwise they'll be convinced it's just some kind of a phase.'

Ethan was nodding. 'It's going to be really hard.'

'Nonsense,' I said. 'You'll have a great time. Just be careful.'

'I'm really scared of . . . you know, doing it and stuff.'

'We all are,' I assured him. 'Doesn't matter whether you're going for the doughnut or the pork sword.'

They stared at me.

'And now I'd like to apologise for that disgusting analogy.'

Justin smiled.

'Well, I'd better get downstairs and back into my double life,' said Ethan with a big sigh. He wiped off his tears in the mirror and reapplied his mascara.

'You're going to be just fine,' I said, patting him on the back.

'Thanks,' said Justin.

* * *

I followed the boys downstairs to the kitchen. Fallon was holding court by the fridge.

'Ooh, Ethan,' she cooed when she saw him, 'come stand by me, baby. I want to feed you some fruit.'

He did, and she fussed and patted round him.

'Ooh, don't stop, darling,' he said.

I wandered into the back garden, to stop myself accidentally kicking her in the tits. Was I old enough to get done for GBH?

The air was heavy with woodsmoke, the residue of a bonfire set up there earlier, which was still crackling away.

Boys were dancing around it at the far end of the gard[...]
swigging heavily from enormous two-litre bottles of che[...]
cider. Suddenly I felt a touch on my elbow. I turned round.
It was Justin.

'Thanks again for . . . in there,' he said gruffly. 'I thought
he was going to have, like, hysterics or something.'

'You sound like the general of the army,' I said.

'What?'

'Nothing. You'll grow out of it.'

He looked at the ground. Then he looked at me, leaning
on his arm against a tree. His big grey eyes were appealing
to me. He smelled of youth; of cigarettes, cheap beer, cheap
aftershave and woodsmoke. It went straight to my head. He
blinked nervously.

'Flo . . .' he said. Then he leaned in, looking at me all the
time, desperate not to misread the signals, constantly waiting
for the confused messages, the outright no, the slap on the
face. There was none. Very tentatively, very softly, almost
trembling with nerves, he started to kiss me. At first I was
shocked, then suddenly found myself desperately wanting to
give in to his soft young lips . . .

'Flo,' Justin was saying, gulping, and grabbing at me with
increasing strength.

'FLORA!' came a shouting voice. The spell was broken
instantly and I jumped back.

'Fuck, that's my brother,' said Justin.

'He's meant to be walking me home,' I said, stuttering,
trying to straighten my top.

'I'll walk you home,' said Justin.

'Um, that's OK,' I said, wondering what Clell might say
to that particular little arrangement.

'Ummm . . .'

'FLORA!'

'I'd better go,' I said. 'I promised my dad.'

Justin kissed me. Then he kissed me again. Then the whole thing started taking off again . . .

'I *have* to go,' I said. 'I have to.'

I kissed him absolutely definitely for the last time. Then once or twice more for luck. Then once more for the road. Then I reappeared, breathless, inside the kitchen door.

* * *

Clelland was standing there looking annoyed.

'Where the devil have you been?'

'Looks like someone's been out behind the bushes,' said Fallon, clocking my fevered cheeks and racing breathing.

'I'm ready,' I said.

'Don't forget your hymen!' sang Fallon gaily.

'Listen, you useless, anorexic sack of shit,' I said, turning on her suddenly. 'You know how when parents divorce they say it's never the child's fault? Maybe in your case you should re-examine that clause.'

She stepped back as if I'd slapped her. I remembered at the last minute that you never ever diss anyone's parents. Fortunately I'm very mature and in control of myself. Equal psychic scarrings for everyone tonight.

'Are they fighting for anti-custody of who doesn't get you?'

'Shut up,' she said. 'Shut up shut up shut up.'

'Well, stop coming it with me, fat tits.'

'Ethan!' she said, her huge eyes wet with tears.

'Oh, hi, Flora,' said Ethan. 'Have a good night?'

'Hey,' I said.

'Watch out for yourself,' he said.

'WHAT?' said Fallon.

I turned round and looked at Clelland. 'Shall we go?' I said.

'Are those teenagers still fighting?' said Madeleine, coming out from behind the door. 'How terribly fascinating.'

'I'm walking these two home,' said Clelland. He looked next to me. 'Oh God, where's the other one? She was here a moment ago.'

'Stanzi!' I yelled. She appeared, staggering slightly, from the coats cupboard, closely followed by a de-spectacled Kendall, looking stunned. I couldn't help smiling, and, smiling too, Clelland caught my eye.

'Right!' he said. 'All out!'

'Uh, Mr Clelland, sir . . .'

We looked at each other again. It was Kendall.

'Yes, what is it?' said Clell, in his best exasperated teacher impersonation.

'Can I walk Constanzia home, sir?'

'Is she staying at yours?' Clelland asked me. I nodded. 'OK. If she's agreeable, you can walk ten feet in front of us, fully visible at all times.'

'Right, OK, great, thanks, mate,' said Kendall, flustered.

'I just went from "Mr Clelland" to "mate",' Clell complained to me.

'Next stop, "wanker"!' I said cheerfully.

'Constanzia,' Kendall was clearing his throat, 'might I ask if I can walk you . . .?'

Stanzi had already leaped on him like a flying red and black bat and we had to usher them out the door glued to each other.

* * *

'Hormones,' Clelland said when we were finally out of the house, walking very slowly behind a stumbling, giggling StanziKendallphant. 'Drive you crazy at that age . . . Christ, I keep forgetting. Hang on a minute . . .'

I was scarcely listening, my pulse was racing so fast. I was still having trouble catching my breath. What on *earth* had I just done? 'What?'

'Are you really thirty-two?'

I couldn't work out why he was asking me. He didn't suspect, surely.

'What do you mean, am I thirty-two? Are you thirty-four? Anyway, how would you know? It's not like you ever attend any of my birthday parties.'

This seemed to put him off the scent and we walked in silence for a while. I snuck a sideways peek at him. He looked relatively unruffled, certainly not angry with me. Maybe I'd got away with it.

'We're walking round the block again!' hollered Stanzi, disengaging suction. We followed.

'I don't think I've ever felt thirty-two,' I said finally. 'I think I've always felt like this.'

'Hmm,' he said. 'Me too, probably. But if everyone behaved like that . . .'

'There'd be a lot fewer wars.'

'Are you joking? You and that gorgeous dark-haired girl would have let off nuclear weapons at each other by now.'

'Oh, yeah,' I said. I hung my head in shame. Could I have behaved any worse than I had tonight? 'Well, boys have no idea what it's like at school. You have no idea how nasty people can be.'

'Are you nuts? Don't you remember me getting my head kicked in for wearing Robert Smith-style lipstick?'

'You were asking for that.'

'That's unfair.'

'Well, yes, but Tom Philmore kicked your head in, and you were playing football with him the next day.'

'So?'

'Girls can make this kind of thing last for months. Also, psychological torture's much worse than physical stuff.'

'I'll ask you about that again next time you're about to get your head kicked in.'

We'd reached the gate. Stanzi and Kendall were enmeshed in each other like a science project. I'd almost managed to clear my head of the stolen kiss.

'Stanzi, we have to go before my dad comes out,' I said. It was near the witching hour of one a.m.

'You tell him, I kill you,' she managed to get out without even coming up for air.

Clelland and I hovered for a while.

'Sorry I lifted you up in the air,' he said.

'God, no. It could have got a bit unpleasant in there. Thanks for saving me from a baying acned mob.'

'Anytime,' he said.

'Plus, I bet you liked doing it,' I teased.

'Only wish I'd thought of it earlier,' he said. I looked at him in the light from the streetlamp. There was a little line between his eyebrows, just the tiniest furrow.

A light went on upstairs in the house.

'Now!' I said to Stanzi, grabbing her. She popped off like a sucker from a car window.

Clelland smiled ruefully. 'Mind you don't miss your curfew now,' he said.

'Hey! I get enough of this shit from Tashy, I refuse to take it from you.'

'OK, OK. Go.'

I looked up at him once again. And he smiled, pulled me over to him and gave me a kiss, right on the forehead.

'Goodnight,' he said softly.

'You know,' I said, 'I'd like to say I had a good time tonight.'

'Hurry up!' said Stanzi as the hall light came on. Kendall had already scarpered.

* * *

I went in, but it wasn't my dad who was there to greet me. It was my mother.

'Oh,' she said. 'I thought it was . . .' Then she choked and turned her face away.

'Mum? *Mum!*' I said, genuinely concerned as her face crumpled up.

Stanzi, silently disappeared to the spare room.

'He's . . . I thought he wasn't going to be so late any more.'

I looked at my watch. 'What do you mean, "any more"? How often is he this late?'

My mother bit her lip. 'I'm not the bitch in this family, Flora. You have to believe that.'

I made her a cup of tea. Her hands were shaking. Then I put my arms around her and I gave her a hug.

'Ssh,' she said. 'It's alright. Go to bed.'

But it wasn't alright. She shooed me up the stairs, where I lay on the bed, curled in a tight ball with my eyes closed, wishing and wishing and wishing this wasn't happening; wishing it wasn't my fault that my mother was going through this again.

At two thirty, the front door opened. There were raised voices, then tears. Voices raised again, then hushed quickly. I heard 'You're never!' and 'Not the first time'. I put my fingers over my ears. The last thing I heard before I drifted off to sleep was my father trying to calm my mother; saying, 'It's going to be alright.' I wondered if she was convinced.

Chapter Thirteen

It is amazing how much you can get away with not mentioning in families. Amazing. And by the time Monday came around, it was a lovely day. What a nice day. Autumnal, crisp. I'd grown to hate lovely days over the last few years, resenting how they made staying in the office even worse, Dean breathing down my neck every five minutes, making sure nobody could have fun just because the sun was shining. It was pathetic how everyone sat in the concrete garden, desperate to eat our Pret à Manger in just a slice of sunlight. Olly and I always meant to go somewhere outside at the weekend, but by the time we'd read the papers and he'd worked and we'd bickered a bit and I'd got to the gym and . . . well, half the time it never happened. Actually, it never ever happened, even when we meant to.

But this was one of those back-to-school days that requires a grey V-neck sweater and some nice fresh stationery. And I had both of those! Mum, quieter than ever, had even made porridge, which I secretly completely loved, as did my dad

– as a consequence of which, she hadn't made it in years. I tried not to think about the fact that I'd glanced at the calendar. And. . .well, I had twelve days till Tashy's wedding. Twelve days till God knows what. Twelve days. And I badly wanted to make the most of them.

'Good party then?' my dad asked me.

My mum glanced up at him immediately. I'd spent the entire day before barricaded in my room, simply so I could read the broadsheet papers without snorts of derision coming from my dad over the *Mail on Sunday* about who was getting all pretentious then, but maybe he thought I was swooning with love for some lad. Oh God. Well, when it came down to it, I had snogged him. Oh God. I was trying to pretend it was all a dream, like the rest of my life. Except – oh, this was ridiculous. I had butterflies. I hadn't had those for years. Yes, his lips were very pink and very soft and he did smell dreamy, but this was just a combination of hormones and nostalgia. Wasn't it? I told myself sternly. YES.

'Yes,' I said. Then I did a reflex I hadn't done for years and would have sworn I couldn't remember what it was. I put my hand up to my neck to check for lovebites.

My dad shot my mother another look, but she wouldn't respond.

'I was very good,' I said.

'Was that sexy counsellor there? They should have sent her to keep an eye on things.'

'Dad!'

My dad had known Tashy since she was six! Kind of.

'I just think she's a good influence on you, that's all.'

'I think I'm going to walk. Gotta go!'

* * *

I dawdled along, kicking leaves up in the air, forgetting for a moment that I was anything other than a kid on her way to school, thinking about English class, walking past Clelland's house as usual. I remembered how I used to hang out, desperately hoping to see him walk past. Now I was trying to scuttle past quickly in case either Clelland brother happened to be there.

Clelland senior was outside the garden gate.

'Um, hi,' I said.

'Um, hi,' he said, looking a bit flustered. I don't know why; I went to school at the same time every day, didn't I? No, no, I didn't. I was an adult with different routines and choices, I tried to remind myself.

'Have you moved back home?' I asked.

'Have you?'

'*Touché*,' I said.

'No, it's just, Maddie doesn't really like her parents thinking we . . . you know. While we're in the country.'

'Are they God botherers?'

'And how. I mean, no, not . . . just Christians, you know, perfectly normal.'

Suddenly Justin came out of the front door. My heart started to palpitate again. He saw me and immediately went red from the tips of his ears to his shirt collar. Oh, for goodness' sake.

'Come on, small bear,' shouted Clelland.

I looked at them both.

'He's not walking me to school,' said Justin sullenly. 'He just won't leave me alone.'

'I've been in Africa for two years,' said Clelland. 'Is a little bit of bonding too much to ask?'

'Bonding, not babysitting,' said Justin crossly. 'And your stupid girlfriend keeps gubbing on about Africa. Are you going or aren't you?'

Clelland suddenly turned a bit tight-lipped.

'Shall we go?' he said.

There was no way round it. I had to walk in between them. Clelland was looking at me with some amusement.

'So what do you have at school today, little lady?'

'I'm selling drugs behind the science block, destroying the fabric of society, failing to vote, expecting the world to owe me a living and sleeping with the PE teacher,' I said grumpily. Justin kept sneaking peeks at me and brushing my hand, and I had no idea what to do about it.

'You obviously love school,' said Clelland.

'Ever since they did away with corporal punishment it's just not the same,' I said.

Clelland laughed down his nose at me and shook his head.

* * *

Stanzi met me at the front gates. She had a gigantic hickey down one side of her neck.

'Stanz,' I said, 'you look like a pram face.'

'I don't care,' she said proudly. 'I've never had one before.'

'I don't think you want to advertise every single stage of your secondary sexual development,' I said. 'Necessarily.'

'Ooh, there's Kendall,' she said, waving furiously. OK. Maybe there were a few long roads of wisdom to womanhood she had to set foot on.

Kendall beamed his head off when he saw her and came running over. Oh. Maybe not.

They giggled and pawed each other quietly and I pretended not to care as we wandered towards English.

* * *

'Miss Scurrison.'

I looked up to see the teacher standing over me.

'Hi,' I said. 'How are you?'

The rest of the class laughed, thinking this was just cheek. I realised I was just trying to be normal. Teachers aren't normal. I was aware that I kept making mistakes like this, like those aliens in science-fiction films who are trying to pass as humans but keep eating the cutlery. Last week I'd been caught listening to early choral music.

'I'm fine, thank you, Miss Scurrison,' said Miss Syzlack sarcastically. 'I'm always fine on Monday mornings after I've spent the entire weekend marking.'

I picked up the essay she'd put in front of me. An A! I'd never had a straight A in my life! I was a compulsive B student. This was great.

'Thanks!' I said.

'Don't mention it,' said the teacher.

'Swotto lesbo,' said Fallon quietly from the back.

I turned round as Miss Syzlack walked back to the front.

'Are you starting?'

She gazed at me for a minute.

'No,' she said sullenly, and went back to doodling on her folder.

'Yes, Flora got the only A in the class,' said Miss Syzlack.

I couldn't help it, I beamed with pride. They should do this at work. If you spend weeks on a report, with proper colour graphs and everything, you should get a big mark for it and everyone should be impressed, rather than leafing through them and throwing them in the bin immediately.

'She's the only person who didn't clearly cut and paste the entire thing from the Internet. It's about original thinking, guys.'

A groan went up from the whole class – including me, when I realised how much time I'd wasted on the damn thing. But I didn't care. I was still glowing. And all I had to do that afternoon was three hours of art, then five of us (including Ethan and Kendall) were off for Coke floats and a lengthy party post-mortem. Hurrah! I'd forgotten that these could take weeks and would involve much embroidery. I was really going to drop Fallon in it this time.

* * *

I escaped at lunchtime. I'd forgotten in all the excitement that I'd arranged to meet Tashy. I was becoming an expert at slipping out of the school gates, but really, sneakily, I'd kind of wanted to catch up on all the gossip, and spread some.

I ferociously wolfed down a cheese toastie and a chocolate milkshake – I was *so* hungry, all the time – while Tashy looked on miserably sitting in the small condensation-filled atmosphere of the little caff.

'Do you remember when I used to be the jolly one and you used to be the worrier?' she said.

I pulled myself back from my obsessive thoughts about having snogged a seventeen-year-old.

'I am worried!' I said quickly. 'I have twelve days before I meet up with myself again and evaporate. Or maybe my other self will adopt me. Can I have another toastie? Have I told you about my A?'

Tashy looked away and let out a big sigh.

'Can we talk about this, or are you just going to stuff your face and act like you have no responsibilities in the world?'

'OK, Tash,' I said. 'Don't marry him. Please. Don't. You'll meet someone else; of course you will.'

'It's not that,' she said.

'People call off weddings all the time. After a few years it becomes an amusing story.'

'It's not that,' she repeated. 'Stop being so . . . so *young*.'

I stuck out my lower lip.

'Do you know what?' she went on. 'I'd almost say fuck the thirteen thousand pounds.'

'Thirteen thousand pounds!' I said. 'Are you nuts? You could have gone round the world sixteen times for that!'

'Yes, thank you. Olly pointed that out too. You try telling my mother to de-invite Aunt Nesta.'

'Well, it's money well spent,' I said hurriedly. 'And Nesta gets drunk and falls over during the speeches.'

'Really? Well, that does make it all worth it, I suppose.' Tashy's tone was hard.

'Yeah,' I said.

'No,' she said suddenly, ferociously playing with the Sweetex. 'It's not that. It's none of that. I see that now. I spent all night crying, just lying beside Max. He'd spent the entire evening on the phone geeking off to one of his friends about computers.'

'Communications skills,' I said.

'And I thought: I can't put up with this. I can't do it. I

can't go to supper with this man, or take him out to meet friends and have him be so dull, and so unsupportive and so un-me.'

I reached out and took her hand.

'Your hand is very greasy,' she said, glancing round in case she looked like a preying paedophile.

'Sorry,' I said. I wiped them on my school skirt, feeling as if I'd been given a telling-off by a grown-up. Then I realised I was being daft.

'OK then, do it,' I said. 'Look at me. It's obvious the world is full of surprises. There are twists of fate every step of the way. You have to follow—'

'Flora,' she said, her tone serious. 'This is important. Do you want to come back?'

This took me by surprise. 'I thought we were talking about your life,' I grumbled.

'I mean it, Flo. This is very important.'

And I thought about it. Hard. I thought about the accountancy firm. And I thought about my thirty-two-year-old body. And I thought about art school. And I thought about Justin. And I thought about Clelland. And I thought about possibilities – to do it differently, to change it. But most of all I thought about my mum and dad.

'Oh God,' I said.

'What?' said Tashy. 'What?'

'Well, yeah,' I said. 'I mean, sure.'

Tashy didn't say anything for a moment, just kept staring at me with an unnerving intensity. Then: 'You don't sound so sure.'

'But my mum, Tash. My mum. I haven't seen her like this . . . I mean, you know her, but you don't have to deal

with her like I do. All those tears, all those calls . . . I think
my dad is leaving – the first time round I left her alone. I
went to university and left her to it. I nearly destroyed her.'

We stared at each other.

'So what are you saying?'

I realised we were both leaning over, desperately sincere
about this. It was serious – very serious.

I thought of Clelland's amused-looking face at my predica-
ments. He would be off to Africa again soon with Madeleine
and I'd never see him again anyway, and I'd be back to Belsize
Park, completely on my own, spinster city beckoning . . .

'Oh God, Tashy, I don't . . . I just don't . . . can't we think
about this nearer the time?'

'In a week and a half?' Tashy seemed troubled. 'Look, Olly
and I have been talking about this.'

'Uh-huh?'

'The thing is. The thing is – I can't call off the wedding.'

'Why not?' I had the feeling I was being a bit slow, but
couldn't quite see where.

'If you can only get back by wishing on my cake . . .'

Suddenly the penny dropped. My mouth opened.

'Oh, no,' I said.

'But I couldn't do that to you,' she said. 'You don't know
yourself. Heck . . .' Her voice took on a kind of strangulated
choking sound. 'What's a small divorce between friends?'

'Please don't marry him.'

'And condemn you to sit your whole life again, in someone
else's world? I couldn't do that. I can't do that. Sorry, missus.'

'It . . . it'll be fine,' I said.

'Unless I get married, it doesn't look like you have a choice
either way.'

I stared at her. 'And Max eats soft-boiled eggs in bed for the next sixty years,' she said quietly.

Then I took her hand and we looked at each oth rily, through tears. All this time . . . I mean, yes, I hated being here, I did, but it wasn't the worse thing that could possibly happen to me, was it? Even if it wasn't where I belonged. Something struck me.

'I should stay anyway though,' I said. 'For Mum.'

'You don't know that. You don't know how you're going to feel on the day. You don't know, OK?' She was angry. 'And if I take that window away, that's it. Game over. Hockey sticks and driving tests till kingdom come.'

We sat in silence, tears dripping down our cheeks.

* * *

'What's wrong?' said Justin, playfully kicking at leaves as he caught up with me as I was leaving school. His feet were enormous in his trainers, I noticed, completely out of proportion to his skinny legs. That made me smile.

'Nothing,' I said, shaking my head. Nothing I was going to inflict on this innocent.

We headed up to the caff. Stanzi, Kendall and Ethan were squeezed into the faded upholstered booth. Stanzi was playing with the big red plastic tomato full of ketchup, clearly delighted to be the centre of attention with two men.

'Hey, hey,' said Ethan as we went in, and I sat down. I looked around. This place was as dingy as I remembered, with tinfoil ashtrays and curtains held together with grime. The cracked tiles were stacked with dirt. But, picking up the sticky laminated menu, I didn't care. Here we were, on the high street, kids on the town, drinking Coke floats. The world couldn't be as bad as we thought, could it? Tash was going to be alright, wasn't she? I looked at Justin, who was buying me my drink from the filthy-looking waitress. Kendall and Ethan were talking about what they wanted to do when they left school.

'Space programme,' Kendall was saying earnestly. 'They need good engineers.'

'They need better ones than they have,' Ethan agreed. 'St Martin's for me, I think.'

'Ooh, me too,' I said without thinking.

'Really? Art college? For you?'

'Are you calling this lovely lady a swot?' said Justin, adding white sugar to the top of his float.

'No,' said Ethan. 'We can discover our inner debauchery together.'

'Maybe not strictly together,' I said.

'No,' said Ethan.

'I'm going to be fashion designer,' said Stanzi. 'All the great designers are Italian.'

'Except for the French ones,' I said.

'I am going to be Di Ruggerio Designs. Fantastic.'

'I don't want to be rude,' said Justin, 'but you wear a Darius T-shirt over your school shirt every single day.'

Smiling, I looked out the window. Fallon was walking past, on her own. She looked annoyed and was kicking a leaf out of her way. I soon realised why: she'd clocked us all, sitting in the window. I stared at her until she lifted her gaze and saw me.

'Come over,' I mouthed, beckoning. She flipped me the bird and I smiled at her. This was nuts.

'Come in!' I mouthed again.

After a pause, she turned into the caff.

Kendall and Stanzi budged up for her, after Stanzi shot me a 'what the hell are you doing?' glance.

'Coke?' I asked pleasantly.

'Diet,' she said.

* * *

It was fun. It really was. It took me out of myself, my choices. We were invincible, we could do anything, we were all ready to take on the world. And as Justin and I walked home in the golden evening sunlight, I really was just a schoolgirl, swinging a book bag, tugging at the tie I once again tied without thinking about it.

'What are you thinking?' Justin asked me.

'Um, I . . .'

But before I could answer, he leaned over and kissed me, right in the middle of the street. It was a stupid thing to do. We were just across the road from his house. In the daytime. Anyone could walk past. My parents, Tashy, Clelland . . . After a second I squirmed out of his grip.

'This is silly,' I said.

'Silly how?' he asked and bent back over.

'Just . . . silly.'

He rolled his eyes and looked surprised.

'Silly . . . how? And he smiled again and gently stroked my neck in a way that felt oddly familiar. I closed my eyes. I could feel he was gradually moving in towards me. I kept my eyes closed. He gently kissed me on the side of the neck. It felt wonderful. The sunny autumn day was reduced to a dazzle behind my eyes as I gave in to the feeling of Justin's lips and his body pressing up against me.

241

I gave myself up to it completely. His soft, young lips, his seventeen-year-old body. I felt the lean hard muscle through his T-shirt, well on his way to becoming a man. His mouth was salty and soft and hard at the same time and tasted as good as . . . as good as . . . no, I was not going to think about the last time I'd been kissed like this, under an autumn sky. I closed my eyes and let the feeling wash over me.

I heard him give out an agonised gasp as he clasped my high young breasts. How long had it been since I'd so excited someone they'd gasped, and kissed me as if they were drowning, or would die if they couldn't feel my body against theirs? A bit bloody long.

'What the hell are you two doing?'

Clelland was storming out of a little black Fiesta that had pulled up to the kerb. Maddie was sitting behind the wheel, looking incredibly disapproving. He was looking from one to the other of us in disbelief.

I swallowed hard. What the hell was I doing?

'Chill, bro,' said Justin. 'Just chill.'

Clelland looked murderous. Then, and you could see it happening in his face, he swallowed heavily as if to draw the anger back in himself. His eyes were black, though, furious and burning. He turned to me and I felt my heart sink.

'Get away from him,' he said.

'Erm, yeah, excuse me, just ignore me, I'm just here for nothing,' said Justin, desperately trying to look unfazed.

'Stay away.'

'I'm sorry,' I said. 'I just got—'

'I can't . . . I can't believe you would do this, Flora. I just can't. I mean, it's like . . . it's . . . with everything . . .'

'I'm sorry! I'm sorry! I didn't . . . I didn't mean—'

'What would this have been like if you were a boy, and he was a girl, eh? Have you thought about that?'

'Eh?' said Justin.

'It would be different,' I said. The tears from lunchtime started to wend their way up again.

'No, no, it wouldn't, Flora. Do you understand?'

'But—' I began.

'You're disgusting. Is this some kind of twisted revenge? On me?'

'No!' I said. 'Definitely not. No.'

'That's not what it looks like.'

'What the hell's going on?' said Justin, looking scared. 'Is there something going on?'

'No!' we said in unison.

'God,' said Clelland. 'You're just . . . I'm just so ashamed of you.'

Justin looked at me, then at him. I was shaking, I really was.

'Come on, Justin. You really don't want to be anywhere near her.'

Justin looked back at me with a longing in his eyes.

'Goodbye,' I said, choking just a little.

'Oh, look at the little girl crying,' said Clelland. 'How deserving of our sympathy. She's only naïve. So new to the world. So many mistakes to make. So fucking many.' He glared at me.

I stared at him, open-mouthed.

'Will you tell me what on earth's going on?' Madeleine had got out of the car and was standing by the door, looking at the three of us.

'Nothing', barked Clelland. 'Nothing you'd understand.'

'You think?' she barked back at him. 'No. Because I don't understand anything, do I, John? Except trying to *do the right thing*, of course.'

She got back in the car and slammed the door. Clelland manhandled Justin towards it, they got in and drove off without a backwards glance.

Chapter Fourteen

For the next four days, as the wedding ticked ever closer I kept my head down in the pillows, crying myself into a teenage frenzy yet again, as my parents worried about me downstairs. I felt alternately sorry for myself and utterly ashamed. Mum brought me up cups of hot chocolate, which made me cry even more, whilst feeling ridiculously grateful for the existence of someone in the same house who would bring me hot chocolate.

No phone call from either of the boys. Well, of course not. What on earth was I expecting? Justin to suddenly transmogrify into a terribly thoughtful grown-up? Clelland to rethink that actually, no, it was pretty cool for a thirty-two year old to cop off with his baby bro? And it hadn't even occurred to me that he ever thought about us for a moment. Not in that way, not at all.

Clelland was right. It was disgusting to snog a seventeen-year-old boy. Or was it? I felt defiant suddenly. Kylie got to snog Justin Timberlake, and she was nearly old enough to

245

be his mum. Rod Stewart was always going out with teenagers. It was just because it was Clelland's brother that he was coming over all Mr 'I'm so protective, wooh!' on me.

I'd been carried away. No doubt about it. But Clelland wasn't the one living in the body of a teenager. And it was him who'd said I had to take this life as a gift, take it and enjoy it to the full, because, more than ever, nobody knew what was coming next . . .

Guess that didn't mean seducing his cute little brother.

I was musing, sniffily, alternating between remembered pleasure at Justin's young limbs and fresh sweet smell, and the absolute conviction that I'd done him no psychological damage whatsoever. Then I thought of Clelland, and what it must have been like to see the girl he used to kiss kissing someone else. Well, he should have thought of that before, I thought, mutinously. Pre Aberdeen might have been a good time.

I wasn't paying attention to anything around me. My mum had gone away to see her sister, and I seemed to manage to avoid running into my dad at all. Maybe this should have set alarm bells ringing.

'You know, marriage isn't easy,' he said meditatively, doling out crispy pancakes on Saturday morning.

Talk to someone who doesn't know, I thought.

'Yes,' he said. 'It's a struggle.'

I eyed him beadily. 'One you're definitely winning,' I said firmly.

He grunted.

My little phone rang to the chimes of 'Colourblind'. Perhaps I should change that. I picked it up warily and headed upstairs with it. It was Tash.

'Don't fall out with me,' I said immediately. 'If I lose

anyone else who recognises me, I'm going to cease to exist altogether.'

'What?' said Tash. 'Why would I fall out with you?'

'Because I'm forcing you into marital slavery.'

'Actually, I'm sorry.'

Her voice was muted.

'You've called off the wedding,' I said, excited. 'It's OK. I understand. You're right, in fact. It's good. I've been farting about for far too long, this way and that way, coming back or staying here. But I should stay here. I've got an application to art college to finish. Fortunately, as I've worked on interview panels for five years, mine's absolutely perfect.'

'Hang on. I haven't cancelled the wedding,' she said quietly.

'Oh. I mean, Max is a lovely man.'

'Shut up. I have, however, bumped up the wedding insurance.'

'That's probably wise.'

'Anyway. It wasn't that.'

'What wasn't what?'

Tash let out a sigh. 'Actually, be glad. I'm very glad you weren't there.'

'Weren't where?'

'Look, Flora, there's no way I could introduce you, and it would have been so awkward, and you would have cramped people's style and . . .'

I almost laughed when the penny dropped and I realised what she was talking about.

'You didn't invite me to the hen night?'

'No,' she said ashamedly. 'I'm really and truly sorry.'

I did laugh. At last I felt distracted from my miserable problems.

'Who gives a flying fuck about the hen night?'

She sighed dramatically.

'OK, I'll pretend to,' I said. 'Were there L-plates?'

'Yes.'

'And cheap polythene veils?'

'Yes.'

'A socially unbalanced mix of people from completely different areas of work and home and family who had to sit next to each other all evening despite having nothing in common except for knowing you, the bridge, and therefore responsible for making sure everyone had a good time, even with Heather organising it and your mum there chain smoking and watching everything you ate and drank?'

'Do you know, I thought it was surprising you didn't bug me more about this before,' said Tash. 'You knew when it was.'

With the untimely disappearance of me, Tashy had been reduced to asking her bitter big sister, Heather, to do the honours. Badly.

'I too have slightly other things on my mind,' I said disconsolately.

'Like what?'

I leaned over. 'I snogged Justin.'

'Justin who?' It took a moment for her to get it. 'NO! That's disgusting! He's a baby! I don't BELIEVE you! How could you not tell me all this time?'

'How could you not invite me to a big celebration of all the closest females in your life? Anyway, I thought you might disapprove and think it was disgusting.'

'Uh-*huh*.'

'I'm a sixteen-year-old girl, I have sixteen-year-old hormones, do you hear what I'm saying here, people? Cut me some slack.'

'What was it like?' she asked suddenly in a low voice.

'Fabulous,' I said. 'We snogged. He smelled unbelievably good. And you wouldn't believe how manly his body felt. Well, boy/manly. In a good way.'

'Was it like kissing—'

'I'm not even considering answering that question.'

'I'm coming straight over,' she said. 'I'll tell you the rest of the hen night.'

* * *

She came straight over. My dad let her in when she told him it was one of our guidance sessions and that she was giving me some counselling.

'Very trusting, your parents,' she said as my dad went off to make her a cup of tea.

'God, I know. Try not to molest me, even though they've given you tacit permission.'

I sat on the floor, leaning against the bed, holding my knees against my chest. Tashy sat on the undersized desk chair. Exactly how we always used to sit.

'Stop sitting like that, then.'

'OK.' I hopped up the bed. 'Tell me tell me tell me.'

She let out a long sigh. 'I'm only glad you weren't there to see it,' she said. 'It meant one fewer person in the world as a witness. Leaving only every female I know, minus one.'

'Tash, you always do this. Always have done. You always think you've done something terribly bad, then you've always just tripped over a pot plant or something.'

'No, it was bad.'

'Worse than kissing a teenager?'

'Yes.'

'Did you kiss the stripper?'

'No,' said Tash. 'God, I wish I'd only kissed the stripper.'

'Dancing on the table with your pants out?'

'God, no, who'd do that?'

'No one!'

She sighed again. 'OK. I . . . um, I had a little meltdown.'

We were quiet for a second.

'Tashy,' I said, 'what's a "little" meltdown?'

Tashy's story, as it came out, was this. About sixteen of them, various friends of Tashy's and some workmates, her mum, her aunt Cath and her sister had been to TGI Friday, another diabolical trick of Heather's, a place designed to induce ennui and existential angst in the most optimistic of brides.

They'd started off drinking vehemently coloured cocktails, called hilarious things like 'Tittiepolitans' and 'Please Waiter Could You Give Me Some Sexual Innuendo-tinis' and, with a kind of dedication to being drunk few people had seen for quite some time, moved on from these, not to the chain's no doubt extensive and tasteful wine list, but to Bacardi Breezers, the natural accompaniment to curly-wurly fries, surf and turf nachos and other such food.

'I don't remember what we ate,' groaned Tashy, 'but all of it was brown.'

'It's sounding pretty good so far,' I said. 'Oh no, hang on. Sixteen to thirty-two. Mental switch. Right. I'm there. Puke.'

'Anyway, Heather starts doing this speech, right?'

'Uh-oh.'

'Uh-oh is right. How hard can it be to stand up in front of a bunch of girls – OK, a bunch of girls completely fucking up the words to "Wooh-oh, those summer nights", but still . . . how hard, just to say, "Well done, sis, I love you"? Something normal families do.'

'What did she do?'

'She flashed her tits at the waiter.'

'Heather has no tits.'

'Have I explained to you again about the cocktails and rum-based devastation?'

'Yes. Sorry.'

'Then she kept going on about, "well, if you must do it", and marriage really shouldn't be something you undertake unless you really feel it's your only option, and remember the inability of men to stay faithful through biology and how—'

My dad knocked on the door and we shut up immediately.

'Here you go, young ladies,' he said jovially, bringing in a tray with chocolate biscuits and everything. 'I hope I'm not disturbing anything. I do realise privacy is very important for teens.'

I rolled my eyes at him in a proper teenage fashion that made Tashy half smile.

'That's right, Mr Scurrison,' she said gravely. 'Well done. You know, when a child is from a stable loving background like here, we rarely have too much to worry about.' She lowered her voice until she sounded like a gossipy hausfrau. 'It's the broken home families we have to worry about,' she whispered.

I was shocked and told her so, after my dad had looked very troubled, briefly rubbed his head, then left us to it.

'What?' she said. 'I'm helping you out, aren't I?'

'Yes, but . . .'

'I know, it's not really my business.'

Suddenly I remembered her those nights when I did try to look after my mother. Tash had always been there, always been sympathetic, always nice to my mother and coming out with us on shopping trips and small treats. She'd been a proper friend.

'It is,' I said. 'And thank you.'

I poured tea. 'So, Heather makes a speech . . .'

'Anyway, meanwhile the stripper is agreeing with everything she's saying.'

'Wait – the stripper's arrived?'

'Yes. He's unbuttoning his shirt quite casually.'

'Doesn't sound like much of a stripper.'

'No, no, well, he's nodding along and then he says, like it's hilarious, "Ladies, you know, it's nothing personal. Marriage just doesn't suit a man. You should see the trouble I have to keep out of for my bird. Those crabs were the last straw."'

'Bleargh!'

'Exactly. So now I have fifteen screaming women on my hands, but they're not screaming with excitement, they're screaming with disgust. But the staff, rather than kick us all out and let me go home, they're like, "Hey, it's so great to see people having fun", with fake American accents. So the stripper doesn't think it's funny any more, and he's talking to himself, saying, "Fuck, don't mention the fucking crabs, you fucking loser," and trying to take his clothes off really fast now.'

'You don't want to see that!'

252

'Well, exactly! Then he gets down to his pants, which are black leather covered in studs.'

'And they thought the studs were—'

'Exactly. The girls are now screaming, "Seafood! Seafood!" And someone threw a prawn from across the room to get us to shut up and . . .'

I shook my head sadly. 'All it takes is one simple prawn.'

'Every time,' said Tashy. 'Anyway, after that, all hell broke loose. There's thousand island dressing on the ceiling.'

'Yeech.'

'Cheesy bacon bits down the front of my Ronit Zilkha. Selina was sobbing in the corner . . .'

'Selina always cries at parties,' I said dismissively.

'. . . my sister is whispering something in the ear of a very panicky stripper . . .'

We paused for a moment to try and work out what that might be.

'Anyway. Then it happened.'

'What happened?'

'Well, everyone else was just throwing food, right?'

'Are we at the meltdown yet?'

'Do keep up.'

'OK. Yep.'

I could hear her swallow hard.

'I dropped a plate on the floor.'

I tutted. 'See! It's always something really minor.'

She ignored me. 'I threw an entire tray of plates on the floor. Just to get everyone to shut the fuck up. Then I screamed, "Shut the Fuck Up!!!" Then I shouted, "Look. All men aren't bastards! So get over it, Heather. And believe me, if you're trying to ruin my wedding, you really don't have to try so hard. Some men are just wrong. And that's just as sad. So cut me some slack, OK? I'm doing a brave thing and all I get is abuse and food thrown at me. And, YOU, go to the chemist's." Only, maybe I wasn't as concise as that. And I swore a lot.'

'What happened then?'

'I was manhandled out the building by the suddenly much less friendly-looking staff. They were no longer interested in my having a good Friday.'

'And?'

She sounded sorrowful. 'I legged it as fast as I could down Haymarket.'

'You're joking!'

'Nope. I was out of there. I was at home tucked up cosily in bed with a cup of tea crying my eyes out by nine thirty.'

'Result! Um, was Max there?'

'He was out on his stag.'

'Oh,' I said.

'He came home at three o'clock in the morning, tried to have sex with me, I threw him out of the bed, he called me a bitch then he immediately fell asleep on the floor. When I got up to go to the bathroom I . . . I . . .'

'What?'

She choked up a little. 'I accidentally on purpose stood on his hand.'

'You did what?'

'It was an accident. Pretty much.'

'You know,' I said, 'when the physical violence starts, that's about time to sort out a few things about your relationship.'

There was a furious knocking at the door.

'Flora! FLORA! DISASTRO!!!!'

'What the hell . . .?' said Tashy, jumping up from her reverie.

I ran to the door. 'What the hell are you doing here?'

Stanzi's face dropped about sixteen miles when she saw Tashy.

'That's my seat,' she said in a small voice.

'Didn't my dad tell you I was having counselling?' I said.

'Your dad, he's just left. In some big hurry for something.'

'WHAT?' Tashy and I jumped up and ran to the front window.

'Where's he gone?' I said, an uncontrollable panic grasping at my throat. 'Has he got a suitcase?' Oh God. What was he trying to say this morning?'

'Shit, what did I say to him?' said Tash. 'Jesus, our entire fucking lives are one big meltdown.'

* * *

Stanzi hadn't followed us out. She was sitting down on the bed, looking forlorn.

'What's the matter?' I said briskly, breathlessly pulling on my coat. Thank God Tashy had the car outside. He couldn't, though, could he? Surely he wouldn't. Not with that girl . . .?

Stanzi stood up. 'It's awful,' she said. 'It's so awful what is happening to me.'

'Oh, petal,' I said, 'will it keep? It's just . . . there's this thing . . .'

'Yes, there is always time for your BIG FAT friend,' said Stanzi hotly. Her face was red and white and she looked as if she was about to explode.

Tashy looked at me.

'OK. What is it?' I said.

Stanzi gulped back a sob. 'It is Kendall,' she said. 'He does not . . . he does not love me . . .'

'Oh, for fuck's sake,' said Tashy, 'can we get going? And I'm not fat.'

'Ssh,' I said. 'This is very important when you're sixteen.'

'I shall *never* get over him.' The tears were dribbling over her hot cheeks. She looked five years old as she started to cry properly.

'Can you tell us about it in the car?' I said, putting an arm round her and propelling her towards the door. 'Someone else is never going to get over something either if we don't get a bit of a fucking move on.'

* * *

I tried to give directions to a frustrated Tashy whilst comforting a frantically miserable Constanzia with the remnants of an old tissue I found under the seat.

'He said we were too young to get serious!' she wailed.

In the front, Tashy snorted. I shot her a look.

'Maybe you are,' I suggested. 'It is possible.'

'You don't understand,' she wept. 'You've never been in love.'

'You'll get over it,' I said desperately. 'Left here. Past the horrible little pink office that looks like a tanning salon.'

Tashy snorted again.

'It does too look like a tanning salon,' I said.

'You're misinterpreting my snort,' she said.

'Look.' I grabbed Stanzi by the shoulders. 'Nothing that happens at this age should be so awful it bothers you for the rest of your life. Nothing.'

Tashy attempted another snort. 'Because if it does,' she

said, twisting her head round to the ball of tears in the back seat, 'you can let it poison your whole life. And when that happens, all hell can break loose.'

'Yes, OK, Buffy the Vampire Slayer,' I said. 'Can you keep your eyes on the road?'

Tashy's phone started ringing.

'It's illegal to drive with your phone,' pouted Stanzi, not too sad to get one in.

'Sssh,' I said. Then I took her in my arms and gave her a big cuddle.

'Hi,' Tashy was saying. '. . . No, no, I'm fine. Look, I can't really . . . I can't really . . . No, it's not a good time.'

'Who's that?' I asked her with my eyebrows. She shook her head at me fiercely.

'No, we're going to see Flora's dad.'

'Shut up!' I yelped at her. Stanzi's tears were wetting my bosom.

'Ssh. No, don't come . . . Don't! No! I mean it. No!' She hung up the phone.

'Who the hell was that?' I demanded as we swerved round a corner.

'Nobody,' she said.

* * *

My dad's car was parked outside his office.

'Shit, I said, under my breath. My dad never worked on a Saturday. Workaholism isn't something you'd think when you looked at him. All I could think of was my mother's face the night I got home from the party.

Next to it was a car, and straight away I just knew. It was something about the prissiness of it. It was a cheap car, but with high-end specs – black leather seats, alloy wheels, all that useless crap. It was red, but not a shocking, bright red. More an orangey hue which hinted at danger without being remotely threatening. It was spotlessly clean. I knew it was hers. I knew it immediately.

Tashy came forward.

'No,' I said. 'Let me. I have to.'

She nodded wordlessly.

'Stay and look after Stanzi.'

'She can fuck off!' shouted Stanzi, still in the back of the car. 'She can't tell me what to do.'

* * *

Well, at least they weren't having sex. I couldn't have coped with that. I would have had a big old primal episode right there and then, and it would have scarred my adult life for ever. Although it might have made a good conversation piece for those future student conversations about whose parents are more of a fuck-up.

My dad was talking to her urgently in the office. She looked like she'd made a massive effort: the roots of her hair were freshly done, and she was wearing a bright flowery blouse. She was a big plain girl, not a tart at all.

'Look, Steph, I don't think—' he was saying.

I summoned everything I had ever learned from *EastEnders* and burst through the door.

My dad's face was a comic picture of shock, as if he'd just won an Oscar or something.

'Flora Jane!'

'Yes, that's right. It's me. Your daughter.' I turned to the woman. 'Hi.'

But I could tell by her face she already knew exactly who I was. She was burning up and staring at the ground.

'Um, Flora, what are you doing here?' said my dad, clearing his throat. He was clearly hoping to carry this off as an innocent Saturday business meeting. Maybe he thought I just didn't have so much insight into the future.

He wanted me to say, 'Mum forgot to tell you to get bananas yesterday, and I didn't know you were working.' He wanted me to say that so much.

'You can't do this,' I said desperately. 'You can't do this to Mum. Or me. You can't. You'll ruin everything. Can't you see?'

'But, I—'

'I mean, after everything Mum does for you . . . for this, this . . .'

I'd been meaning to say tart, or slag, or whatever word I felt like about this woman who was condemning my mother to a life of clinging, desperate misery, daily fretting, terrifying loneliness; and her daughter, the same way, jumping about, never able to make up her mind; to settle, to be happy and make someone else happy.

But then I looked at her and the heavily applied makeup, and I just saw an unhappy-looking woman. Who had missed the boat and knew it. Who had (I knew this later) been married to a horrible man; divorced and alone, conscious of her clock ticking out and her looks nearly gone completely. Could I really blame her for grabbing her last chance? Her kind, jovial, fundamentally decent last chance, and damn the consequences, because this was her life, the only one she had, and she just couldn't bear to face it alone, unwitnessed, unattended and going out slowly like an untended fire? But he was ours first.

'Dad,' I begged. 'Please.'

259

'Look, Flora, you have to believe me,' my dad said, wild-eyed. 'I came here to break if off, honest.'

Stephanie looked shocked

'That is a coincidence,' I said, my heart beating wildly.

'Ever since you . . . started going off the rails a bit . . . I've been speaking more to your mother, and I realise, you do need me, you both need me. More than anything.'

I looked at his face. He was choking on each word as if he was spitting out glass.

'I'm so sorry, Flora,' he said.

He was crumpling up like a little boy. Does no one ever grow up?

'I don't blame you, Dad,' I choked.

But as I said it, I realised that I did blame him. I always had, for far longer than I should. I'd taken that summer and made it into the story of my whole life. I couldn't commit because Daddy had left. I couldn't get over Clelland because I was all alone. I couldn't do the things I wanted to do because I had to look after my mother. I had taken their commonplace everyday tragedy and turned it into my great Grand Guignol; my defining cause; my explanations for my own unhappiness. One normal, average, weak man who happened to be my dad, and one lonely, average girl, who just wanted to be loved, here in the shoddy setting of a local office, pink pinboard detailing rotas and instruction dates; tawdry carpets and a smell that didn't seem as non-smoking as it ought to have done. So small, after all.

Oddly, I suddenly felt strong. This wasn't my fault. It wasn't my problem. It was just one of those things that happened. And it had happened to me, and I'd let it screw up my whole life. I'd used it as an excuse to stick with men I didn't love;

to refuse to grow up. I pitied my first-time-round self again. And resolved: whatever happened, whether I was here for good, whether I got to go home; whatever happened, I was going to be alright, and I wasn't going to end up like this.

'Bastard,' muttered Stephanie under her breath, looking between us. I was moving towards my dad, and I realised I wanted a hug, very badly.

'What?' said my dad.

She swallowed hard. 'You never meant to leave them, did you? You were lying all this time, weren't you?'

'I wasn't lying, Steph, I promise.' He looked absolutely wretched. 'But my family needs me.'

'My family needs me,' she mimicked, staring hatefully at me. 'Right. And plain old Stephanie will be just fine. Of course. I'll just go home and drink a pint of tequila and take the sleeping pills on my own, shall I?'

'Stephanie,' I said, moving forward.

She showed a residual flash of anger. 'Don't talk to me, you little witch. OK, you won, with your boo-hoo eyes. Don't need to fucking gloat. You've got your whole life ahead of you. And you've left me with nothing. Hope you're proud of yourself.'

'He would have left us for you,' I said to her, and meant it. 'I promise. He would have. If I hadn't bugged him so much. He did love you.'

She sniffed heavily.

'And my mum. I had to do it for my mum.'

She looked from me to Dad.

'Oh, fuck it all,' she said, and pushed out of the room.

* * *

261

My dad was actually crying. And he kept saying sorry, over and over again. I hated it and didn't know how to get him to stop.

'You've done the right thing,' I said. 'You have. I promise. You'd have been unhappy later.'

He looked at me. 'I'm unhappy now.'

'Well, talk to Mum about it. Do something about it. Nobody promised middle age was going to be a walk in the park, did they?'

He looked at me through red-rimmed eyes. 'You know, Flora Jane . . .'

Whatever he was about to say, he changed his mind. Instead he sank down on to a chair. 'Let me tell you something about being a grown-up.'

And I gave him a hug. Just a small one, just enough to let him know everything wasn't entirely lost.

* * *

I left him there – I couldn't face it, and he had to go and see Mum on his own.

Outside, the car was gone. Stanzi was sitting on the kerb of the road, looking more petulant than ever.

'Where's Tashy gone?'

'Your made-up guidance counsellor went off with a man,' she said. 'For no reason. Just to be mean to Stanzi and say everyone has man, even dried-up old lady.'

'Who?' I said, surprised.

'Fat. Bald. Old.'

I creased my eyes. 'Her dad?'

'Maybe,' Stanzi shrugged.

'Did she know him? You didn't let my b—' I nearly said best friend. 'You didn't let my friend get abducted, did you?'

'I think unless very perverted, abductor would want me first.'

'Didn't she offer to take you?'

'Yes. I say no thank you. I care about you. I wait for you.'

'Ah,' I said. 'The thing is, I really need to go somewhere . . .'

Chapter Fifteen

My feet couldn't carry me fast enough. I dashed through the streets, tripping over my stupid, stupid wedge heels. When I got my hands on some money, the first thing I was going to do was buy myself a better pair of these fucking shoes. Please let him be in. Please. I had wanted to talk to him, I always had, and I had to say sorry.

Justin opened the door.

'Hey,' he said, a mixture of confusion, fear and pleasure passing over his face. His hair was wet, so he must have been just out of the shower. Probably staring in the mirror, prodding at things, if my remembered teenage life was anything to go by.

I stopped short, suddenly feeling bashful and shy. 'Hi,' I said, staring at the ground.

He looked ruefully at me. 'Sorry about the other day. John's a dick. He thinks I'm still nine years old.'

'He can't help that,' I said. 'Actually, is he here? I wouldn't mind a quick word, if that's alright.'

Justin looked a bit perturbed at this. 'Why?'

I had to make something up.

'Oh, my mum asked me to give him something. It's boring. Grown up — some recipe or shit.'

'Oh.'

He didn't look entirely convinced, but it would have to do for now.

'Um, yeah. S'pose. He's just watching the football. But do you want to . . . go for a walk or something? My mum won't let me borrow the car. But they're out. So we could . . .'

'Why won't she let you borrow the car?'

'Doesn't matter. Actually, I'm a very good driver.'

'I'm sure you are,' I said, smiling. 'Maybe later?'

He stared at me for a while longer, then obviously remembered himself.

'Want to come in then?'

'Thanks,' I said nervously. I stepped over the threshold carefully.

'JOHN!' shouted Justin. But he was already there, standing darkly shadowed in the hallway.

'What do you want?' he said gruffly.

'Um, my mum says we have to . . . talk,' I said.

He looked stupefied. How come the teenager could see through such an obvious ruse and the adult was just padding around?

*   *   *

We sat in the kitchen, at the back, looking out on to the autumn leaves drifting across the garden. Justin hovered around, trying to listen in, but Clell told him to scram and soon he was back in the front room, happily shouting at the television football.

'I'm really sorry,' I said first.

Clell was up spooning coffee into mugs. 'No filters, I'm afraid,' he said gruffly. 'My parents don't believe in 'em. Milk and two, still?'

'No,' I said. 'Just water, please.'

'Don't be a fucking coffee snob!'

'OK. White and two. And by the way, before, when you weren't listening. I said I'm sorry.'

The kettle popped off, and he started to pour water into two beige mugs with harvest corn patterns that were as old as his parents' marriage. He took his time carefully pouring out the water, added milk and sugar and set them down carefully on the table. Then he exhaled and pushed a hand distractedly through his thick black hair. I found it profoundly irritating. And a little bit sexy at the same time.

'I heard you,' he said.

'Good,' I said. 'Perhaps now you can stop pretending you're Mickey Rourke in a film.'

'Well, if I'm Mickey Rourke you're . . .' He thought for a minute. 'Some incestuous child molester I can't think of at the moment.'

I stood up, flushing hot.

'I came over here to talk to you,' I said. 'Is that a waste of time?'

He stood up too.

'OK. No. Sit down.'

I sat down. We played around with blowing on our coffee a lot. I started stirring the sugar in the bowl, smoothing it down like one of those Japanese rice gardens.

'You and me,' I started, swallowing nervously, and trying not to look him in the eye in case I got blown off course completely. 'It was a long time ago.'

'I know,' he said.

'I don't know why I never got over it.'

'I didn't know you didn't get over it.'

'I realise that.'

'Until I saw you again.'

At first I thought he meant at the wedding. Then I remembered he'd never seen me at the wedding, because the wedding hadn't happened yet.

'Because we've never met!' I exclaimed, realising suddenly.

'Um . . .'

'As grown-ups, I mean. In my head I think we've met as grown-ups so I assume you know certain things about me so you know . . . so you can see what I'm really like. But you haven't.'

'I'm confused.'

'We meet at the wedding. As adults.'

'OK . . .'

'You think I'm just this little lost girl who never grew up, trailing the streets looking for you.'

He looked uncomfortable.

'You think I'm just some manifestation of arrested development.'

'The thought had occurred to me.'

'I'm not, you know! I'm a proper grown-up! I have a flat, and a life – a good life but now, you know now, you have no idea what it's like for me,' I said. 'I'm performing every day of my life. Every day is a whole new test which I have no idea whether or not I'm going to pass or fail. I'm acting the entire time. Almost no one has the faintest idea who I really am.'

Suddenly I felt I was going to cry. 'I am the only person in my class who can even remember Britpop. I'm the only one who ever used francs or lira, or remembers life without a remote control, or mobile phones or email or satnav.'

'Or what?'

'I don't know! I don't even know what that is, but they keep talking about it!'

Clelland tore off a piece of kitchen roll and handed it to me. I thanked him and carried on.

'I'm the only one who knows how to change a plug or make a fucking restaurant reservation. I'm the only one who . . . I'm the only one who's had their heart broken. You know . . .' I was openly sobbing now, those big painful ones that come from deep down. 'Our history teacher was talking about 9/11. And she said had anyone been to the World Trade Center. And nobody had, because they were all fourteen years old and don't even remember it that well. Except I have. There's a picture of me there, and now it never existed. And I couldn't even say how much I loved it and how much we all cried. And I am so alone.'

Clelland was rubbing me on the back. 'Ssh,' he said.

'I'm not a little girl,' I said. 'I'm not.'

'No,' he said.

'I'm caught between two worlds. Umm, Like Britney Spears. And I was looking for comfort. And I'm sorry.'

'I know.' His mouth was very close to my ear. 'I'm sorry about what I said.'

I made a strangulated noise.

'You're not the only one who took a long time to get over it, OK?'

There was a sudden, perceptible change in the room. Justin was standing in the doorway, in his stocking feet, a bottle of Coke in his hand. He was looking at us, astonished.

'What's going on?'

Clelland didn't react. He just kept looking at me.

'You'll be growing up again soon then, won't you?' he said softly. 'I'm sure everything will be fine. Now we've sorted that out.'

I gulped, hard. 'Yes,' I said. 'Yes.'

He checked his watch. 'OK. I'm late for Madeleine. I . . .' He seemed about to say something about that, then didn't. 'OK, well, um, will I tell Tash and Olly you've decided?'

'To go back? I have to,' I said. 'I can't bear it.'

He stood up, giving Justin and me a meaningful look.

'You two behave yourselves.'

Then he left.

Justin continued looking puzzled. 'Is he still giving you a hard time?' he said.

I nodded. 'He's not so bad.'

'He can be a right dick, my brother.' He offered me the Coke. I drank it, making heavy swallows. 'He's making me come to this stupid bloody wedding thing on Saturday too. I don't even know these people.'

'I'll be there,' I said.

'Will you?' His face brightened momentarily, then briefly coloured. Justin hadn't quite learned proper diffidence yet.

In that moment I realised something, something I must have known all along. That I was leaving and I wanted to give him a gift. Something that would hold him in good stead. Something he could use for ever. Something I'd never given his brother.

'Come over here,' I said.

* * *

He felt so beautiful; so lean and strong. His body was almost hairless, and his surprise exceptionally comical. When I had not only accepted but welcomed his skirmishes at my breasts, his eyes had popped open, widened as I gently showed him exactly how I would like him to caress and squeeze them, and how I would like it to go.

'God,' he sighed, and immediately I had felt him up against my leg. I pulled off his T-shirt, and I was going to take my bra off for him too, then realised that wouldn't be terribly helpful for him in the future. So I took his hands and guided them into unclipping the clasp. He would have lain us both down on the linoleum floor at this point – blind with need, there is very little he wouldn't have done at this point, I suspect – but I took his hand and guided us upstairs to his bedroom, which, as well as being comfortable and warm had the added bonus of giving us a few moments if anyone arrived back unexpectedly.

As Justin, his sweat smelling sweetly on his body, buried his soft curls in my neck, and I could feel his disbelieving hands roaming everywhere, I couldn't stop thinking of Clell and me, in this very same room. The same probing hands, but with me, anxious and uncomfortable, holding back, making us both embarrassed and frustrated and uneasy. I couldn't think about that, and I certainly couldn't think of what he might be like now. I had business to attend to.

'What you're looking for,' I whispered tenderly in his ear,

'it's here. Give me your hand.' And I guided it between my legs.

I laid back, revelling in the sweetness of my young body; feeling no urge to hide before his eyes, which were drinking me up like a dying man in a desert. I could tell what he was doing. He was desperately trying to imprint the sight of me on his memory banks in case he never saw another naked woman ever again.

'Do you like it?' I asked teasingly.

'You're . . . you're the most beautiful thing I've ever seen,' he stuttered.

I had never been the most beautiful thing anyone had ever seen. But I knew he would never forget me.

'Come here,' I said. 'Have you ever put a condom on before . . . ?'

* * *

I hadn't for a second thought that I would enjoy it. And I hadn't thought I would feel pain. But both things happened. I was so tight – and Justin so unbelievably hard – it took a little while to get everything arranged just so. But once we did, the fit was unbelievably snug and perfect, and the sheer joyful plunging enthusiasm of him, the feeling of his strong young muscles under my hands; his inability to keep from muttering his astonishment into my hair. It was all so different, so old and new at the same time, and as he came, hard and fast, I took off with him, and felt myself bite his shoulders, pull him in and, eyes tight shut, squealing as he let out a depthless cry somewhere between a sob and a roar.

* * *

He couldn't stop staring at me in some kind of wonder, as if I was a figment of his imagination.

I checked down the bed. 'Look,' I said, in astonishment. 'There's blood.'

His eyes widened. 'Was that your first time?'

'Erm, yes, obviously,' I said. 'Not bad, eh? No wonder school keeps telling us not to do it.'

He leaned over. I was cradled in his arms.

'It was my first time too,' he whispered confidentially.

'Really?' I said. I snuggled into him, smiling that broad smile you get like a happy cat after sex. I kissed him on the chest.

'It was special,' he said.

'It was special to me too,' I said, propping myself up on one elbow and tracing his beautiful young chest with my fingertips.

He grinned. 'Can we do it again?' Even as he spoke I could sense him rearing up under the covers.

'No,' I said regretfully. 'I have to get back.'

'Oh . . .' Then he remembered his manners. 'OK.' And he got out of bed, and I struggled not to laugh. Very important, not laughing the first time in his life a boy gets his penis out.

He held on to me like a drowning man at the door.

'I feel like everything's different.'

'It is,' I said. 'You've kissed it all better.'

And I walked home with a spring in my step, aware of his eyes on my back all the way down the road.

* * *

I had to swallow it for Tash on the phone.

'My dad's coming back,' I said quietly.

272

'Oh, thank God. We're . . . I'm so relieved.'

'Who picked you up? Stanzi couldn't tell.'

There was a long pause on the end of the phone.

'Tash?'

'Um, Max. He was passing. Yes. It was definitely Max.'

* * *

I looked around me. Was this my last day at school? It was Friday, the day before the wedding. I walked in. Justin and Ethan met Stanzi and me at the front gates. Stanzi was walking with her head held high, all tear-stained, 'I Will Survive' defiance. Kendall was nowhere to be seen. Ethan and Justin came up to join us, both of them grinning so broadly I couldn't help but immediately guess that Justin had told him.

'Don't tell the whole school,' I said in a warning tone of voice.

'That you're a really hot mama?' said Ethan.

'Shut up!' I said, but I couldn't stop smiling.

'It doesn't matter,' said Justin, reaching in to tickle me. 'Because you are mine, all mine.'

I couldn't help shrieking as he lunged at me, and swung my schoolbag round to catch him in the stomach. Laughing uncontrollably, I was out of breath when I shortened up to see the imperious figure of Fallon standing right in front of me. She was curling her lip.

'Having fun?' she said.

'Oh God, Fallon,' I shouted. 'Really. Actually, yes. I am having fun. And you should have some too. Because nobody really gives a shit what you think, so you should just learn to enjoy yourself. I know you think you're sixteen going on

thirty, but you're just a kid really. And you should let yourself behave like one once in a while.'

'Exactly,' shouted Justin, more kiddish than ever now I'd
made a man of him. 'Tag!' And he jumped up and tagged
her on the shoulder.

Then he, Ethan and Stanzi all made themselves scarce.
After a second of realising what they were doing, I ran too,
for my life. And after a second of everyone's eyes upon her,
Fallon realised she had no option but to do the same. So,
running extremely gracefully in such high shoes, she plunged
in, rushing up and tagging Ethan immediately, who picked
one of the pretty younger boys, whereupon all hell broke
loose. Leaves were flying everywhere in the early autumn
sun, and the whole playground was a screaming mass of
running, yelling kids. The younger kids were absolutely
delighted to see the so-called grown-ups playing a game and
rushed around relentlessly. I was so worn out and hysteri-
cally overexcited I still couldn't stop laughing when Justin
grabbed me down into a pile of leaves behind a tree.

'Oh God,' I said, still giggling, listening to the mayhem.
'I don't want to go.'

'Go where?' said Justin, propping himself up and tick-
ling me on the nose with a leaf.

I caught my breath. 'Nowhere,' I said, looking at his
lovely open face, and feeling dreadful. 'Nowhere. I mean,
leaving school.'

'Course you do,' he said, kissing me on the stomach.
'There's tons of good stuff coming up.'

'Pff,' I said.

'I love you,' he whispered.

'*What* did you just say?' I sat bolt upright.

'Nothing! Nothing! I didn't mean it! I've just . . . I've never said it before. I just wanted to see what it was like.'

'It's a big old week of firsts for you, isn't it?' I said.

'Uh-huh.'

'Try not to say it unless you mean it,' I said.

'Uh-huh,' he said.

* * *

'Well done,' said Miss Syzlack, looking up and down my marks.

I'd lingered at the end of the guidance session. I wasn't even quite sure why.

'You've caught up much better than I thought you would with the art.'

'People can, you know,' I said. 'Sometimes, academia isn't the only thing you should be pushing people towards.'

'Are you trying to tell me how to do my job, Flora Jane?'

'No, miss,' I said. 'When you started out, did you think you were going to hate it?'

She smiled and I remembered those awful tears and discipline problems.

'I'll let you into a little secret,' she said. 'When I started, I hated it.'

'I know,' I said.

'You don't,' she said. 'It was awful. I used to cry in the classroom.'

'Did people used to lock you in cupboards?'

'Yes!' she said. 'It was dreadful. I wanted to give up every day. I couldn't sleep. My doctor was going to prescribe me something.'

'You're much better now,' I said. 'What happened?'

'Well, I realised that we only have one life. And that this

was what I'd chosen. And that it is a good thing to do, it is worthwhile, so I'd better just make the best of it. And I found once I'd done that, I started to get better at it, and I even started to enjoy it. I know what you're thinking, Miss Scurrison, but there are a lot worse things I could be doing. Stuck in an office all day, for example. I couldn't bear that.'

'Didn't you ever . . . you know, want to get married? Have your own family?'

She laughed. 'You know, I was thinking you were an old head on young shoulders, Flora, but I'd at least have thought you'd have been up on school gossip. I've been living with Miss Leonard for ten years.'

'The gym teacher?'

'Run along now, little girl.' And she shot me a big smile.

* * *

'Has Tashy called?' I asked, for the nineteenth time.

'No,' said my mother, looking over. My dad was helping her cook. Wonders would never cease. There'd been another afternoon of shouting, tears, and my mother slamming doors, while I hid upstairs, eyes tight shut.

Then finally, amazingly, it was like the clouds had parted and the world had become calm. They were definitely, *definitely* making an effort – to talk to each other, for him to do things for her. I was keeping my fingers crossed that my mother just might have a willing slave for life.

'You better not have annoyed your guidance counsellor,' said my dad.

'What are you going to do, get me into trouble?' I said. 'I'm her bridesmaid, Dad, OK? Just checking.'

* * *

Stanzi looked at the large Galaxy ice cream I'd bought her with undisguised suspicion as we sat on the wall outside the house.

'You try to make me fat so no man will ever love me again so I never get sad no more, yes?'

'No,' I said. 'Can't I do something nice for my friend?'

'Your best friend you always leave behind.'

'My best friend,' I said, sending up a silent apology to Tash, from whom I'd heard nothing since our phone call days ago. I'd called her again, but she wasn't in work or picking up her phone. Or at least, picking it up to me. She must be lying low. Or just panicking. But I'd have thought, before her wedding, she might have wanted to talk to me. Maybe she was just too furious that I was making her go through with it after all, that I wanted to go home.

'You're the best friend anyone could ever have,' I said. 'And I am so, so sorry for leaving you behind.'

Stanzi sighed. 'Life is hard.'

'It is.'

'I hate him.'

'He won't be the last.'

'No. You're right. I shall hate all of them.'

'You won't,' I said. 'Wait and see.'

'We will find nice boys together, yes?'

'Uh-huh,' I said. 'Come here.' And I gave her a big cuddle, just in case I was saying goodbye.

'Friends for ever?' she said.

'Yes,' I said. 'For sure.'

We ate the ice cream. Then I went home and cried for two hours.

Chapter Sixteen

The rain was beating down on the windscreen as my dad damply tried to navigate the wet road.

'I think it's up here,' I ventured.

'That's right, you'd know,' he said gruffly, although he had been driving from London for six hours.

'Don't be nasty to Flora, dear. It's wonderful she's a bridesmaid.'

My parents were over the moon. They couldn't imagine anyone connected with education liking me enough for this to happen, so they were all dolled up. I was panicked. Torn so completely. Nothing seemed right. Staying here, in the wrong (albeit pretty nifty) body; having to go through God knows what all over, watching my friends get older and settled and leaving me alone with a bunch of dirty art students . . . or back to that damned accounting firm; back to my poor parents, living unhappily on opposite ends of town, not knowing that they could get over it, that they could get on. Oh God, I felt sick, and that was even before

I thought of poor Tashy, walking straight into this thing for her friend.

'I'm going up to see her,' I said, as my parents busied themselves looking for — yuk — our family room.

'Are you sure you should?' my mum said. 'Don't be a bother, Flora.'

'I won't, I promise.'

The *déjà vu* was overwhelming. The same hotel, the same wooden staircase. Possibly even more chintz than last time? I couldn't be sure. I even ran up to Tashy's room and banged on the door and wished I'd brought some Baileys.

'Just a minute!'

'It's OK, it's only me!' I said, bursting in — but carefully, still mindful of the wedding dress hanging on the back of the door.

Tashy was sitting on the side of the floral-patterned bed facing the window, and sitting next to her, with his arm around her, was Olly.

'Bloody hell!' I said.

'This isn't what it looks like,' said Olly, jumping up immediately.

'No, I know that. One of you's getting married in the morning, and one of you's you. I was just surprised to see you, that's all. I thought you had work to do tonight.'

'How would you. . .never mind,' said Ol. He looked flushed.

Tashy turned round to face me, and I gasped. Even in a week, she was thinner than I'd ever seen her, and her face was streaked with tears.

This was my fault. A month ago, she was maybe a bit ambivalent, but nothing like this. This was the face of Kate Winslet trying to throw herself rather prematurely over the back of a big ship. What were we doing? What on earth was going to happen?

'Tash!' I ran to her. 'I'm so sorry! I'm so sorry. It's not too late to cancel.'

She shook her head, shivering. 'I'm going to be fine,' she said. 'I am. I can do it.'

'You won't.'

'I will.' She looked at me. 'Look at you. If you didn't want to come back, you wouldn't have been here. You'd have been down the Dog and Duck, trying to hang out with local musicians.'

I grimaced. 'That's not the point.'

'It is, love.'

Olly stroked her hair, and I squeezed her even tighter to show I was her bestest friend, not him, even if they were born in the same decade.

'I'm going to bite you until you agree to call the whole thing off,' I said.

'Listen,' Tash said. 'It's not just you, I promise. I don't have the guts. I just don't. I'm getting on a bit, and I've been planning this for a year, and, partially with you, for twenty years. I am not going to let my mother enjoy some victory whilst pretending to feel sorry for me, or have Heather nodding her head sagely about how things can never work out. I can't, and I won't, Flora. Don't you see? You're the brave one. You can take the chances. You're the one that takes the risks.'

I avoided looking at Olly, and he avoided looking at me.

'Don't end up like me, Flora. Please. Promise. Promise you'll go off and study something fun and have a great time and do everything you want and stay a free spirit and never, never compromise.'

280

I looked at her, and vowed that I would. I'd change the job — I'd changed the man already — I wouldn't be afraid. I would just go out and live life, properly.

'Well, what if I just start now?' I protested. 'It'd be much easier to change from age sixteen. And that would mean you don't have to get married!' I said.

She looked at me, and I saw the awful truth in her eyes.

'No,' she said. 'You were only ever an excuse. I was always going to do it anyway.'

* * *

Just as before, the rain of the night turned into a beautiful morning; sunny and warm for so late in the year. Perfect, in fact. Just as Tashy had always dreamed it.

I'd had a restless night. That was something of an under-statement. I don't know how I'd got through it. Between my dad's snoring and my mother's peculiar noises, and the endless, endless circling in my head, it had been very hard to get anything straight at all. But here I was, reflecting in the mirror, twirling in the early autumn sun. The dress was so lovely; a kind of regency high-chested thing, which made me look like one of the naughtier sisters of a Jane Austen novel.

'Doesn't she look grand?' said my mother, smiling happily.

I gave them a twirl. My dad smiled back at her. Then he looked a bit choked.

'You're lovely, pet,' he said to me. 'Doesn't seem so long ago since she was just a baby, does it, Joyce?'

My mum shook her head. 'Time goes so fast.'

'Next thing you know, it'll be her getting married.'

'Oh, I wouldn't worry about that quite yet,' I said.

* * *

I sat beside Tash as we got our hair and makeup done by one of those slightly snotty girls who are better-looking than you, and I think do makeup so they can compare your face with theirs in the mirror and feel good about it. She was shaking, I swear to God. I felt like one of the handmaidens of Lady Jane Grey.

'Did you see Clelland?' I murmured faintly, as the makeup lady desperately tried to put a blush into Tashy's deathly pale cheeks.

'Yes,' said Tash, glancing dispiritedly at the bouquet. The florist had told us to keep the stems immersed in water to keep its spirits up. I briefly toyed with the idea of immersing Tashy in water.

'How was he?'

She looked at me. 'Weird.'

'Weird how?'

'Hard to say.'

'So are you two sisters?' asked the makeup woman in as uninterested a manner as possible.

'No,' I said. 'Just friends.'

Tashy sniffed loudly.

'So, are you looking forward to getting married?'

'Now that is a long story,' said Tash.

* * *

We clung to each other as we limped down the stairs, trembling. Tashy's daffy mum was at the bottom, having a sneaky fag. Next to her was Heather.

'Oh, I see she finally got into that dress,' she said snidely. 'I'm Heather,' she said to me. 'Natasha's sister. Who are you anyway?'

282

Mind you, Heather used to pretend we didn't exist when I did know her.

'I'm Tashy's boss's daughter,' I said quickly, before remembering that Marshall was gay. All six Blythe eyebrows shot up, then down again, in case they were being impolite or telling Marshall's daughter something she didn't know.

'Do you know when Dad's getting here?' said Tashy.

'Christ, you are nervous,' said Heather, with a slightly bitter laugh. 'It must really be the best day of your life.'

I'd always liked Tashy's dad; he was such a gentle soul. He didn't look at all himself, coming up the hotel path, wearing a stiff morning coat and looking ruffled.

'Hey, Mr Late,' said Tashy's mum, who insisted on being nicer to him now they'd broken up than she ever was at the time.

'Yes, yes,' he said. 'Where's my angel . . . ahem, I mean, my littlest angel?'

Heather stood aside sulkily, and Tashy went up to him. She hugged him for just a bit too long, and he patted her on the back and made 'there, there' noises. The way he cuddled her made me wonder if he knew a bit more than he let on. He stood back and looked at Tash, who was highlighted in the morning sun streaming through the door, and looked gorgeous.

'Thanks, Daddy,' she said.

He looked sad for a moment, shook his head a little, then caught sight of me.

'Good God!' he said in alarm. 'Tash, this girl looks exactly like—'

Our confusion was offset by my delight that someone else knew who I was – who, I guess, loved me. I wanted to run up and hug him.

'No, no,' Tashy jumped in. 'I know, she looks a bit like that girl Flora who I used to know, but she's Marshall's daughter.'

Mr Blythe stared at me. 'Extraordinary.'

I couldn't help it, I winked at him. He blinked rapidly a couple of times and turned back to Tash.

'We want to be getting to the church, love,' he said. 'Don't want to keep Max waiting too long. You know what a stickler he is for timing and all that.'

She nodded mutely.

We must have looked an ungainly sight, stumbling out to the beautiful vintage Bentley; Tashy practically being held up by her father, her other hand gripping mine, followed by the ugly sister. The driver, who presumably had seen every form of marriage imaginable, simply tipped his cap and closed the doors tightly behind us.

* * *

The first time I tripped over Tashy's delicate ivory train, I realised walking into the church whilst keeping my eyes shut was simply not an option. We paused at the church door.

'I'm sorry,' I said, for the millionth time.

'Don't be,' she said bravely. 'Everything's going to be just fine. I'm sure of it.'

We peeked into the church. Sure enough, Max was down the front, his back to us, deliberately not turning round.

'Because it's against the rules to spoil the surprise,' said Tash. 'He'd hate that.'

'OK?' said her dad. Then, *sotto voce* to me: 'And I'll be keeping my eye on you.'

'OK, Stan,' I said.

'How does she know my name?' he asked Tashy.

'Please shut up,' said Tashy, as the familiar Trumpet Voluntary struck up. 'Right.'

'Right.'

I squeezed her hand tightly one last time. Oh God, it was really happening. And I was going to have to make a choice.

'Don't we have a plan B?' she asked.

'We definitely should have had a plan B,' I said.

She walked out onto the red carpeted aisle.

* * *

At least, being a bridesmaid, I could keep eyes front, and not look at a thing. Also, ever since Fergie did that awful bug-eyed, saying hello to all her old chalet maid chums in Westminster Abbey thing, it's quite OK for a bride to smooth her way up to the altar being far too grand to look at anyone. So we held it together. Tash said her vows in a quiet low tone, different from the way she'd giggled through them the first time I'd heard her. I felt another stab of remorse. And the worst was yet to come. There was – as usual – a pregnant pause when the vicar charged them both, if either of them knew of any impediment why they may not be lawfully joined in Matrimony to confess it, and I definitely felt a wince.

Then it was all said, the register signed, and we turned back, Tashy smiling as gamely as she could for the photographs. I couldn't see through a wash of tears. People were shouting my name, I could hear that for certain, but as the confetti flew and the cameras snapped, I willed myself into keeping them out of focus.

'I'm going to cut the cake as soon as possible,' she

announced as they headed for the car to take them to the reception. 'Don't you think?'

I nodded frantically. Then I could make my wish and get the hell out of here and . . . well, I suppose I could worry about the rest later.

'Well,' said Max, dragging her along, 'we have to say hello to everyone first. Then there's a two-hour champagne reception. Then there's dinner, of course. Then there's the speeches – I think you'll rather like mine – then I think we all break for coffee and then I suppose it's the cake.'

'Why don't we do the cake first?'

'You're my crazy firecracker, aren't you, baby? Always trying to be different.'

'Wild and crazy, that's me,' said Tash through gritted teeth. 'Always defying expectations.'

'You look lovely,' he said. 'Doesn't she, short bridesmaid stranger?'

'Yes,' I said. 'Lovely.'

And he smiled and looked happy as they got in the car, flashbulbs going off, and I felt worse than ever.

* * *

I didn't know bridesmaids had to stand in receiving lines. This was stupid. Particularly next to Max's very unprepossessing fat best man, who was half-heartedly trying to chat me up with the air of a man who knows he's completely unattractive to women his own age but reckons he might have a shot with someone extraordinarily naïve and is trying to work out just how naïve you are.

'So, you like Big Events?' he was whispering.

'As long as they're very hot and exciting,' I whispered

back, making him break out in a slight sweat. God, this is boring. Plus, I was going to have to duck for cover if we saw Tashy's gay boss, whose daughter I was pretending to be.

Olly's eyes bored into mine as he made his way down the line. He was clearly furious with me.

'I hope you're not going to say this is all my fault,' I said when he got to me.

He planted a very unaffectionate kiss on my cheek and tried to smile whilst saying, 'Who else's could it be? Everything was fine before you did all this.'

'Yes, you believe that,' I said, stung, but he had already passed on.

He held Tashy out at arm's length. 'You are the most beautiful thing I've ever seen,' he said, his eyes drinking her up and down. 'That dress is absolutely perfect.'

Tash got some real colour in her cheeks for the first time that day.

'Thank you,' she said. She bit her lip and looked at the floor. Then she reached up and kissed him. 'Thank you.'

Olly touched his cheek.

'Max,' he said, overheartily. 'You're the luckiest man in the world.'

'Looks like it!' said Max.

'No. You are,' said Olly quietly. With another look at Tash, and a quick flash of annoyance at me, he crossed the room to inspect the food. I spotted him upending a glass of champagne down his throat in double-quick time, a very unOlly thing to do.

* * *

'You look like Little Miss Muppet,' said Justin.

'Who even let you in this line?'

'Oh, come on, I had to, didn't I? Give us a kiss?'

He looked delicious, in a navy-blue suit, with a lighter blue shirt and tie.

'Is that your first suit?'

'Why, what's wrong with it?'

'Nothing, nothing.'

He was so cute. I wanted to put my hand on his curls, but his brother was right down the line, so I thought maybe best not.

'It's my interview suit,' he said gruffly.

'For what? Court?'

'College actually.'

Clelland hoved into earshot.

'Given any thought as to where you're going to go?' I said.

'No,' said Justin. Then he looked at me again. 'Maybe I should stay close to home.'

'Justin, sweetie, thanks so much for coming,' said Tashy. She dragged him over to her by the sleeve, obviously keen at least to look him up and down all over. 'You have grown so much.'

'That's because you knew me when I was two,' said Justin sulkily, as Clelland took his place.

'I talked him out of Aberdeen,' said Clelland. 'Gets a little cold up there.'

I looked at him. 'You can say that again.'

He shook his head. 'This is a rum old business, isn't it, Flora?'

'Where's Madeleine?'

288

He looked down. There was a long pause. 'She's gone. Had to get back to Africa. I was meant to go too.'

'She went without you? When?'

He looked even more uncomfortable.

'*When?*'

'People there need her more than I do.'

'Was it on Saturday?'

He nodded. So when I was in bed with Justin he must have been . . . Oh God. This didn't bear thinking about.

He looked at me. 'You look lovely. Are you sure you want to come back, child?'

'Don't call me child,' I said, swallowing hard. Did I want to go back? Did I?

'OK. Are you sure?'

'Fuck, no,' I groaned.

'I should never have gone to Africa, you know.' He looked a little misty. 'I should have stayed on, got my PhD. Science, maybe . . . discover something a lot more useful to a lot more people.'

'I was thinking more about maybe going to art college,' I managed to squeeze out. OK, Madeleine had gone, but here he was, advising me to go off and sit exams. Like a child.

'Oh, yeah. Oh God, you'll have so much fun.'

'Stop it,' I said.

'OK.'

'Look what Tash is putting herself through for me.'

'*OK.*'

He stepped sideways, put his arms round Tash and gave her a massive squeeze. 'Hey,' he said to her softly. 'You've done an amazing thing. You really have.'

'Don't talk toss,' she said, slightly muffled.

He put her down. 'You'll be fine. I know it. I just do.'

'Goodness, no one can keep their hands off my woman today, it seems,' said Max in that slightly stiff way of his. 'I thought wearing white was supposed to keep all that under control.'

'It's cream,' said Tashy.

'Oh,' said Max. 'Well then.'

Clelland smiled, shook Max as briefly as possible by the hand and disappeared into the throng. I noticed, with a horribly sick *déjà vu*, that Justin was having a conversation with Oliver about the food, waving a sausage covered in sesame seeds.

'There you are, darling!' It was my mum. 'We thought you were great up there.'

'A true pro,' said my dad. 'Effortless. Although you could have smiled a bit more for the photos.'

'My mouth was tired,' I said.

'Look at all this!' My dad nudged Tashy. 'Gosh, you guidance counsellors must be making more money than I thought!'

'Dad!' I tugged on his arm. 'Don't be embarrassing.'

'Mr Scurrison,' said Tashy, turning it on with a huge big smile. 'How lovely of you to come. Wasn't Flora magnificent?'

'We're so proud of her,' said my dad. He swallowed and glanced at me. 'Almost made us remember our big day, eh, Joyce?'

'Ooh, it was a long time ago!' said my mother, but she blushed a little, nonetheless, and he pushed her on the shoulder.

Tash raised her eyebrows at me. Then she redoubled her efforts.

'Hi,' said a character to me. 'I'm Marshall. Isn't this fabulous?'

'Hi, Dad,' I said, without prompting.

* * *

That was the longest dinner of my life. A dinner, too, I'd already eaten, so I was denied the pleasure of guessing whether the salmon would be cold or pan-fried. Between us, Tashy and I ate about enough to sate a very small mouse who'd spent the morning at a cheese and wine party.

The speeches were interminable too. Oddly, whilst Max's was exactly the same – and, for me, even worse, because I could wince now even longer before we got to the far-approaching punchline – her dad's was somehow different. He seemed less proud, less sure of himself; less confident all over. This wasn't good.

I was on the top table, and glumly watched my parents urge each other to try different foods, and giggling and glancing at each other throughout the toasts. At one point they even clinked glasses. My dad was trying too hard. Oh God, I couldn't do it. I couldn't go back. They needed me here, they really did. How could I take this away from them? I was dreading it. But if I didn't, then all this around me was a waste. A waste of lives, a waste of money, a waste of everything. I looked at my mum's smiling face and thought back to when she sat here before, nervously checking with me in case she had to pay for anything, or whether or not it was OK to take second helpings. Olly, on another table, spotted me looking at my mother – who, of course, had not the slightest clue who he was. He smiled ruefully then raised his eyebrows.

At last, at last, with the coffee still warm in my mouth, the caterers looked as if they were starting to clear the tables away. I had to get out. I had to clear my head. I needed to think. I looked at Tashy.

'I'm going out . . .'

'Run,' she said. She was drinking rather heavily for a bride. 'Run as fast as you can and never look back.'

'I was thinking more of a walk around the garden.'

'Whatever,' she said dully. I took off like a bolt of lightning.

* * *

Oh God, here it was again. I'd forgotten about the stupid effing fountain. I walked around it, resisting the urge to kick it. Such a beautiful day. In the distance, I could see my parents too, taking a little walk in the sunshine. Were they holding hands? Oh, crap. Maybe I shouldn't go. Maybe I had to.

I sat on the side of the fountain, idly lifting my skirt, and stretching my legs out in front of me, twirling my skinny ankles, admiring the sheer, unfreckled whiteness of my legs, the lack of wrinkliness in the knee. Who knew you got wrinkles in your knees? Not me.

'Here!' Justin looked triumphant. 'John's bloody watching me like a hawk, but I managed to sneak away and I got these.' He handed over two bottles of pink Bacardi Breezer. He must think it was my favourite. 'Cigarette?' he proffered me a Benson & Hedges.

'God, no. Don't even think of it, stinky boy.'

He rolled his eyes. 'Whatever.'

He stretched out on the grass. 'This isn't too bad after all, now, is it? Lift your skirt up again.'

I smiled. 'What do you think this is, lapdancer central?'

'I cannot wait till I'm twenty-one,' said Justin dreamily. Then he remembered himself. 'Not that they'll be as nice as you.'

'You're probably right,' I said.

I had been having slight second thoughts about everything we'd done before. Maybe he would think all girls were as easy as me and get turned into some kind of daytime TV presenter sex fiend. But, watching him as he smiled lazily, completely relaxed, getting grass stains on his new suit, half closing his eyes against the late afternoon sun, I figured he'd be alright.

'You'll be alright,' I said out loud.

'What're you talking about?' he said, blinking.

'You'll be fine.'

'Uh, yeah. Maybe you shouldn't drink so fast in the hot sun.'

'Hey!' shouted Clelland, striding over the lawn. His tie was loosened and he'd unbuttoned his shirt a little. It made him look adorably ruffled.

'We were just talking,' I said, trying not to look guilty.

'I hope so.'

'We were.' I was blushing again.

He looked at me, and I melted.

'Well, anyway . . .' he said. 'Are you smoking?'

'No!'

'Oh. Right. God. No, it's just . . . they're about to cut the cake.'

'Flora! Flora!' It was my mother's voice. 'They're cutting the cake! You should come to see it.'

'Yes, yes,' I said. Olly too was now running out of the house, running for me.

'They're cutting the . . . !'

He was shouting, and I suddenly felt very tender for him, looking out for me; tearing across the short grass just to make sure I was alright.

'Cake cutting?' said Justin, closing his eyes again. 'That sounds boring.'

'You're not needed, squirt,' said Clelland.

'Fine,' said Justin. 'I'll stay here. Come back soon, Flo.'

I looked at him, and suddenly a lump welled up in my throat. I was frozen to the spot.

'I don't know,' I said.

'Flora,' said Clelland, softly.

I looked again at Justin, lying stretched out on the grass, like one of those beautiful boys from pictures of Edwardian house parties, not long before they all went off to Belgium to get slaughtered.

I clutched Clelland's arm.

'You don't have to,' he said.

'I don't know,' I said again.

'You'll be fine,' he whispered.

'Don't be long,' murmured Justin, but he already sounded as if he was drifting off into sleep.

* * *

The room looked eerily, horribly similar. Tashy was standing at the cake, her face completely fixed. She was staring at me.

'Get on with it,' somebody shouted. She didn't move. I walked forward until I was facing her.

'We're going to cut the cake now,' she said weirdly, as if she was announcing it on television. She was standing in front of Max, almost obscuring him in her pure dress.

'I know,' I said, equally stiffly.

I could feel Clelland behind me, standing as if to steady me.

'Are you ready?'

'No.'

'Don't,' said Tashy.

Max nudged her. 'Erm, can we get a move on?'

I looked around. My parents were there, smiling anxiously, hopefully; at me and each other; holding hands. Tashy was standing, so beautiful and defiant. Olly was lurking sullenly in the background. And in the garden, perfect and dreaming, a boy, young and guileless, without a care or a fear in a world under a golden sky.

The two hands joined on the knife, and pressed down.

Chapter Seventeen

Nothing happened.

Chapter Eighteen

I'd expected – I don't know, a blackout. A disappearance. Maybe a blinding flash of light? Or a jump to the next morning, or something. Something.

I had done it. Instinct had taken over. My eyes had focused on the cake, the wish bubbling up – and I had spoken it, I must have. Stupidly, I was tempted to say, 'I wish I was twenty-five again,' but swallowed it at the last minute. I had said, 'I wish I was my own age again.'

Maybe that's why it had worked badly! Maybe it thought I just wanted to stay sixteen! Olly was right: I had arrested my development so completely I would be staying here for the rest of my life! Or would go round it over and over again! Or nobody would remember anything about it and I'd be confined to an insane asylum like Sarah Connor!

All this flashed through my mind as I concentrated on the two hands on the cake, cleaving it through to the bottom, and all around me there was applause, and flashbulbs went off and people cheered. Tashy and I stared at each other, and her eyes were wide and shocked. Then I blinked, several times, and let my field of vision expand to take in the whole scene. Tashy was still in front of Max, but as they started to move, my focus shifted and became blurry. It couldn't be . . . it just didn't . . .

The person standing behind Tashy suddenly wasn't Max. It was Olly.

* * *

Tashy's face of shock widened as she realised whose hand she was clasping so hard. Then she turned round, and her mouth dropped in delight, and she shrieked and jumped up, wrapping herself around him and almost knocking his ears off. His face too was comical, his eyebrows fighting each other like quotation marks, his ears pink as a pig's.

'You know, for such a short courtship, I never thought it would work,' I heard somebody – probably her mother – say behind me. 'But they certainly look happy enough.'

I wanted to rush up to them, run into them, but they were clearly in a private moment of such joy and intimacy it would be sacrilege to interrupt them. All those secret meetings; discussion about me, my arse! They were falling in love! No wonder Tashy had been so tragic these last few weeks.

I grinned from side to side, then realised what this might mean. Oh God, I had to get to a mirror. Now. I looked down. I was wearing the same Karen Millen trouser suit I'd worn first time round. I stumbled out, hearing voices calling my name, but ignoring them so I could rush into the bathroom, breathing heavily, my heart pounding at a thousand miles an hour. I leaned my face against the cool tiles, counted to ten and tried to will myself to look in the mirror. Oh God. Oh no.

It was me, alright, the first touch of tiny wrinkles under my eyes. I looked really tired. My teeth seemed yellower. But, in a funny way, I was so, so pleased to see myself again. This was . . . this was me. Not an unformed me, barely touched by life. But a me I was quite happy to see. A me who had clearly smiled a lot in life. A me who had her curls under control. I lifted up my under arm and felt it flop with a dispiriting wobble. But still: look at my nicely curved breasts, blooming up under the well-cut Karen Millen suit. I looked pretty much OK. No, I looked good. Holding up well. In fact, I felt better about the way I looked than I had for a long, long time. All that wasted energy, thinking that if I was old again, I'd be a complete hag.

My heart plummeted suddenly. Oh God, my poor mother. I had offered my mother the chance of happiness then dragged it away from her. I blinked back the tears from my eyes. But that wasn't my world to live in, was it? Was it? I would be so, so good to her now . . .

'Flora?' It was my mother's voice.

'Yes?'

'Nothing, you just looked a bit sick there, and your dad and me wondered if you were alright.'

She came into the bathroom. I stared and stared. Was this my mum? She was older again too, but not in the same way; not a bit of it. Her hair was nice and set, and she was trim and shapely-looking, not horribly bent over and skinny. She was wearing her wedding ring.

'MUM!' I burst into tears and flung my arms around her neck.

'There, there,' she said. 'You've done so well, pretending you don't mind your best friend marrying your ex-boyfriend, but I know there must be some strain, eventually . . .'

'I really don't mind,' I said honestly. 'I'm chuffed for them, I really am.'

'Don't worry,' she said. 'It'll be your turn next.'

'You always say that,' I said.

'Well, me and your dad, we always want the best for you. Come on out, he'll be worried about you, and we don't want to worry him, do we?'

'No,' I said. I let her guide me out of the bathroom like a small child.

'Hey, pet,' said my dad, looking more rotund and jovial than ever. 'Here's my two most beautiful girls, eh?'

My mother mock slapped him down.

They were interrupted by Olly coming up and grabbing me in a huge bear hug.

'You,' he said in my ear, his voice choking with emotion, 'are the best wolverine in the whole world.'

'Yeah, yeah,' I said.

'You're not pissed off with us? Not that . . . I mean, I really didn't know this was going to happen.'

I grinned so wildly my face hurt. 'It's been that kind of month. Twice. Oh, Olly, I'm so chuffed. I'm so . . . I had no idea you two were in love.'

'That's because you were a self-obsessed teenage idiot,' said Olly.

'Oh, yeah.'

'And I'm the luckiest man on earth,' said Olly. Then he

hugged my mother. 'Mrs Scurrison, you are gorgeous as ever.'

'Get away with you,' said my mother. 'And you be as good to that young lady as you were to Flora, now, do you hear?'

We all sobered up a little at that.

'I'll try,' said Olly.

'You'll succeed,' I said.

'Go see her,' said Ol. 'She's in floods of tears, eating cake. Um, happy tears.'

'She hasn't eaten for six months,' I said. 'The cake probably got to her just in time.'

'Go.'

'Just a minute,' I said. 'There's someone I have to see.'

As I left, I could hear Oliver announcing to the crowd, 'My wife and I . . .'

As inconspicuously as I could, I left through the French windows. And there he was, still lying asleep in the grass by the fountain. Still beautiful and, gosh, so young. He stirred as my shadow fell upon him.

'Er, yeah?' he said, springing awake and jumping up. 'Uh, sorry, have I missed something? Just dozed off for a second . . .'

Fully standing, he stared at me. I don't know what I expected. Well, I did. But just for a second I thought he might . . .

He looked as if he almost did.

'Sorry, you look really familiar to me.'

Of course, he'd said that before. He'd guess in a minute.

'Maybe you were having a dream,' I said.

'Huh.' He shook down his new blue suit. 'It was a nice dream.' He coloured slightly.

'How nice?' I asked.

'Um, er. Hi there.' He stuck out his hand. 'I'm Justin Clelland.'

I nearly laughed. To keep from crying.

'I know,' I said. 'I'm Flora Scurrison.' I paused. 'I'm a friend of your brother's.'

His brow furrowed. 'That sounds familiar. Didn't you used to live near us?'

'Something like that,' I said.

'Well, nice to meet you.'

'Yes,' I said, swallowing hard. Then, there was a gentle touch on my shoulder, as the fountain tippled away endlessly, round and round for ever, in front of me.

* * *

'You know,' said the low voice behind me, rather similar to the one in front of me. 'You haven't changed a bit.'

* * *

I looked up at him, his wonderfully familiar face looking into mine, and felt a huge rush of relief.

'Justin, scrammify,' said Clelland over my shoulder.

'Yawn yawn yawn,' said Justin, and wandered off, muttering about not wanting to spend time with a couple of oldies anyway. I watched him go.

'God, he seems such a baby!' I said. Then, just at the last minute, he whipped round and stared at me. His face was a picture: quizzical and delighted. He stared at me. Then he raised an eyebrow. I winked at him. He stared for one more second then walked on, shaking his head in confusion. He knew.

'So were you.'

'Oh, yeah.' I felt myself blushing, and smiling.

He put his hand up to my face, then retracted it, as if it would be too intimate.

'It's OK,' I said.

'It's just . . . it's so incredibly weird. Really, I haven't seen you for sixteen years. Are you *taller*?'

'I can't believe you never ever contacted me. Not once, after all that time.'

He shook his head. 'Me neither. Life . . .'

'And . . . Jeez, things have changed.'

We started to walk away from the fountain, away from the formal garden.

'Have you spoken to the bride and groom?' I asked.

'They are the happiest people in the history of the world. I think we're agreeing to keep the whole thing quiet.'

'I think that's a good idea. Where's Max?'

'Oh, he's at home. Tashy phoned him, just to check. Says some really young girl picked up the phone, so she reckons he's getting over it.'

'And it goes on,' I said.

'What about you?' he said. 'Have you changed?'

'Apart from the crow's-feet and the rather nifty trouser suit?'

'Yeah,' he said. 'No, I mean, in yourself. Everyone else has.'

'Have you?'

'Oh, yeah. No, not really. But I was practically perfect to begin with.'

'Hmm. But I don't know.'

'Check your wallet.'

'Why?'

'I don't know, but Tashy's had a picture of Olly where Max's used to be.'

'Yeah, but I bet she's had that for ages.'

Nonetheless, I pulled it out of my small bag – with, bliss of blisses, my house keys and my credit card. Oh, I could never have dreamed of being so happy to see plastic and metal.

'What's this?' I said suddenly, loudly, drawing a card out of my wallet. I held it up to the light. 'Fuck! Clell, it says I'm a nut!'

On the card, it did, in big black letters. N.U.T.

Oh God. Was this a mental hospital? Had I dreamed the whole thing? Was I having psychotic episodes? Was Clelland my doctor? I mean, what had happened . . . it was impossible. Maybe I was in maximum security. Maybe . . .

'Calm down,' said Clelland, examining it, and seeing what was going through my head. 'You're not a nut.'

'Are you sure? Maybe I'm babbling right now.'

'You are. And just wait till you see this.' He handed it over. 'Look at it carefully.'

I did. Clelland was eyeing me closely, waiting for my reaction. It started the birds from the trees.

'National Union of TEACHERS!!!!'

He started laughing.

'I'm a TEACHER!!!!??????'

'Beats accountancy, for sure.'

'I'm a TEACHER!!!!????'

'Oh, come on, think of the holidays.'

He felt for my hand and took it as we strolled in amongst the trees.

304

'I'd better be a fucking art teacher.'

He giggled. 'You'd better stop flirting with your charges.'

'Fuck!!'

My phone rang. The ringtone was 'Colourblind'.

'I think you've got one of your student's phones.'

'I think not,' I said, promptly switching it off. 'He's a doctor and a Persian king, you know. Good mix.'

He smiled. 'Well, beats an old charity worker like me.'

'Who's old?' I said.

I glanced behind us into the twilight. The entire wedding party, it seemed, were out looking for us. Tashy's gown was catching the last rays of the light of the Indian summer evening. I could see Justin in the distance. He was chasing Kathleen, Tash's little niece, obviously restored to brides-maiding duties in the lovely empire dress, through a meadow. Their screams of laughter reached us. I smiled at him and suddenly felt peaceful. I'd spent all this time being torn in two, between two lives, between two worlds, between two sets of people, between family and friends.

There were two of us here. But I didn't feel torn at all.

'Fancy a little bit of hide and seek?' I winked at him.

'Yes, miss!'

So we hid behind the tree. And he took me in his arms and I didn't object. And then I kissed him, and was kissed, properly. Like a grown-up. Without guidance and without restraint, just with sheer, perfect, fitting-together passion, without need for talking; without even a need to think. To paraphrase the Spice Girls, a band Stanzi didn't even remember: two became one.

Later, for sheer naughtiness, and because it's what teenagers do, we carved our initials on the tree. So they'll still be there this year, when we go back. For a special occasion of our own. That I'm hoping is going to be just as special as Olly and Tashy's but in a very, very, *very* different way.

I think I'll stick to profiteroles.

Working Wonders

Jenny Colgan

Laughs, love, office life. And a little touch of magic . . .

Gwyneth Morgan loves her job. And she's good at it – she's never faced a challenge she can't handle – until she meets Arthur Pendleton and his motley crew.

Gwyneth sets Arthur a challenge that makes his heart sink. His team can't even work their swivel chairs, let alone win a prestigious competition.

Pitted against his ex-girlfriend, as well as his love rival and deadly enemy, Arthur is forced to break the law and overcome massive obstacles as he embarks on his quest to achieve the impossible – and maybe, just maybe, win the heart of the enchanting Gwyneth.

As Gwyneth learns some surprising revelations about the man she'd once considered just an inept colleague, she's forced to reconsider. Is it possible that Arthur is her knight in shining armour?

'Will melt even the hardest of hearts.'   *Red*

'Funny, magical and moving.'   *Time Out*

'Hugely entertaining and very funny.'   *Cosmopolitan*

ISBN 0 00 710555 X

Amanda's Wedding

Jenny Colgan

Mel and Fran can't believe it when their old schoolfriend Amanda, Satan's very own PR girl, pulls off the ultimate publicity stunt in getting herself engaged to a Scottish laird.

Who cares that Fraser McConnald has worn the same pair of Converse trainers for the last three years and that his castle is a pile of rubble with one Calor Gas heater – she'll be titled.

Something must be done . . .

Gentle, decent Fraser is clearly ignorant of her wiles, and Mel and Fran, still smarting from the memory of all the mean things Amanda put them through in their days at Portmount Comprehensive, set out to sabotage this mismatch of the century.

So between fighting off the attentions of a love-crazed accountant, keeping Fran's deadly manoeuvres with the opposite sex under control and trying to win her own war of love with the elusive but gorgeous Alex, Mel finds herself attending a wild Scottish stag night, a hen night from hell, and preparing for a wedding that's everything you'd wish on your worst enemy.

ISBN 0 00 653176 8